PRETTY POLLY

Abby Davies

PRETTY POLLY

Published worldwide by Apple Loft Press

This edition published in 2024

www.abbydavies.com

For Gran

Also by Abby Davies

Mother Loves Me

The Cult

Arrietty

Her No.1 Fan

The Girl Who Heard Maggots

Come Polly come Polly come go along with me
Before we are married some friends for to see
He led her ore hills ore valleys so deep
At last pretty Polly sat down for to weep

O Billy O Billy you have led me a stray
On purpos my innocent life for to stay
Polly O Polly O that is what I have
I was all the last night a digging of your grave

She went a little farther as she did spy
A grave being dug and a spade standing by
Her lilly white hand in sorrow she rung
Begging for mercy cries what have I done

A Murder Ballad
Douglas MS (NY) c.1845 Thompson

Prologue

She is evidence of an ugly death. Her body lies broken and battered behind a rusted tractor in a field long abandoned to nature's mercy. She is covered with mud and straw, skull cracked open, sunny side up.

Wind whips up soil, sweat and blood, carrying it across the barren fields toward the city. It tugs at the straw stuck to her skin and plays with her blood-drenched hair.

In time, someone will find her.

Flies, maggots and crows will have had their fill by then. Only her teeth, hair and bones will remain. Even the marks on her skin will be erased, stolen by weather, time and hungry little mouths that enjoy the taste of human rot.

The person who finds her will wonder what happened. A shudder will creep into their veins and the horror will spin through their mind like a carousel of the dead. They will feel afraid. Especially when they hear about the second body.

Locals will fear that there is a serial killer on the loose.

Police will discover they are right.

When officers find the third body, fear will escalate to terror, because this killer does not play by the rules. This killer does not leave a defining signature.

They do not content themselves with staging or posing.

They do not crave infamy.

They do, however, possess the dark triad of personality traits: Machiavellianism, narcissism, and psychopathy. They are manipulative, egotistical, and totally self-centred with a callousness that is beyond belief.

As serial killers go, this monster is a new breed, which presents a problem, because almost every trace of evidence has been eaten.

Chapter One

Tension vibrates in the air like a poised quill, the future yet to be written. Outside my office, the sky is papery and dull; as lifeless as the teenage girl opposite me.

While Polly George completes the medical form, I take the opportunity to consider her. She wears minimal makeup and smells clean and fresh. Her school uniform is unwrinkled and bears no tears or stains. She is striking – breathtakingly beautiful in fact - but unnaturally pale; a symptom no doubt of her troubled young mind.

I think of Michael when he was fifteen. Scrawny and splattered with acne, but always smiling, always positive. Fortunately, puberty gave him an easy ride and somehow, despite what I did, he's never struggled mentally. I smile at Polly, try to communicate to her that my office is a safe space, that I'm here to offer help and guidance. Deep down, I know that if Michael ever felt the need to do what this young girl has done, my logical approach would go out the window.

"Polly, before we get started, I want to let you know that everything we talk about is confidential. The only exception is if you tell me that you're going to hurt or kill yourself or someone else or that you know of a child or elder who's being abused."

She doesn't react.

Light streams through the window casting her in an angelic glow. Her face is so symmetrical and enchanting, as if it's been carved out of white marble by a sorceress.

"I know you're taking anti-depressants now. Would you say they're helping?"

Instead of answering my question, her eyes flit to mine and away. She wraps her arms around her torso and hugs herself tightly. I wait for her to answer but she continues to stare at her knees. She looks so small and helpless. Silence stretches on. I hold my tongue, give an encouraging smile. I mustn't pressure her. She'll speak in her own time.

"Alone together," she says, her voice soft, sad.

"Yes, we are alone. Are you pleased it's just the two of us, Polly?"

She nods but doesn't look up. "My mum's finding things difficult. It's hard to be around her right now."

I lean back in my chair. 'Can you talk to her about how you feel?'

Her gaze drifts to a faraway place. Moving like an old woman, Polly rises from the sofa. "I'm beginning to worry about her."

She looks around my office, takes in the bright walls and oak furnishings, the bonsai tree that Michael gave me for my birthday. Her posture is ballerina-like, complexion as pure as china. She homes in on the bookshelf at the back of the room. I know what she's going to do before she does it. With a shy smile, she walks toward my books, most of which are psychiatry tomes I haven't touched since university. A shiver passes through me as she trails her fingers across their meaty spines.

"Have you read all of these?" she says.

"Most of them, yes. I wonder if you could sit down now so we can talk properly?"

She spins around, eyebrows raised as if startled, a deer in headlights. "Oh yes. Sorry."

Polly moves back to the sofa but doesn't sit down. Instead, she stops in front of my desk, hitches her weight, and picks up the framed photograph of my sons. It's relatively new. A stranger took it at my eldest son's graduation last year. A sharp pain ripples through my heart as I think of James wandering around Thailand, so far away, so unprotected, and not back for another six months. At least Michael's still in the country…

She holds the photograph up to her face and strokes the glass. Discomfort scratches but I push it away.

"Are these your sons?" she says.

"Yes."

"What're their names?"

"The one in the graduation gown is James. The other is Michael."

"Michael's very good-looking."

I reach out my hand, gesturing for her to give it back. "Thank you."

She hesitates and a small frown – the first I've seen – crosses her doll-like face. For a split second, I question her behaviour; is she playing some sort of game? Trying to get under my skin? What purpose that would serve I'm not sure, but sometimes, our actions aren't driven by conscious decisions. Of course, often they are. Perhaps she's testing me.

She hands back the photograph and returns to the sofa with a small sigh.

"You said a moment ago that your mother is struggling. Could it be because she's worried about you?"

She nods. Murmurs, "It's all my fault."

"Why is it your fault?"

She glances up at me. Tears transform her eyes into glass pebbles. She drops her gaze and fiddles with her sleeve. "Because I hurt myself."

"What were you thinking when you did that?"

"I was thinking…I don't know what I was thinking." She shakes her head, twists her fingers.

Observing her distress, I dismiss the idea of game-playing, for now.

At this moment, I want to offer her physical comfort. It's clear how much she's hurting. But I can't. It's not my place.

"It's okay, Polly. You're doing really well. Talking about these things is never easy. I want to ask one thing though -

do you feel like you might hurt yourself again?"

A scuffing sound rises from her lap, drawing my eyes downward. She's scratching her bandaged wrist. I fight the urge to tell her to stop.

"Polly?"

She doesn't look up. I hesitate, take a deep breath. She continues to scratch at her skin. The sound and thought of what she's doing makes me wince. I imagine blood oozing from torn flesh. The air feels too hot, the walls too close. Though I work hard to keep my face expressionless, my mind swirls with theories and curiosity. I lick my lips, remind myself to be patient.

Polly looks up and manages to meet my eye. In a trembly voice, she whispers, "I bet you have secrets, haven't you Doctor?"

"Er, yes. I have secrets. It's a normal part of being a human being."

I take a sip of water. "Could it be that you have a secret, Polly?"

She bites her lip.

"Would you like to talk about it?"

Her eyes widen and she shakes her head fervently. The wispy hairs that have escaped her bun quiver like dandelion feathers in a violent wind. Tears roll down her cheeks and her shoulders cave inward. She buries her lily-white cheeks in her hands and shakes her head more gently. Her body trembles.

"Polly?" I say softly.

She sniffs and peers up through teary eyes that can't focus on mine. The shadows below are purple, her skin too white. Vampiric almost. She slips her left thumbnail between her teeth and bites. Her nails are painted black. I listen to the hard click as her teeth snap through keratin.

I soften my tone. "Polly, are you okay? Talk to me."

She stops biting. Silence envelops us in a tense embrace as she hides her face in her hands once more. I ache to come out from behind my desk and hold her, but remain motionless: the observer. If there's one thing I dislike about my job, it's this.

"Polly? Perhaps if you try to tell me how you're feeling, you'll feel a little better."

She sniffs. Her voice is muffled as she says, "I don't think anything will make me feel better. Not now."

"Can you tell me what happened last month? Can you tell me why you hurt yourself so badly? Remember, I'm here to listen, not to judge."

Her shoulders sag lower and she begins to gnaw at the tender skin around her thumbnail.

"I, I can't. They won't let me."

"Who won't let you?"

"They…they want me to keep our secret. They'll do something even worse if I tell."

Even worse? Even worse than what?

"What secret, Polly?"

She shrugs. "They always seem to know. And they're bad and when they get angry, they do bad things. Terrible things."

"What sorts of things?"

"I'm sorry – I can't. They'll never forgive me. They'll hurt us."

My blood pounds. "Who do you mean by 'us', Polly?"

She opens her mouth to speak, but before she can utter a sound, her eyes roll back to form white pearls, and she falls onto her side on the sofa.

I jerk to my feet and run to her. A faint like this has never happened to me before. Mind whirring, I watch her breathe, watch the tears dry on her cheeks, and wonder how to proceed.

I am, some might argue, out of my depth. Something odd is going on with this poor girl. I have older, wiser, more experienced colleagues who could take on Polly and help her faster and perhaps more effectively than I can.

There's Bobby Falcon, my old dissertation tutor. We message each other once or a twice a year, and he's very well-regarded. With thirty years under his belt, he ought to be. I look at my laptop, think about emailing Bobby later, then turn my attention to Polly. As I watch her pale face, I realise I already feel responsible for her. She and her mother chose me. I can't rely on someone else to solve this problem – can't foist Polly and Mrs George onto someone else simply because I'm out of my comfort zone. I did that once before and the young man in question didn't get the help he needed. Instead, Roman took his own life.

Regret ripples beneath my spine.

I'll never forget the abject misery on Roman's mother's face. The pure torment of being unable to save her son, even though she turned to professionals. I should have treated him myself, not ferried him along to another colleague, but I was afraid I'd fail.

There are steps I can take to solve this mystery faster.

I check my watch. Only two minutes of the session remain. I frown, irritated that we don't have longer, but aware that Polly has almost certainly had enough for one day.

She begins to stir, and I help her sit up.

"You fainted. Here, sip a little." I raise a glass of water to her lips and she drinks thirstily, thanking me in a tiny voice that makes my heart twinge.

"I'm sorry," she says.

"Sorry for what? For fainting?" I smile.

She offers a tremulous smile then winces and raises her hand to her right temple. Her sky-blue eyes meet mine.

"Can I see you again, Doctor England?"

I nod. "Of course. Same time next week, if you like?"

She nods shyly and I escort her from the room, unable to stop myself staring at a long, white scar under her earlobe and wondering how she got it.

Most of all, I wonder what Polly's secret is and who will

hurt her if she tells.

Chapter Two

My home is empty and soulless. Without the boys and with their father long gone, the building is too big for me. But after what I did, this is what I deserve. I deserve to be alone.

I eye my father's butterfly collection, which he gave me shortly before he died. Michael and James wanted them to stay because they reminded them of Grandpa Harry. I loved my dad too but I'm not too fond of his butterflies. Displaying perfectly preserved dead bodies in little glass cases doesn't feel right to me. It also reminds me of a terrifying thriller I read a few years ago called *The Butterfly Garden*. Still, the boys wanted them to stay, so they stayed.

With a groan of relief, I kick off my heels, dump my bag and coat on the sofa, trudge to the kitchen and pour myself a small G&T. At least tonight I have a mission. Tonight won't be a case of making my meal-for-one then watching evening tele alone, my mind wandering to James' and Michael's adventures – or misadventures, as the case may be - because tonight I have research to do.

It's not normal practice to research my clients but I want to. The idea that someone will hurt Polly if she tells me her secret is frightening. Who could want to harm her? Is she talking about herself? Has she got a personality-type disorder, or is there a real-life person in her life she fears?

I begin by googling 'Polly George'. First up is a handmade ceramics website called PollyGeorgeCeramics. I search 'Polly George' on Facebook, and it takes only a few seconds for my Polly George's picture to appear, but when I log in and try to view Polly's pictures, her privacy settings won't let me. Good girl.

I return to my Google search. On the third page I spot

a news report with Polly's name in. The article was written ten years ago when Polly was five years old. A photograph shows a pretty, fair-haired boy with his mother – who is a much more attractive, younger-looking version of the Mrs George I met today – and an adorable, fair-haired little girl. Mr George is nowhere to be seen. I read with growing horror and concern; why didn't Mrs George tell me about this when she booked Polly's first session with me? Early sibling loss can have devastating ramifications, especially when the lost one is a twin. Is this the dark secret Polly was talking about? Suffering a traumatic experience at such a young age could certainly be partly to blame for Polly's depression and recent suicide attempt. But why would someone hurt her if she told me about this? It's not a secret that her brother disappeared ten years ago. The media made sure of that.

I slurp my drink and read on, bending over my laptop to ease the ache in my lower back. The hairs on my neck prickle. On 1st February, Polly's five-year-old twin brother, Benjamin, went missing. Horror floods in, thick and bitter as bile. To this date, he has never been found, alive or dead. I shake my head. The thought of something like that happening to Michael or James is gut-wrenching. Being apart from them for more than a week is tough – in fact, I know I'm battling Empty Nest Syndrome - but forever…it doesn't bear thinking about, and yet I can't stop imagining the horror Mrs George – and Polly – must have gone through. The horror they must still be living with, day in day out. Because the grief never goes away. And the not-knowing must be dreadful.

The need to de-stress soars. I down my drink, go to the kitchen and pour myself another, doubling up the gin, telling myself tomorrow's a Saturday so a slight hangover won't be the end of the world.

Back at my laptop I read on, desperate to know more.

The Georges were living where they live now when this

happened, which is only a short drive from my house. A memory stirs: I do remember this happening – I would have joined the search, but back then I was dealing with my own big, dark secret, and too self-focused to help.

I picture Polly's tearful face. Now that I know that she lost her brother as a child, I need to encourage her to talk about it. Dredging up the past might seem counterintuitive but talking about her feelings will help her return to normality, so to speak. Of course, even that might not work. She's incredibly fragile and there's something she's hiding. I'll need to tread very carefully.

Hunkering over, I scour the net for every report related to missing Benjamin George. The more facts I can assimilate, the more prepared I'll be for my next meeting with Polly. I also decide to call Mrs George and ask her if I might pop in to talk to her when her daughter's not around. This might not be normal practice, but something warns me that if I don't act quickly, someone might hurt her or she might take a pair of nail scissors to her wrist again, and this time she'll be successful.

I can't let that happen. Not after poor Roman.

Chapter Three

Mrs George invites me over at midday, saying Polly is revising at a friend's house. I'm pleased to hear that Polly has someone she wants to spend time with and something to occupy her. It also means I can see Heather privately.

The sky is morose, the November air damp and crisp when I pull on my yellow raincoat over a navy wool dress and jump in my car. The drive to Mrs George's house takes less than two minutes. By the time I arrive, the heavens are weeping. I yank up the hood of my raincoat before jogging to the front door of number 12 Sycamore Lane, a Victorian mid-terrace smothered by creeping ivy that almost entirely masks the red brick walls. Spider webs lace the corners of the porch and the windows appear not to have seen a cleaner for at least a year, but the house has character and charm – far more than mine does anyway.

I ring the bell and wait, tucking my already frizzy brown hair behind my ears. Mrs George answers a beat later and I wonder if she's been hovering by the door awaiting my arrival. She bursts into a speech full of gratitude and relief – how glad she is that I'm coming over to talk to her, how generous it is of me to give up my free time.

She leaves me sitting on a rather uncomfortable brown sofa in the living room. I admire the original brick fireplace and the homely, warm feel generated by framed photographs of Mrs George and her daughter, or just of Polly on her own. The most recent photograph of Polly has her dressed in a pretty polka dot sundress standing in front of a glimmering ocean. Their last summer holiday perhaps. In the picture the girl looks happy and her eyes sparkle like the water behind her. I move closer to scrutinise her young face. Her smile matches her eyes; she seems genuinely happy. People with depression can experience moments of levity. Perhaps this was one of those moments. Or maybe something bad happened to Polly after that holiday. An incident or trigger that pushed her over the edge.

I sit back down and scan the room, seeing candle after candle and porcelain figurines of birds – Mrs George's treasures no doubt. With unease, I notice there isn't a single photograph of Mr George. There's just one photograph of Benjamin – a school portrait - which must have been taken shortly before he disappeared.

I notice a frame lying face down on the mantlepiece and move toward it, but Mrs George hurries into the room apologising for taking so long. I take the proffered coffee and place it on the table to my right. The smell of strong coffee blends with the room's overly sweet aroma of vanilla, making me feel queasy.

"Your home is lovely."

Mrs George brushes hair out of her eyes and tries to smile. She looks washed out and wears the same clothes as yesterday. Her dirt-blonde hair is lank and greasy. "Thank you. Please call me Heather, by the way."

I nod. "Call me Jessie. Much less of a mouthful than Doctor England."

"Is your coffee okay?"

"Perfect, thank you. So, Polly's at a friend's house revising?"

"Yes. She's at Dana's. They've been friends since nursery."

"Have they got mock exams coming up?"

"Just before Christmas."

"And how do you think Polly's coping with the pressure of exams?"

Heather George sighs heavily. "I don't really know, to tell you the truth. She doesn't open up to me – hasn't for a long time now."

"How's she doing at school?"

"Well. Really well. She's predicted all 8s and 9s. She took her Maths GCSE last year. Got a 9. She's a bright spark. Doesn't get it from me, mind."

"And no concerns have been raised by any of Polly's teachers?"

Heather looks down and shakes her head. When she looks up, tears glitter in her eyes. Unlike her daughter, she has dark green irises. "I'm such a terrible mother. I should have noticed something. I should have…"

She swipes angrily at the tears on her sallow cheeks. I long to comfort her, but her body language tells me to stay where I am.

"You're not a terrible mother," I say, "Young people are surprisingly good at hiding how they're feeling, just as we are. And I know what happened is awful and you feel, albeit irrationally, guilty about it, but you have to realise that this was Polly's cry for help. Now that she's made us aware that she's struggling, we can help her, and that's a very positive thing. That's what we have to focus on now. Polly needs our help and she wants our help, and there are many things we can do to help her get better."

"No. You're wrong. I am a terrible mother. I -"

I wait for the woman to continue but she stops abruptly and her eyes dart to the left making me wonder what she's holding back.

"Heather?"

"Nothing. It's just…I should have noticed something, a sign, something to suggest she was feeling so desperate, but what with work and everything, I think I just…" She gives a helpless shrug.

"You mustn't blame yourself," I say as firmly as I can. "No mother is perfect."

Inside, I cringe at the irony of my words.

"I can't bear it anymore. First Benjamin and now Polly. And Rich has left us. It's just…it's too much. And now I'm turning all self-pitying. I'm pathetic!" She laughs bitterly and my heart goes out to her. The poor woman has been through so much. Too much. It's a wonder she's still managing to keep going. I tell her so, then take a deep breath. She's mentioned her lost son now, giving me the perfect opportunity to bring up the subject.

I give her a moment to compose herself. After a minute or so, her fingers stop trembling and she meets my gaze. "I'm sorry."

"There's no need to apologise. Heather, this is a difficult subject I know, but I need to ask you about the time Benjamin went missing. What were the exact circumstances? How much, if anything, was Polly aware of at the time?"

"Why do you need to know about that? That was ten years ago." There's a sharpness in her voice that almost makes me jump.

"When a child experiences the loss of a loved one at a young age it can take years for this experience to resurface in the form of anxiety or depression. To help Polly I need to understand what went on at that time, what she saw, what she was told, how she reacted, that sort of thing."

Heather sighs then nods. Her eyes take on the faraway expression of someone remembering the distant past, and she gazes through me as she speaks, her voice expressionless, hands clenched so tightly on her lap that the ends of her fingernails turn yellow. Outside, hail clatters against the windows and the sky morphs into a sour colour turning the cream living room walls a sickly shade of yellow. Shadows settle on Heather's lined face and I wish she'd turn on the living room light, but she's too wrapped up in remembering to notice the darkening of the day.

"I woke up because Polly was knocking on my door. Not knocking actually. It was more like hammering. Yes. She was hammering her tiny fists into the door and crying. It was only five thirty in the morning. Rich had already left for work. I opened the door and she tried to speak but couldn't because she was crying too hard. She was muddy and wet-through, said she'd gone outside to look for Benjamin. I remember it was a stormy night; I'd woken up several times but never left my room.

"Anyway, I picked her up and ran into their bedroom. Benjamin wasn't in their bedroom, of course. I ran into the spare room, but that was empty too, then I ran downstairs screaming his name, but there was no answer. I searched every room. There was no sign of anyone having broken in or any damage, and Benjamin was gone. I rang the police then Rich, who said he'd just got to work but would turn straight back and come home. The police were here within minutes. They searched high and low, questioned all the neighbours, but no one saw anything. They even searched Rich's car, checked his alibi. Fortunately, someone at work had seen him drive into the car park then speed back out of it, which was what cleared his name. For a while the police had him as their prime suspect."

"That's terrible," I say, knowing most of what she's told me already. "And Polly? Did she see anything?"

Heather shakes her head. "At the time I thought Polly was trying to tell me something but it was wishful thinking. All she knows is that when she woke up, she noticed Ben's bed was empty so she went and looked outside then came and got me."

I lick my lips, take a sip of now-tepid coffee. "What made Polly wake up?"

"What? Oh, I don't know. I think she said she had a nightmare. Or maybe it was the sound of Rich leaving for work."

"I see. How did Polly react to the disappearance of her brother in the days and weeks following the event?"

Heather hesitates. She swallows, and looks me in the eye. "She went very quiet and clung to me. She wouldn't leave my side. I couldn't even get her to go to school for the first three or four months after it happened. It was awful.

But she gradually got her old self back – or at least I thought she did."

"And did she ever speak about what happened?"

"No. And neither did we. After the first year with no answers, Rich said we had to move on, not mention it, or it would be the end of us and Polly would have a terrible childhood. I had to go on anti-depressants, but Rich was a rock. He was our rock, for the first few years anyway. Then something changed."

"Oh?"

A faint blush comes into her cheeks. "Yes. He started seeing other women. Thought I didn't know about it, but there were signs. Polly never knew though – she still doesn't to this day."

"Did you confront him about it?" I say, thinking that perhaps Polly did – and does - know about her father's disloyalty.

"I did, finally, about a year ago. He got angry, blamed me for being so distant and negative all the time. And he, he hit me."

My heartbeat speeds up. "Did you report him?"

"No. I couldn't. I couldn't bear the thought of losing him too. I told myself now that I'd confronted him, he'd stop doing it, but I don't think he did."

"Does Polly know he hit you?"

Heather shakes her head. "No. I don't ever want her to know. Anyway, he only did it once."

A tremor in her voice and her sideways glance betray her lie. I've dealt with abused women before and the signs are here, all too obvious now. The low self-esteem, lack of care about her appearance, inward body language, timid voice, inability to make eye contact.

"He never hit you before, Heather?"

"No. No, he didn't." There's a sharpness in her tone again but a moment later, she glances up at me, an apology in her eyes. An apology that's asking me to understand.

Needing me to.

I nod. "And Richard left with no warning?"

"Yes, well, sort of. I told him I'd had enough, that I wanted him to leave," she exhales heavily, "and since then there's been no note, no text, no voicemail. I know you'll be thinking 'good riddance', but he's Polly's father and she needs him and…"

"Do he and Polly have a close relationship?" I say.

She meets my gaze and I'm shocked to see a steely coldness in her expression. "Yes. They have a good bond. And no, before you ask, her father's never laid a hand on her. Not once."

I hesitate. "Do you think Richard's departure led Polly to hurt herself?"

Heather's gaze drops to her hands and she sighs. "I don't know. Maybe. It was only five days after he left that she did it, but I just don't know."

"Have you tried to find him?"

To my surprise, she shakes her head. This is a strange revelation. After what Polly did to herself, calling her father would have been the first thing I'd have done.

"He'll come back when he's ready. He always does."

"You've called him, though?" I say, trying to make sense of this strange decision.

Heather nods absently. "Oh yes. I've called several times."

"And he hasn't responded at all?"

She shakes her head, picks at her nails. "He's probably lost his phone or something. It wouldn't be the first time he's gone off and not been in touch for a while."

"So he's done this before?"

"Yes. When Polly was younger."

The hail abruptly stops and silence invades the room, broken only by Heather's breathing. I find myself hating this man I've never met. Becoming selfish due to depression is one thing, but abandoning his family repeatedly…Could Polly's secret be something to do her father? Is he the one she's afraid will hurt her if she tells?

I hesitate, knowing the poor woman must be drained already. But I need this one last thing from her. It could help me understand Polly's motivation. I know it's unlikely, but where there's a 'could' there's always a chance.

"I'm so sorry to ask this, Heather, but there's one more thing I'd like to know before I go, and trust me, hard though this has been, what you've told me is really helpful."

She tries to smile. "Thank you for saying that. What is it?"

"Can you show me where Polly was when you found her?"

Heather nods and stands, her face devoid of colour. "I thought you might ask that. She was in the upstairs bathroom."

Chapter Four

I follow Heather into the narrow hallway, and we climb the stairs to the bathroom at the top of the landing. She hesitates outside the door as if bracing herself for the memories that are sure to attack the moment she steps into the room.

She turns to me and murmurs, "I heard a thud and came running up." She pushes the door, which opens with a long creak. "Luckily, we don't have a lock on this door. The shower was running so I knocked, but there was no answer. I raised my voice, and she still didn't answer so I went in, and she was lying there, passed out. Blood was everywhere. It was the worst moment of my life since…"

She doesn't need to complete the sentence. Since Benjamin.

I stare at the white floor tiles and picture Polly lying there, her wrist cut open, blood pooling around her young body. A shudder grips me and I suppress it. The urge to cry is strong. If I found James or Michael like that, I can't imagine how I'd cope. The worst thing that's ever happened to either of my boys is a concussion and a broken wrist, and that was hard to deal with. Seeing my babies in pain was too much and their pain wasn't even self-inflicted. Despite my profession, I'm not sure how well I'd handle it if either of my boys suffered like poor Polly. Am I a hypocrite?

Yes.

You've certainly been a hypocrite in the past.

I bite my lip and try to block out memories of my biggest failure, irritated for thinking about myself at a time like this.

Stop it. Be professional.

I concentrate on the smell of bleach and the cold, damp feel of the air, and try to think objectively. The entire bathroom is white; white bath, white toilet, white sink, white blinds, white hand towel, white-rimmed mirror. The contrast between the scarlet of Polly's blood and the white of the room must have been striking. And so awful.

I stare at the mirror for a second. The question pops out of my mouth before I can stop it.

"Which way was she facing when you found her?" I try to make my voice as casual as possible.

"This way," Heather says, moving to stand in front of the mirror and darting a look at her reflection.

"So, she was facing the mirror and used nail scissors, is that right?"

Heather shudders. "Yes. And, um, there was something else. Something strange. I haven't told anyone else about it but, maybe it will help if you know."

"Know what?" I say stepping into the room, inhaling an acrid sting of bleach.

She bites her lip. "As if the whole scenario wasn't horrible enough, there was," she clears her throat and gives me a pained glance, "there was, uh, blood on the mirror."

My eyes follow hers to the mirror above the sink. Our eyes lock, but she glances away quickly.

"Blood on the mirror? What, splashes of blood?"

"No...not splashes. There were letters. Three letters, written in blood."

"Was there blood on Polly's fingers?"

"Only on one. On the tip of her index finger. She'd been trying to spell out something but only got the first three letters done."

"What were they?"

"M, o, n," she breathes.

"Do those letters have any significance to you or Polly?"

"I've been thinking about this a lot and, well, I suppose

that they could be the first three letters of Dana's brother's name. He's called Montgomery. Monty for short. Or..."

"Or?" I prompt.

Heather gives her head a shake. "It's silly. I'm sure it's not him she was writing about..."

"Who?"

"Mr Monroe."

"Mr Monroe. A teacher?"

"Yes. The girls – Dana and Polly – I've heard them talking about this 'young, hot P.E. teacher'. Apparently, all the girls at school fancy him."

"Oh. I see. And Monty. Are he and Polly close? Have they ever been involved?"

Heather's eyes widen at the suggestion. "Oh no. No, I don't think so. I'm pretty sure Monty's gay."

"Oh really? What makes you say that?"

"His mum, Carol, thinks he is."

"Ah," I pause, trying to gather my thoughts, "and there's no one else, no one else at all you can think of with those letters in their name who you or Polly – or even Richard - know?"

Heather shakes her head and closes the bathroom door.

"Thank you, Heather," I say as she leads me downstairs. "This has been extremely helpful. It really has."

And I'm not lying.

As I drive away from the house, I feel exhausted but high on adrenaline. I am going to solve Polly's problems. I'm going to find out if Polly's teacher has anything to do with this. Maybe he's the person she's frightened of.

Chapter Five

Before going home, I do my weekly shop and run a few errands in town. When I get back, I pour a large glass of wine and run a bath, tipping in a generous portion of Epsom salts. At the weekend, 5 o'clock is wine o'clock. After the day I've had I deserve something to take the edge off.

On leaving Mrs George's home, I felt so ready to take on this challenge, but now doubt creeps into my mind like the devil's mistress. If I mess this up, the result could be disastrous.

An image of Polly lying in a pool of blood fills my mind. I squeeze my eyes shut, take a deep breath and dunk my head under the water. Think about James. Think about Michael. They're probably having the time of their lives.

My sons' smiling faces bring a small smile to my own, and tension seeps out of my shoulders. I think about seeing Michael at Christmas and a frisson of excitement and warmth melts away a little of the day's horror. An urge to ring Michael grips me but I tell myself no. It's Saturday. He'll be having a few beers with his friends in preparation for one of his big nights out. No. I'll call him tomorrow, like normal. Sunday at 7 pm; one of my weekly highlights.

My smile dies on my lips as a rough male voice penetrates the walls. The voice is coming from outside my house. The man is ranting and raving, screaming, "Come out WHORE! Show yourself BITCH!"

Every muscle in my body clenches. I tell myself he's not directing his vile language at me, but he shouts, "ENGLAND, YOU BITCH! SHOW YOURSELF!"

I get out of the bath and hastily towel-dry before whipping on leggings and a baggy jumper. Did I lock the front door? Who is this man? What have I done to him? Is he a client I didn't manage to help?

My heart races as I jog downstairs and rummage in my handbag for my phone, but it's not there. Fists hammer on the front door. I grab my keys off the kitchen counter, run to the door and lock it. With a sigh, I stumble backwards as he screams more obscenities.

"OPEN THE DOOR BITCH!"

The front door's locked. I should be safe, unless he decides to smash a window. I dash along the hallway into the living room. The curtains are closed. I drew them when I got in. The man continues to pound on the front door. He carries on screaming, his voice loud but growing hoarse. I try to work out if he sounds drunk. He pronounces each word clearly, though his voice betrays a northern accent. Sheffield, I think. I'm familiar with the accent from studying at Sheffield University. Of course, he won't be adding the endearment 'duck' to the end of his sentences like the university librarian always used to. I rack my brain trying to recall anyone I may have upset back when I was at uni. I come up empty-handed. It also seems highly unlikely that this man is from that time in my life, given that I completed my BA twelve years ago, and is it my imagination or does he sound too young to have studied when I did?

The knocking stops. My heart bangs and I listen, straining my ears, eyes on the living room curtains. The windows are double-glazed. Not that easy to smash. I wait another moment then gasp – the back door.

I race out of the living room, up the hallway, through the kitchen and into the utility room. I grab the back-door handle and sigh with relief. Locked like always.

The hammering begins again at the front of the house. I hurry into the kitchen and search for my phone. The surfaces are empty. Where on earth have I put it?

"WHORE! BITCH! LYING SLUT!"

For the life of me, I can't remember where I've put my

phone. The hammering stops for a beat then commences again only this time it's louder, more aggressive. It sounds like he's kicking the door now. Even though I know the door's made of oak, I cringe at every kick. I try to conjure anger but fear has settled in my bones. Whoever he is, he's not giving up. And if he's as crazy as he sounds, he's bound to find a way to break in sooner or later. I need my phone. Where the hell is my phone?

"LET ME IN YOU FUCKING BITCH!"

I run into the hallway and stop two metres from the front door. Taking a deep breath, I wait for him to pause then I shout, "I've called the police! They'll be here any second!" Believe me. Please believe me.

Silence, then a different voice. A voice I recognise; my elderly neighbour Charlie Jenkins – a sweet, eighty-year-old ex-marine on his last legs. From the sound of it, Charlie's trying to reason with the brute outside. Oh God, please don't let this crazed man hurt Charlie. I hesitate, take a couple of steps forward, try to listen in, but Charlie's grumble is too low. A moment later, I hear a normal-sounding knock on the front door.

"It's me, love. He's gone." Charlie's voice has never sounded so sweet.

With shaky hands, I unlock the door and usher him inside, darting fearful looks into the darkening street behind him.

"You okay, love?" Charlie says, placing a gnarled hand on my shoulder.

"Yeah, just, that was so strange. I don't even know who he was. I don't have a clue what I've done to make that man act like that. I was terrified he was going to break in. Thank you so much."

Charlie winks. "One look at my ugly mug and he scarpered."

"Did he say anything to you? What did he look like?"

"Nice-looking lad, truth be told. Could smell the beer

on his breath."

"Lad? How old was he?"

The old man tips his head to the side. "I'd say no younger 'n twenty, no older 'n twenty-five. Skinny one too."

"Did he say anything when you confronted him?"

Charlie shakes his head and pats my shoulder again. "No, love. And listen, he won't be back, I can tell you that for sure. Know why?"

I shake my head, glad to feel myself starting to calm down.

"Told him I'm an ex-marine with three sons who are current marines and if he dares comes back again my sons'll hunt him down and rip him a new piece."

A laugh bursts out of me at Charlie's brazen lie and I throw my arms around his small, blocky frame. "Thank you. That makes me feel a hell of a lot better."

"You should have seen the look on the lad's face!" Charlie chortles.

"I wish I had," I say. "Hey, you didn't manage to take a picture of him by any chance?"

Charlie grimaces. 'Sorry, love, no. Silly of me, really. Left my phone inside."

I internalise a groan and say, too brightly, "No worries. I'm sure you've scared him off for good, whoever the hell he is. Fancy staying for a cup of tea?"

I find myself hoping he'll say yes. I don't fancy being alone after what just happened.

"Sorry, love. I'd be dead keen to but I'm entertaining right now. Got an old mate next door waiting for his sausage and mash."

I smile and thank him again then lead him to the front door. After he leaves, I lock it then go into the living room and collapse on the sofa, trying to work out who that man was, but unable to come up with a likely suspect.

My yellow raincoat catches my eye. It's draped over the top of the sofa still damp with rain. With an eye roll, I remember where my phone is: in my coat pocket.

Chapter Six

Diary,

If I didn't have you to confide in about my fears, I think I'd go crazy. As it is I'm worried I'm dangerously close to losing my mind altogether. Today, when Polly's therapist was asking about Richard hitting me, I felt like picking up my porcelain eagle and clubbing her over the head with it. There was something in that woman's eyes and voice, a knowing look that told me she knew what I didn't and in that terrible moment, I got this urge. The need was fleeting, but...it scared me. It also reminded me of my old self, the one I need to leave behind. It reminded me of Polly too.

I hate thinking this way about her, but I need to be honest. I love her to bits but sometimes. Oh God. Sometimes she makes me nervous. There's this look in her eyes that's so alien. This wild, faraway expression. I didn't tell Doctor England this, but she had that look when I found her, after she'd – you know. She hadn't passed out, though she looked to be about to. But when I went in the room and found her there on the floor, she looked up at me with this strange smile. At the same time her cheeks were as white as my porcelains and tears stained her perfect skin. Then she said something I didn't quite catch. I've been going over and over it in my mind trying to work out what she said. It sounded a bit like 'otter' which makes absolutely no sense at all. She said it several times, her voice growing weaker and weaker, and I grabbed the hand towel and wrapped it round her little wrist. She didn't move, just stared at me with those wild eyes. Eyes I barely recognised. Even her irises seemed a different colour. Paler. It must have been all the white of the room. In that moment I hated the whiteness of that room. All that blood seemed magnified by those horrible white walls. All that blood. And the blood on the mirror. I wanted to throw bleach all over the walls and scrub it away. And the letters. Oh God. It was like a nightmare made real.

Sometimes I wonder if it's all my fault. But I thought I was protecting her by burying the truth. I really did. Part of me still thinks I did the right thing, but that part seems to be fading, because when I look at Polly, I know she's changed and she's still changing, transforming from a caterpillar to a uniquely strange butterfly – one with asymmetrical wings – and I find myself wondering – fearing – what's going to become of her. Maybe if I'd told the truth all those years ago she'd be a happy, normal teenager now. I don't know. And then I tell myself all teenagers change, but Polly's different to other teenagers. I want to believe it's because she's special. She's so beautiful, and practically a genius after all – I still can't wrap my head around the fact that her IQ puts her in the top 1% of the population – but...there's just something...I can't find the right word for it. It's on my tongue. I know the word, I just can't bring myself to write it down. It's like a betrayal to think that about her. And then there's how I think about myself, and what I know but keep hidden, and I wonder if I'm distorting reality, deluding myself to find some semblance of peace. But peace will never come because this constant, gnawing grief will never go away. Benjamin isn't coming back. My only hope is that I can make Polly – the healthy Polly – stay.

Sometimes, all this thinking makes me feel so tired I just want to get in bed and stay there forever. But I can't do that. Not when she needs me. And she does need me.

At least one thing's for sure: I've done the right thing by sending her to see Doctor England. In fact, Polly wanted to see her. She chose her. I wonder what made her choose this therapist. Is it because Doctor England's a woman and attractive? She can't be more than forty and she looks good – great – a million times better than I've ever looked. But I shouldn't be so shallow. I'm sure the woman knows what she's doing, and she really seems to care already. Also, the fact that Polly chose this woman has given me a tiny spark of hope. It makes me think that Polly wants to get better and be normal again. I think it's this hope that's keeping me going, because there's nothing else, and I've nothing left to give.

The thing I fear the most, of course, is that Polly will talk too much. I've taught her that honesty is the best policy, but in this instance, I can't have that.

H

Chapter Seven

"Hi darling. How're you?" It's five minutes to seven; I couldn't put off ringing him a second longer.

I'm lying on my bed in my navy cotton pyjamas, curtains drawn tight, room dim. My bedside table lamp offers a soft glow, casting black silhouettes onto the duck-egg walls. I'm usually comfortable with the shadows of my bedroom, but today they morph into strange men with sinister intentions.

"Hi Mum! Good. Lit, in fact. Guess what?"

I try to smile. This was a favourite game of mine and the boys when they were little.

"Um. Let me see. You got a first for your Shakespeare essay?"

"Ha! Nope. Two one. Three percent off a first, but never mind. Guess again."

A yawn escapes me and I smother it with my hand, holding my mobile away from my mouth. After what happened last night, I barely slept a wink.

Michael's excited voice interrupts my thoughts. "Guess again!"

"Um. I know. You got into the first rugby team?"

"Nope. I wish. One more try."

I rack my brain, but nothing comes to my mind; nothing will come, not when thoughts of last night continue to drift in and out of my consciousness like dark spirits.

"Sorry, darling. I'm absolutely stumped." I laugh then wince at the emptiness of the sound. I've already decided not to mention last night's incident to the boys. Knowing Michael, he'd rush back from Sheffield to see me, make sure I'm okay, and I can't do that to him, not after what I put them both through before…no, I need to look after myself. I can't rely on my boys. I can't rely on anyone but myself.

Michael laughs and blurts, "I've met someone. A girl."

I laugh and it feels more genuine. "Not a boy then?"

"Ha ha. She's proper lit. Studies in Nottingham. Maths. Uber-brainy. Uber-lush."

"What's her name?" I say, trying to sound excited but feeling my heart sink a little; will this mean he won't come home for Christmas – will he be going to her parents'?

"Kiera Jones. She's eighteen too, and funny and cool."

"Kiera. That's a pretty name. How did you meet? And when?"

"It was only two weekends ago. She was visiting a friend in Sheffield and we bumped – literally – into each other in a pub. I'd gone for lunch with the guys. I wasn't too far gone luckily – it was only two in the afternoon - so I went for it and we chatted for the whole afternoon and she gave me her number. We've been texting each other nonstop for the last two weeks and then yesterday we met up again for lunch. You'll love her, Mum. She's so lit."

"Lit. I gather that," I chirp, aiming for enthusiastic. "I'm so excited for you, darling. When can I meet this 'lush' girl?"

"Not for a while yet, Mum. That would be weird. But I'll keep you updated."

"Have you arranged to see each other again?"

"Yep. Next Saturday, same time, same place."

"So you're not going to Nottingham to see her?"

"I offered, but she said she'd rather come to me. Said she'd tie it in with seeing her friend – her friend's just had a baby and she's got post-natal depression so Kiera's trying to support her as much as possible."

"That's very kind of her."

"I know. That's what she's like. Seriously, Mum, you'd love her."

"Hopefully I'll meet her one day." I pause, think about suggesting he bring her for Christmas if they're still together then.

"Anyway, how's work?" Michael says, and I can sense he's not particularly interested, but he's trying, and I love him for it.

"It's fine. Light on clients at the moment but took on a new one this week. Interesting case. Something I've never dealt with before."

"Cool. And your love life? Decided to give it a go yet?"

I roll my eyes. "No. I'm happy being on my own, thank you, Mr Matchmaker."

Michael laughs and the sound warms me. I decide to end the call, knowing he's got far more fun things to do than talk to his boring old mum, but just before I hang up, Michael surprises me by saying, "Mum, what do you want for Christmas?"

"You. All I want is you."

"Mum! So cheesy. Seriously, what do you want?"

I sigh inwardly. My first answer was the real one. An idea pops into my head. "A manicure. That would be perfect."

It's been so long since I've had one. Memories of when I used to regularly get them flit across my mind, reminding me of other, less savoury things I was doing around that time.

Chapter Eight

Ten Years Ago

Claire was his girlfriend and he loved her. She was funny and she let him eat her sweets. Claire told him a big secret in the playground at morning play. She whispered it in his ear and he giggled because her hair tickled his face.

She told him not to tell anybody, not his mum, not his dad, not even his sister. But Polly was watching them and when Claire ran off to play on the swings, Polly walked over. She was wearing her not-nice face and she made him tell her the big secret. Benjamin thought that Polly would like the secret and want to help him, but she laughed at him. She said it was a load of baloney. He didn't know what that word meant but he didn't think it was very nice. Like Polly. Polly wasn't very nice. She pretended to be nice but she wasn't, not really. Sometimes she would play with him and he would start to think she was a nice sister and he would try to tell her he loved her, then she would turn all funny and say not-nice things. He always told Mummy and Daddy. They would tell Polly off and she would cry and everything would be okay again for a bit. Then she would do it again. He didn't know why she was like that. He just wanted them to play together nicely. It made him feel sad and when she laughed about Claire's secret, he felt really bad. But being sad wasn't going to stop him from doing what Claire said he needed to do if he wanted to see the big secret. Which he really did.

That was why he was lying in bed wide awake, waiting for Mummy and Daddy to go to bed. He could hear the television through the floor and he could hear Polly breathing. She slept on the top bunk.

Downstairs went quiet. Mummy and Daddy had turned the television off. They were going to bed!

Benjamin lay as still as he could and listened to Mummy and Daddy's footsteps coming up the stairs. He almost giggled – they sounded like big, fat elephants.

The light outside his bedroom flicked on and he heard Mummy laugh her tinkly laugh. His door was not closed properly. A thin line of light ran into the room across the carpet toward his bed. He held his breath. His tummy felt like it was full of flutterbies.

In the gloom, Benjamin smiled when he heard the toilet flush. Not long now and he would get to see the big secret. He didn't care if Polly thought it was silly. Claire thought it was cool and Claire was his bestest friend in the whole wide world.

Chapter Nine

I'm in the office at 8.45am, regular as clockwork, despite the fact that my first and only appointment of the day isn't until mid-afternoon. But there's no spring in my step today at all. I barely slept. Unable to get the savage young man's words out of my head, I replayed them over and over throughout the night like some kind of masochist. His voice was a stuck record that scratched mercilessly at my skull all night long. Nothing would make him disappear; even conjuring up Michael's and James' smiling faces wouldn't work. I woke with a blinding headache and grainy eyes. And this morning, no amount of under-eye concealer could hide my shadows.

Eimear Blithe, my secretary, is already in reception typing away behind her desk with her ridiculously long nails, looking as fresh as a daisy. She pauses and grins at me over her laptop. She's wearing a bright pink blazer over a low-cut top which flaunts her cleavage. A black velvet choker digs into her fleshy neck. White musk perfume fills the air – a scent I've grown to love over the four years Eimear's worked for me.

Her Irish lilt calms me as she says, "Mornin' me dear. How's Mikey?"

Eimear may be only five years younger than me at thirty-three, but she seems permanently chirpy, not dragged down by the responsibility of being a single mum of two feisty girls, Pippa, six, and Rosie, eight. I often wonder how she does it. I usually conclude that it's because she's not haunted by her past like I am.

I force a smile. "He's fine. Great actually. He's met someone. Seems smitten already."

"For real? Wow, that's fab news. Ain't that somethin'?"

It's something all right. If Michael doesn't come home for Christmas, I don't know what I'll do.

"Yeah, it's great," I say, feigning enthusiasm. I ought to be happier for my youngest son but something's niggling away at me; it feels selfish and anxious. Close to fear.

"'Bout time you followed suit, wouldn't you say?" Eimear says, swivelling her laptop around to face me.

I raise an eyebrow. "What the hell is that? Oh no – no you didn't! Eimear, you…"

She holds her hands up in defence, making the bangles on her wrists jangle. "Hey, wait! Hear me out! Look, I've only set you up a basic profile and you don't have to talk to anyone you don't want to and the best 'ting is you won't get any messages from creeps 'cos I've ticked the 'Only interested in a relationship' 'tingy – so you ain't going to get some arse of a loser messaging you a pic of his teeny tiny ding-a-ling, okay?"

I fix a cross expression on my face but her use of the word 'ding-a-ling' combined with her ridiculous 'I surrender' pose makes it impossible to hold. I roll my eyes. Smile. "You're a nutter, you know that don't you?"

"Promise me you'll give it a try? Just for a week and if you don't like it, you can cancel your membership and what've you lost? Nothin'."

"Maybe."

She hands me a pink post-it note. "I've written your username and password down for you."

"Thanks," I mutter, "I'll think about it, but I'm not making any promises."

Eimear grins and swivels her laptop back around. "Fancy a cuppa?"

"No, I'm good thanks."

I escape into my office, and my haven of books, sensible, solid furniture and much-needed peace and quiet. The need to be alone with my thoughts is all-encompassing. For a few moments I hover beside my bonsai tree and think of Michael. I sit at my desk and check my emails, try to concentrate, but now that I'm back in this room, it's hard not to think about Polly and her mother.

The room feels stuffy so I open a window and breathe in the cool city air. As I gaze unseeingly at the concrete playground below, my thoughts turn to my conversation with Heather George and I replay her words in my head. And her lie. The more I think about it, about her expression, her tone of voice, the way she glanced down when she spoke, the more I realise that her husband was worse than she made out. How much worse is hard to tell, but there's no denying Heather George looks like a beaten woman. A person who's had the fight knocked out of her. From my experience of treating abused women, I've learnt they have a tendency to blame themselves. They take the blame away from their husbands and absorb it like a sponge, and all too soon this sponge becomes drenched, sodden, too full for any human mind to bear. Rational thought abandons people like this. They lose self-esteem and begin to believe that everyone hates them – everyone but him, the one, ironically, who is to blame for making them feel like this in the first place. But it's worse than that. These victims begin to hate themselves as well. They lose the will to fight and turn inward. But this doesn't mean they stop loving their children. And Heather George's love for her daughter shone through in her need for my help. Though the poor woman barely met my gaze, she got her message through to me loud, clear and urgent. Please help my daughter. Please save her. She's all I care about in the whole world. A sentiment I can certainly relate to. Michael and James are my everything.

The more I think about it, the more relieved I am that Richard George is out of the picture. It must have taken Heather great strength not to try to track him down. In her distorted mind, she still believes he loves her. Still thinks she loves him. But her focus has shifted onto Polly and rightly so. Polly needs her right now, more than she probably realises. She needs me too.

The poor woman snapped when I asked about Polly and her father's relationship; was this because I hit too close to the truth? Has Polly's father hurt her too? Did he have anything to do with her twin brother's disappearance ten years ago? The girl's behaviour was slightly strange. It didn't fit with the typical behaviour of a depressed young woman who has recently tried to take her life. Perusing my shelves and showing interest in my sons was unexpected. And then there's that scar on her neck. Could she be hiding a history of paternal abuse? Is this her dark secret? But she said 'they'…could she be referring to her mother and father? Maybe the answer lies somewhere else entirely. Is she being groomed? On the mirror, she wrote MON in her own blood. Is this Mark Monroe teacher involved somehow? I told myself I was going to investigate that man, so I need to do it. But the sensation of being defeated by uncertainties drags me down. I need to be proactive and act fast before fear of failure prevents me from taking any action at all.

Turning away from the window, I stare at my neat, organised desk. My thoughts slowly de-frazzle.

Polly needs my help. Heather needs my help. Stop being a waste of space and do something.

Maybe it's my early morning coffee kicking in or a surge of adrenaline kick-started by picturing Polly taking a pair of razor-sharp nail scissors to her delicate wrist, but I feel a burst of energy and determination.

My feet start to move. I know I shouldn't do this but can't help myself. The need to investigate him is too strong. My bottom finds my chair and my fingers tap my keyboard and I open Google and begin to search. Mr Monroe. P.E. teacher at Kingston Secondary School. M. O. N.

It doesn't take long to find out about the man. His online presence is pretty transparent and, to my disappointment, he seems extremely normal. He's definitely a looker, but isn't as young as I'd expected, at twenty-eight years old. I'd been expecting him to be fresh out of university, all bright-eyed and bushy-tailed, but in his picture he looks his age, perhaps a little wizened around the eyes, the gangly leanness of youth gone, the muscles in his shoulders and arms large and defined, indicative of a rugby player or someone who works out. His skin is a dark caramel colour, suggesting mixed race, and his dark hair and lashes make his pale green eyes look quite mesmerising.

Could this be the man in the mirror, so to speak?

I can see why the girls at Polly's school fancy Mark Monroe. Even I feel a small pull of attraction, which is ridiculous given I'm a decade older than him.

I close my laptop knowing what I need to do. I don't have to be back in the office until two o'clock. I have plenty of time.

As I mumble a lie to Eimear about where I'm going, I try – and fail - to ignore the rapid beat of anxiety pulsing in my chest. I'm going beyond my professional boundaries and risking my career, but if I'm going to help Polly fast, I need to know the truth.

Chapter Ten

There's a thrill of adrenaline rippling around my body that I recognise from before. I know I ought to hate this feeling because with it comes hot, sweaty guilt, but there's something in this surge of adrenaline that makes me feel more alive than I've felt for a long time. Even my skin feels different. Hot and tingly. My breaths come short and fast. My palms sweat. I know worry ought to make me change my mind, but it doesn't and I don't.

I get out of my car, yank on my jacket and stare at the building, lies circulating my mind like rabid dogs chasing their tails. These lies have been building since before I left the office. And, horrid though it is to admit, I'm good at lying. I always have been.

The school is an ugly, concrete block with nothing going for it. Even the sign wedged into a small patch of grass just beyond the front doors looks old and battered, the school's name chipped and scratched, the red logo faded and resembling more of a squashed tomato than anything of significance.

My hair whips into my eyes and the wind whooshes at my ears. It's a cold, biting wind. More January than November. Winter's come early this year. I shove my hair behind my ears, take a deep, steadying breath, and walk toward the school entrance. My jacket flaps around me and the frosty air nips at my face and fingers, so it's a relief to step inside the heated reception area where I'm immediately hit by the smell of school; of plastic and play dough, pencils, sweaty plimsolls, gymnasiums and school dinners. It takes me back to fun times when before Mum fell ill. Before I got pregnant with James at seventeen. Before I got married. Before I finally went to university and discovered freedom. Before I made the greatest mistake of my life.

I walk over to the reception window and wait for a plump, grey-haired lady with zany glasses to finish her phone call. Her voice is high and fast as a finch's morning chatter, and drills into my taut nerves. She finishes her call and turns, giving me a warm smile.

"And how may I help you today?"

My stomach clenches. Lies echo around my mind like voices in a cave. I may be good at lying but that doesn't mean I like it. "I'm thinking about sending my daughter here. I've a tour of the school booked for nine o'clock."

The receptionist frowns, clearly puzzled. "Really? We usually do our tours on Thursdays and Fridays."

I raise my eyebrows. Shit. "Oh really? Oh, well, er -"

She holds up her hand and laughs. "No worries, dear. Let me check the book. We've a new girl back here. Only started a few weeks ago. I expect she's the one who booked you in."

She waddles to a shelf at the back of the room, picks up a red A4 book and flicks through. I hold my breath, knowing she won't find a booking in there, preparing for my next lie.

The woman frowns again, tuts and shakes her head. "Oh dear. Looks like she's forgotten to write you in. Never mind. I'm sure I can get one of the older students to take you round. Can't have you trekking all the way here then being sent away, can we?"

I smile, "That would be brilliant. Thank you so much."

She scribbles something in the book then asks my name and car reg. I have a name prepared. First name same, second name my mother's maiden. "Jessie Hartley."

The woman writes down my details, snaps the book shut and picks up the phone. I zone out as she twitters away, happily arranging for a student to come down to reception to give me a tour.

I turn my back on the receptionist and take in my

surroundings. Inside, the building is more modern and far less drab. The walls are painted a warm cream shade and an array of students' artwork is showcased in glass cabinets. I'm drawn to a Picasso-esque face painted in various shades of blue, green and grey. There's a deep sadness in the portrait's distorted eyes. Glancing down at the name below, I start: Polly George. What are the chances? I bark out a laugh.

"Amazing, isn't it?" a pleasant young voice says.

I turn and see a tall, angular girl dressed smartly in a black skirt and blazer. She must be a sixth-former. Her face is blitzed with freckles and frizzy orange hair fires out in all directions around her thin face like a lion's mane. She holds out her hand and I shake it. Hers is cold while mine is hot and still, embarrassingly, a little on the sweaty side.

"I'm Georgia. I'll be your tour guide this morning. Follow me."

Out of politeness and the need to keep up my pretence, I allow the girl to lead me around various parts of the school. Again, I'm impressed by how modern everything looks. I nearly sent James and Michael to this school, but at the time St Peter's Secondary had an outstanding Ofsted report while Kingston had a good report. I didn't bother to visit the schools. Perhaps I should have, but James started at secondary school ten years ago and I wasn't in a good state of mind at that point. It was my own doing of course, but luckily both James and Michael enjoyed St Peter's.

We visit the art block, science labs and the library before my patience begins to wear thin and I blurt out another lie.

"My daughter's really into sport. Could I see the gymnasium and the sports' fields?"

"Yeah, of course. That's cool. Which sports is she into?"

"Hockey," I say quickly. It's the first one that jumps into my head, probably because it was my favourite sport when I was at school.

"That's good 'cos we've got a great senior hockey team. We made nationals last year."

"Wow! I'm sure my daughter will be excited to hear that."

We leave the warmth of the library and cut across a courtyard onto a walkway lined with more grey concrete buildings. My tour guide wraps her arms tightly around herself and I do the same, feeling a pinch of guilt at making the girl go outside, but knowing in my gut that I need to follow this lead. Dewy grass and wet earth scent the air.

We reach a field full of screaming girls wearing a navy and white P.E. kit. There's a hockey game going on and despite the bitterly cold wind the girls all wear short navy skirts and white T-shirts. The girls on the field look younger than Polly. Twelve years old at most. They appear to be enjoying themselves as they cry out to each other and sprint around the rough field. A chubby girl sits out on a bench holding something to her ankle, a school jumper pulled on over her kit.

I scan the field for the P.E. teacher and spot a tall woman standing over the other side of the field with a whistle dangling from her lips.

Georgia smiles at me and we walk on.

"I think the boys are playing rugby in the other field," she says.

I follow her, struggling a little to keep up with her long, quick strides. She's almost a head taller than me. Must be verging on six foot while I'm five foot five, which is quite a nice height for a woman, I've always felt. Not that I'm in the business of caring much about that anymore.

Wishing I'd worn an extra layer, I shove my hands into my pockets and up my pace as we pass a red brick building that Georgia identifies as the new changing rooms, the fresh paint thick and cloying. The sound of young men's voices greets my ears before we reach the playing field. I look up and scan the area. This pack of youths are doing drills, dodging around brightly coloured cones on their tiptoes and doing short sprints. These boys are older than the girls playing hockey, more like sixteen or seventeen years old, their voices gruff as they hurl banter at each other through the crisp air.

I quickly spot the man I'm looking for. Bingo. M.O.N. Could it be?

Mark Monroe stands on the same side of the field as me and Georgia, only about ten feet away. Despite the cold, he wears only navy tracksuit bottoms and a navy hoody, no jacket or gloves. For the most part he remains a quiet observer barking out the occasional order to the boys in a clear, deep voice.

"Is he their coach?" I say, nodding in Mark Monroe's direction.

Georgia nods. "Yeah. That's Mr Monroe. He's quite new here. Only started last September."

"Is he good? A good teacher, I mean?"

"Yeah. Everyone loves him."

I watch the girl carefully when she says this, but can detect nothing but admiration.

"He's quite young for a teacher," I say, desperate to eek information out of the girl.

Georgia shrugs.

I hesitate, question whether I should say what's hovering on my tongue. What the hell? I'll never have to see this girl again.

"He's very good-looking," I say, giving the girl a grin.

She laughs, taking me by surprise. "Everyone fancies Mr Monroe. Even some of the teachers!"

I join in with her laughter and try to think of something else to say that might elicit more gossip, but I can't think of anything else. A gust of wind whips my hair in front of my eyes. I swipe it away and look up, shocked to see the man in question striding towards us.

"Morning ladies. What brings you out here on this lovely sunny day?" he says with a wide grin, eyes shining.

"I'm giving, um, the lady a tour," says Georgia. A sideways glance at the girl tells me what I thought I heard in her voice; she's blushing. A lot.

"I'm thinking about sending my daughter here," I say.

"Well, I can safely say Kingston's a great school full of great teachers. Especially the P.E. staff. Not that I'm in any way biased."

His voice and smile are all charm and I wonder for a fleeting second if he's trying to flirt with me, because his eyes are lingering on mine, scanning my face. And is it my imagination or did he just look at my lips?

No. You're reading too much into it, just because you want to think he's dodgy.

I clear my throat, a little uncomfortable with the directness of his gaze yet attracted by the strange green shade of his eyes.

"I expect you've got to get back…"

Monroe chuckles. "Nah. Leave them to it for a while. They're practically adults anyway. To be honest, they know what they're doing. I just stand at the sidelines and try to seem important." He glances at Georgia. "Hey, Georgia, why don't you go back inside, let me finish up the tour? You look bloody freezing."

Georgia smiles with relief and rubs her pink nose. "Thanks, Mr Monroe. It was nice to meet you, er…"

"Jessie," I say, surprised to hear the teacher say 'bloody' in front of a student – or me for that matter, given that I'm a 'prospective parent'.

The girl smiles more broadly then rushes away leaving the two of us alone beside the sport's field. The wind swishes my hair across my face, and I hold it back with one hand and look up at Monroe. I can smell his aftershave. It's a nice smell, one I don't recognise, but he seems to be wearing an awful lot given he's just a teacher with no-one to impress. Of course, there could be a female teacher he's interested in. Maybe he's involved with a colleague.

He interrupts my thoughts by asking what sports my daughter likes.

"Hockey," I lie. "What other sports do the girls play here?"

"Everything really. We even have a girls' football team. Seniors only. I coach that one. Got some fantastic players. How old's your daughter?"

"Fifteen."

"Really? You don't look old enough to have a fifteen-year-old."

I smile, unsure whether to acknowledge the compliment, but he breezes on, "So, she's fifteen - that'd be perfect then. Has she played football before?"

"A little," I say, beginning to worry about the lies I'm weaving.

He smiles and steps a little closer. He's really a very attractive human being. He's hot on eye contact too. I can feel myself blushing.

"I'd better get going," I blurt.

"But I said I'd finish your tour, and it's nearly break time. The boys will be going in to change in a couple of minutes, so I'll be free to take you round."

"No. Really. Thanks, but I've got a patient to see."

"Oh, are you a doctor?"

The truth slips out before I can stop it. "Yes. A psychiatrist."

"Wow. Can I have a card? I've got a friend who's thinking about seeing a therapist."

Caught by surprise, I find myself digging into my handbag and pulling out a rather crumpled business card. I hand it to him and our fingertips brush. To my dismay, my tummy flutters at the contact.

"Thanks, Jessie," he says, waving the card and slipping it into his pocket.

"Thank you for taking the time to talk to me," I say backing away.

"The pleasure's all mine. Really."

I hurry away, telling myself to grow up. As I rush along the path, I'm sure he's still watching me.

Mark Monroe didn't seem like a predator, but could he be hiding behind that charming smile and those undeniable good looks?

Maybe M.O.N doesn't stand for anything at all. Maybe I'm wasting my time following this supposed lead. Maybe I ought to focus on what I'm trained to do and get back in my office.

As I exit the car park I glance in my rear-view mirror, surprised to see Mark Monroe standing outside the school watching me leave with his arms crossed over his muscular chest.

Chapter Eleven

"Night night darling ones," Mummy whispered.

Benjamin opened his mouth to say 'night night' back then he remembered he was pretending to be asleep. He kept his mouth closed and listened as Mummy walked away. He heard her open the big bedroom door. She closed it. He listened to her climb into bed. The bed made a squeaky sound like it did when Daddy got in.

Daddy was snoring. It was funny. Benjamin had never heard Daddy snore before. It sounded like a pig snorting. Benjamin giggled then put his hand over his mouth. He had to be as quiet as a mouse. If Polly woke up, she would tell on him and he wouldn't be able to see the big secret.

His tummy fizz-popped and he grinned and began to count. He couldn't do anything until Mummy was fast asleep. He could only count to twenty-five, so he started counting. When he got to twenty-five, he started again. He counted three more times then pretended to be a dog. Dogs had really good ears. They could hear much better than people could. Benjamin knew this because Mummy had told him. Mummy said they were going to get a puppy soon. Benjamin was so excited about getting a puppy. So was Polly. But Polly wanted a girl puppy called Rose and Benjamin wanted a boy puppy called Zack. Mummy said they could do Ip Dip Sky Blue if there was a boy and girl puppy at the puppy place. Benjamin hoped it would land on him and they could get a boy puppy. A boy puppy called Zack with soft, brown hair and a waggy tail and really good ears.

Benjamin imagined he was Zack the puppy. He made his ears go up like a puppy's ears and he listened very carefully. Daddy was still snoring, but Mummy was quiet.

Benjamin counted one more time. He listened and listened, and Daddy snored and Mummy did nothing. Pleased they were both asleep, Benjamin peeled back his duvet and swung his legs round.

His heart banged hard. Lots more flutterbies whizzed around in his tummy. He knew he shouldn't be doing what he was doing, but Claire said this was the only way he would get to see the big secret. Seeing the big secret was almost as exciting as getting a puppy called Zack.

Chapter Twelve

The week possesses the pace of a slug, leaving its slime trail all over me in the form of a nasty head cold. Part of the week's sluggishness is down to anticipation. Since abandoning my less traditional methods and attempting to go rogue, sitting in my office seeing clients has made time slow down. Boredom writhes inside me like a needling maggot, and my desire to see Polly George again niggles and gnaws.

I've just got in from work. One more night's sleep before I can sate this odd curiosity that's got me in its grips. One more sleep before I can help her.

I blow my nose and consider my face in the mirror. I look a state. My nose is dry and red, and shadows ring my eyes. Despite washing my hair this morning, it's frizz-bombed, turning as dull as a muddy puddle – like the many that drench the roads outside.

Rain slashes my bedroom windows and the wind whirls around tempest-like. The forecast says Hurricane Alice is on her way. Flooding has already affected the Somerset Levels.

I change out of my work clothes, relieved to take off my bra and get into slouchy loungewear. A bath would make me feel better, but I can't be bothered to run one. Gone are the days when my husband got in from work, sensed my exhaustion and ran me a lovely hot bath. Gone too are the days of bedtime cuddles and silly nicknames.

I feel my thoughts taking me downward to a dark, forbidden place so I think about tomorrow and seeing Polly. Our second session. I'm excited, there's no denying this, but I'm also affected by a sense of foreboding. *What if you can't help her?*

I roll my eyes at my self-doubt and remind myself I've got twelve years of psychiatric practice under my belt. I've set up my own business, which has brought in enough profit to enable me to recruit Eimear and pay her a decent wage for the last four years. I might not earn much but it's enough to cover the bills and help James and Michael every now and then.

I leave my bedroom and go downstairs. Popping a microwave meal in, I turn to see my laptop on the dining room table, and Eimear's voice pops into my head telling me to go on the dating website. Give it a go. What have you got to lose?

I stand barefoot in the kitchen and stare at the silver machine allowing my imagination to roam. An image of a tiny erect penis enters my mind and I surprise myself by barking out a laugh. I can see Eimear's smiling face, picture how happy she'd be if I told her I'd at least given it a shot. I've nothing else to do to make the evening pass other than work myself into a state about my session with Polly, so, after pouring a naughty glass of Merlot – telling myself I need it to get me through this new experience - I sit down at the dining table and open my laptop. The post-it note with my username and login are in my bag, so I retrieve it from the front door then settle down and type my details into the website.

I quickly become immersed in filling in the details of the profile Eimear has left untouched like my hobbies and interests, in which I put reading and shopping, adding cooking and yoga as an afterthought to make myself sound slightly less boring. I used to love cooking and yoga, so it's not a complete lie. Then it comes to filling in a large box with a description about me, and I sit back and frown. When it was filling in facts I could cope, but now I'm stuck.

My chest tightens and I realise I don't want to do this anymore. Anything I write about myself will sound false because I'll leave out the truth. I'll have to sound bubbly and energetic and full of life, and that's just not me. Not anymore. A wave of sadness washes over me.

The microwave beeps. My mouth finds my glass and I drain the contents then go to the kitchen to get a refill and my cottage pie for one. I never drink during the week, but tonight is an exception. Tonight, I need a little something to steady my nerves and help me sleep. I return to the dining room table and close my laptop. If Eimear asks, I'll tell her I forgot all about it.

I trudge into the living room with my meal and wine and sit on the squishy leather three-seater with my leg tucked up under me and a cushion on my lap. I balance my plate on the cushion with one hand and take a slurp of merlot with the other, feeling tension evaporate as a delicious airiness floats behind my eyes. Wondering what to watch, I place my glass on the coffee table and pick up the remote control, and that's when I see it.

My heart jolts and cold sweat breaks out under my arms. I jerk forward sending my dinner crashing to the carpet. Wine slops onto my lap. Time seems suspended as I force my eyes to focus on the coffee table. My gaze darts to the wall. My father's butterfly cases are gone.

I question for a second whether what I'm seeing is real or imagined, and for another second I'm unable to believe my eyes until I reach out and touch the wooden surface of the table and feel the scores beneath my fingers. Scores that have been scraped into the wood by something very sharp. I pick up the torn pieces of butterfly wings, their fragile texture like paper-thin velvet. My heart pangs as I recall how much my father admired their intricate beauty. I look down and beyond the table. On the carpet lie the remains of the shattered glass cases. Someone has pulled every frame off the wall, stamped on it, ripped out the butterflies, torn them to pieces and scattered them over the coffee table around the vicious message that they have gouged into the wood. It is wanton destruction. Home invasion. A personal violation and a silent act of aggression designed to strike fear in my heart.

I sat in this very spot the previous night and saw nothing on the coffee table. The butterfly cases were on the wall, untouched. Since last night someone has broken into my house and done this. They had a wide window in which to do it; nine hours while I was at work, but how could they have gotten in? There are no signs – none I've noticed anyway – of a break-in, so how…unless they came in when I was here, at home, when the door was unlocked. But I always lock the door, front and back. Did I lock the front door when I got in tonight? I jump up, step over the mess on the floor and check the front door. It's locked.

I try to think. I hardly ever use the back door because the bins are round the side of the house, and I let the back garden go haywire in the winter. I haven't touched the back door since Saturday when that horrible man came screaming abuse.

A shiver passes through me, and my eyes find the message scratched into the coffee table and the shredded butterflies. Could the same man have come into my house and done this as well? It certainly carries the same sentiment. Anger. Violence. Hatred.

I grab my mobile out of my bag, eyes fixed on the destruction. The police might be able to dust for prints, find out who did this. I go through what I'll say to the operator and begin to realise it sounds silly, but before I can talk myself out of it, I dial. If I feel threatened, it ought to be a no-brainer: get the police involved.

As I describe what's happened, I can't take my eyes off the message that has been scraped into my coffee table by someone who has come into my home uninvited. Someone with serious problems. Someone I probably know, because this feels personal.

LYING BITCH DIE

Chapter Thirteen

Feeling like I'm being watched, I drag myself upstairs, yank off my jumper and pull on a bra then whip my jumper back on. I change out of my wine-splashed joggers, pulling on a pair of jeans that make me look more civilised. I'm shivering so I grab a woolly cardigan out of the wardrobe and pull that on too. I hurry back downstairs into the living room and take out my half-drunk glass of wine and the spilled plate and cutlery, retrieving a bucket which I fill with hot, soapy water, a Tesco carrier bag and a wad of kitchen roll. I yank on a pair of marigolds then dash into the living room. My breathing is fast and for some unknown reason I feel like I have to clean up the mess I've made before the police arrive. On my knees, I grab handfuls of cottage pie and dump it into the bag then scrub the carpet and stamp it dry, making the soles of my feet damp.

I thought cleaning might make me feel more normal but I'm still shaking when someone triple-knocks on the door. I jump, pull off the marigolds and quickly deposit the remains of my meal and the cleaning stuff in the kitchen before smoothing my hair behind my ears and going to the front door. With a shaky breath, I unlock the door and try to smile at the male and female officers standing on my doorstep. Both officers tower above me. I feel edgy on seeing them, despite the fact I've done nothing wrong. Mumbling hello, I invite them in then lock the door. In response the large female police officer raises a too-thin blonde eyebrow. The male officer, lanky with a large roman nose, offers me a thin-lipped smile.

"I'm Officer Firth and this is my partner, Officer Black," he says, tilting his head to the side.

"Thank you for coming. I – er – would you like a cup

of tea? Coffee?"

Both officers shake their heads. Neither say 'no thank you', which irks me. They seem cold and unfriendly, too business-like and they smell of MacDonalds. The female officer surprises me by telling me to sit down, her voice soft and kind compared to the harshness of her expression. Eased a little, I perch on the edge of the two-seater, offering them both a seat, which they decline.

"It's there. On the coffee table," I point to the table, and both lean over to inspect it.

Officer Firth withdraws a phone from his pocket and takes four pictures of the message and butterfly carnage. He pockets the phone and looks at me, his expression serious but softer.

"When did you first notice this?" he says.

Officer Black takes her phone out and begins to jot down notes as I explain what happened less than half an hour ago.

"I see," he says, tilting his head to the left, "do you have any idea who may have done this? Anyone who may feel a grievance against you, however unjustified?"

I shake my head. No one knows what I did in the past. That secret is safe so there can't be anyone from that time seeking some kind of delayed revenge. And anyway, that sounds like a movie plot, not a real-life story.

I shrug, "I'm a psychiatrist so I've dealt with challenging clients. To my knowledge, none of them harbour any resentment toward me. But," I pause, trying to find the right words, "last Saturday, a man stood outside my door screaming similar things at me to what's written on there."

Both officers' eyebrows rise.

"Tell us exactly what happened, if you would," Officer Firth says.

Again, I explain and Officer Black taps away, jotting down words I can never take back.

When I finish, the woman looks up and says, "Why didn't you report this at the time?"

I bite my lip and shrug. "I don't know. Charlie seemed to think the man was drunk and it sounded like he'd given him a good scare. I didn't want to make a fuss, especially as I didn't know what he looked like."

"But this Charlie, your elderly neighbour, he saw the young man?"

"Yes."

"All right," Officer Firth says, "I think we're finished here. We'll pay your neighbour a visit now, see if he can give us a description of the man's appearance."

They turn to leave, and I rush to unlock the door, then stand in their way. "I'm sorry, but what do you suggest I do?"

Officer Black's eyes are soft when she speaks, but her voice remains hard. "You say there were no signs of a break in?"

"None," I confirm.

"Then he must have slipped in while either your front or back door was unlocked or climbed in an open window. All we can advise is that you are extra vigilant about locking your doors and windows the moment you get in. If you still feel unsafe, you could stay with a friend or invite someone to stay over to keep you company."

I nod, too embarrassed to admit there's nobody I could stay with. Eimear lives in a small house that's just big enough for her and her daughters to squeeze into. I briefly consider asking Eimear to stay over but quickly crush that idea as thoughts of the hassle it would cause her erupt in my mind. When you have two young children you can't just up and leave at a friend's beck and call. And I don't fancy having two lively little girls haring around the place at the moment. No. I decide leaving my home or inviting someone to stay means the person who's doing this to me has won, and I won't have that.

I stand aside, thanking them for their time and holding the door open for them, wondering how much of a description they'll be able to get out of Charlie who I know has cataracts.

As soon as there're off my driveway, I close and lock the door then sink into the two-seater sofa with my head in my hands racking my memory for anyone I may have upset recently or further back. I upset my husband, but he's gone now, married to another woman over in Australia – and he's never been a volatile man. Greg's been living there for four years now. He visits the boys once a year and pays for them to visit him every year, but we never speak and as far as I know he's happy and doesn't want anything to do with me, which hurts but is what I deserve. I never had any boyfriends before Greg and fell pregnant with James when I was just seventeen, much to Mum's unconcealed horror and disappointment. At least Greg had the decency to stay with me, try to make it work, and after a time, it did work and he seemed to genuinely love me, for a while...

I look up and my eyes land on the coffee table. The words scraped into the wood, though upside down, taunt me, crawling under my skin and scraping at my nerves. The decimated butterflies make me feel sick. I grab the dustpan and brush and clear up the papery bodies and broken glass cases, empty the debris in the kitchen bin then hoover up the remaining splinters of glass. Unable to bear its presence, I grab the table, lug it upstairs and shut it in James' old room.

A moment later, sirens blast the air. They're getting closer and closer, and I tense, waiting for them to pass and quieten, but the blaring noise becomes so loud that I run downstairs to the living room and yank open the curtains, shocked to see an ambulance pulling up outside my house. A police car follows, parking outside Charlie's house. My gut clenches as two men jump down from the front of the ambulance, go around to the back of the vehicle and pull out a gurney. I watch, unable to tear my eyes away as they drag the gurney up Charlie's driveway.

Chapter Fourteen

Diary,

I remember the first time Richard left us. It wasn't long after Ben disappeared. That was the first time of many, of course.

At the time I put it down to grief, told myself he needed some alone time, some space – but when he came back, I don't think I could forgive him for leaving, not when Ben was missing, presumed dead by everyone – except me, it seemed. I said some awful things, I know that now. I did that thing where you fire out every resentment and hurtful comment you can think of. Afterwards of course, I apologised. I think I even grovelled. But he drew away from me, further and further away. And he had this look in his eye I'd never seen before. I'll never forget it. It was a glare of pure hatred. I don't know if he's ever forgiven me for the things I said. And worst of all, I know Polly heard me say them. When I stormed upstairs, she was there, perched on the top step, her eyes full of tears. Tears and something else. Something hard to name. She was only five at the time but sometimes that strange look is still in her eyes, and it makes her feel like a stranger. It also makes me feel nervous, which, don't you think, is a really odd way to feel? Especially about your own daughter. Sometimes I worry she has too much of me in her.

But I shouldn't be writing this about Polly. She's been through so much. I need to be supportive. And stronger. If I don't hold it together, what will become of my little girl?

My little girl who's no longer a little girl. Not really. Not by the sound of her diary...

I know I shouldn't have looked but it was sticking out from under her pillow when I went into her room to put away her clothes. I tried to resist, I really did, and then a thought occurred to me – her diary could give me an insight into her state of mind, which seems like a wedge of concrete to me right now. And I thought, maybe, just maybe, in that little red book, there might be something written down that she's not telling me, something I need to know. Something Doctor England needs to know. Something we both need to know so we can help her get better. More importantly, I need to know if she's told the doctor something that needs to stay hidden.

So I pulled it out from under her pillow and started to read.

I still feel consumed by guilt for looking inside. I know I shouldn't have done it. I'm not even sure it helped me understand her any more than I already do – which isn't much at all. In fact, the short snippet I read has worried me a lot. More than a lot. A ton.

I only read a page. Polly wasn't back from school yet, but I knew I didn't have long. I'd only read that one page, was about to turn over, when I heard the front door. I re-positioned the diary exactly where it'd been and left her clothes folded on the bed then dashed into my bedroom and pretended to be tidying up. I felt bad, really bad. Still do. I never thought I'd be one of those mothers who reads their own child's diary. Then again, I never thought I'd be such a useless mother, did I?

Anyway, enough about me – I need to write about what I read in that book. Try to make sense of it, because right now the things I read are making me feel more worried and confused than enlightened, and there's no one I can talk to. No one at all. I couldn't talk to Richard about this even if he was here. No, I can just imagine his reaction and it wouldn't be good. It would be terrible. And I would suffer the consequences. That's why it's better to have him out of the way.

And so. Polly's diary.

The first thing I noticed was that her writing looked different. It wasn't neat and small like when she does her homework. It was large and spiky, really ugly, truth be told. Not my Polly's lovely work at all, which made me think that when she wrote it, she was probably feeling moody or distressed, or maybe she was rushing to get her thoughts down, like I do sometimes when I write in here. I mean, my writing isn't that neat right now, is it? And everyone's writing goes to pot a bit when they've been scribbling for ages, and the page I flicked to was the most recent thing she'd written, so she could have been writing for pages on end without a break before she got to this page. Suffice it to say, I was surprised but not overly so, given everything. Also, Polly probably types more than she writes by hand, so she must be out of practice.

After being struck by the look of her writing, I started to read, and it didn't even sound like Polly. Not the Polly I know. The words sounded...I don't know how to put it. Different, I suppose is the best word to describe it. Different and more self-assured. Surprisingly confident, veering towards cocky. And she sounded so old. Far older than her years. More like an adult than a teenager. Maybe this should make me worry less but it was what she was describing that's worried me.

Because – oh God, right, breathe. Because, she wasn't exactly describing having sex with someone, but there were hints she had, or that she was going to soon. It was hard to work out because I read so little. But she's only fifteen! She's still a child. If it wasn't for how cool and calm - how confident she sounded - I'd fear this older man was pressuring her into sex, but – and this is hard to write – but, if anything, it sounded like it was the other way around. In fact, she described him as her 'present and future conquest'. Conquest. Such a strange word to use and so un-Polly. The whole thing just sounded so wrong. So unlike her. So unnatural. Horrible.

I've thought about asking her if she's seeing someone, trying to get her to open up, to talk to me, but I know it's pointless. She's a closed book. She won't tell me anything. She even pretends she's okay when I ask her how she's feeling, even though I know she isn't. She can't be. Not after what happened. I wasn't even sure she should go back to school so quickly, but she insisted. Said she couldn't miss her lessons because of her exams. And she does seem a little more upbeat, more so than the week leading up to the incident. Maybe it's because she's met this man. Maybe I need to just steer clear of the subject, and hope and pray that he doesn't take advantage of her or get her pregnant.

I'm just so confused. I only read it last night and Polly's seeing Doctor England later today. I've got to pick her up early from school and take her there. I keep thinking about telling Doctor England about what I've read, but what would I say? None of it's clear. And is it my place to say anything? I don't know. I just don't know.

If this man's making my daughter feel more positive about life, that's a good thing – even if he is older than her. And he might not even be that much older. He might only be in the year above. Although, thinking back to what she'd written, it sounded like he wasn't at school anymore.

God. My stomach hurts just thinking about it. And writing all this down doesn't seem to help clear things up, and I have this terrible urge to go into her room this very second and read some more. Maybe that's what I should do. I need to put my mind at ease, find out what's really going on, and what she's been telling Doctor England.

H

Chapter Fifteen

My drive to work passes in a blur of worrying. Worrying about the man who screamed at my door, the message scratched into my coffee table and my father's destroyed butterflies and, more importantly, Charlie, who the police found last night unconscious at the bottom of his stairs, his leg twisted at an awkward angle, breathing laboured. Poor old Charlie. I'll visit him soon. His condition is stable, thank God.

I know I ought to be getting my thoughts in order in preparation for my second session with Polly George, but anxiety is spreading all over me like a rash. It's in my head and in my heart. I can feel the past rushing up and flooding my body with cortisol, the vile stress hormone I've fought so hard to quell over the years. Last night's message has sliced open the past with the brutality of a serial killer slicing open his still-breathing victim's skin. But I'm not a victim. Not really.

I close my eyes for a beat and think about what I did. What I can never forgive myself for. Maybe what someone else can't forgive me for either. To some, it might not seem that bad; to others, it might be terrible. Up until now, I'd remained so sure that my secret was just that: a secret. A secret held between three of us. But now I'm not so sure. No matter how hard I rack my brain, I can't think of anything else I've done that could compel someone to seek the kind of revenge they're now seeking.

So this has to be linked to my past. It just has to be.

What eludes me is who that person is. And why they've waited a full ten years to strike. Could they have only just found out that I'm the guilty party? Or have they been biding their time, watching me, waiting for the perfect opportunity to act? To strike. Because that's what this feels like. This feels like an attack – a personal attack on me. There's nothing subtle about that message. There's a clear desire screaming out: DIE. This person is out to get me. To kill me. It sounds dramatic, but it's there, in the brutalised butterflies and terrifying message, gouged in my table, scraped into the hard wood by someone with a powerful reason to hate.

There are four basic reasons people kill: love, lust, hate and money. As far as I know, nobody loves me enough, no one lusts after me – not anymore, unless I have a stalker I'm unaware of - and I don't have masses of money, so it must come down to hate. And, as far as I'm aware, I've only ever done one hateful thing. The big question is: do I deserve to die for what I did? In this person's mind, the resounding answer seems to be yes.

I gnaw my thumbnail to the quick. What consequences did my actions cause? Did I destroy someone's life? Terror clutches my heart as a thought occurs, jagged and piercing and frightening in its realness: this person may have been dwelling on what I did for a whole decade. They may have been nursing it - obsessing over it - and obsession's a very dangerous thing, especially in the wrong person's mind. It swells and multiplies like maggots on a dead body. Once the compulsion takes hold, nothing can allay it, and sane, rational thought vanishes into the ether. I ought to know. I've tussled with obsession before. In fact, some might say I'm in the throes of it right now with my mission to help Polly. It's an obsession I can't explain. All I know is that I need to save her, just as I need to save myself.

Chapter Sixteen

Benjamin was afraid of the dark. Luckily, the bedroom was not completely black because a gap in the curtains was letting in a bit of light from the street.

He slipped his feet into his teddy bear slippers then tiptoed to the door. He looked back over his shoulder to check Polly was still asleep. In the gloom, all he could make out was a lump where her body was. He smiled. She was fast asleep. He would be gone and back and his sister would never know he had left their room.

A shiver of excitement shook his little body as he reached out for the door handle. Gently, he pulled the door towards himself. It usually creaked but this time it didn't make a sound. Heart racing, he slipped out of the room and tiptoed along the landing.

There was less light out here and he didn't like it one bit. He trailed his fingers along the banister rails and inched his way forward. He hurried past Mummy and Daddy's bedroom door, suddenly sure one of them would poke their head out and tell him off for getting out of bed. But the door didn't move, and no-one came out to tell him off.

He slowed down a bit, worried he might trip and fall and make a big crashing sound that would wake everyone up.

Sticking his tongue out in concentration, he tiptoed forward. The carpet under his feet was soft and his slippers were fluffy, so his footsteps didn't make a peep.

He made it to the end of the banister and used the edge to guide his feet around toward the top of the stairs. This was the tricky part. The stairs were creaky. Sometimes they sounded like they were alive - like they were angry at being stepped on. The stairs were very dark as well. He couldn't really see the steps, so he had to be really careful, or he might fall.

Benjamin gulped and wiped his forehead with the sleeve of his pyjama top. He felt hot and shaky but excited at the same time. He grabbed the banister with his right hand and carefully lowered his foot onto the first step. Phew. No creak. Taking another breath, he lowered his other foot onto the same step. This time a tiny creak came. Benjamin's heart pounded. He tried to go down another step, but he felt too scared. He thought about how brave Harry Potter was. Mummy was reading Harry Potter to him and Polly at the weekend. He loved it. When he grew up, he wanted to be a wizard just like Harry Potter. A wizard with a dog called Zack.

Benjamin nibbled his lower lip and told himself to be like Harry Potter. Harry Potter was brave and fast and clever. Harry Potter would be able to get downstairs quickly and quietly.

Using the banister for support, he lowered his foot onto the next step. No creak. He brought his other foot down. No creak. Phew. He repeated the same routine again and again and the steps kept their mouths shut for him. He smiled and stepped down again. This time a really loud creak came. Benjamin gasped and held his breath. Eyes wide, he waited and listened. He listened and listened and listened, sure Mummy or Daddy would come. Daddy's snores carried on. He waited another twenty-five seconds then pretended to be Harry Potter again and lowered himself onto the next step - the bottom of the stairs! He almost jumped up and down, but remembered he had to be quiet.

Using the wall, he shuffled towards the coat rack. In the shadowy shadows, he felt for the fat bulge of his puffy blue coat. With slow movements, he pushed each arm into his coat and tried to zip it up, but he couldn't do it. Mummy or Daddy always zipped him up. It was a fiddly job, as Mummy said. Too fiddly for little fingers like his.

Benjamin shrugged and told himself it didn't matter. It was cold outside, but his coat was very thick and warm. It would keep him warm even if it wasn't done up properly.

Chapter Seventeen

Pulling into the car park comes as a surprise; the journey here having passed without my knowledge, and I fleetingly wonder how on earth I got to work without crashing into anyone.

After doing battle with the virulent wind, I slam my car door shut and hurry toward the white-washed building that houses my office, thinking the only way to protect myself is to try to find out who my attacker is. If I can find out – if – perhaps I can work out a way to stop this person before they go too far. They've already invaded my personal space and given me a death threat; I have to wonder what's next.

A trickle of ice passes over my skin as I picture my own ashen face and cold, stiff limbs. My dead, staring eyes. Michael and James standing over my bloodless corpse tasked with the heinous job of identifying me. Dead at thirty-eight. In my vision James is holding it together – just – whereas Michael is a complete mess. I've never had a favourite, but of the two, James has always been the stronger, more independent one. Michael has always needed me more.

Tears sting my eyes. Keeping my head down, I blurt a quick hello to Eimear and rush past her desk into my office, not wanting - not able - to chat. Guilt nips at me as she rises in her seat, her smile freezing on her face. She's clearly eager to talk, but I feign ignorance and shut the door behind myself, closing myself off, shutting my friend out. She can't help me, so what's the point in weighing her down with my worries? No one can help me. I have to deal with this on my own. After all, I've brought it on myself. This is my problem to solve. My mess. My karma.

Relieved to be alone, I snap the door shut behind my

back and lean my head against the hard wood. My heartbeat ought to slow, but it doesn't. Instead, my pulse races: my office isn't a safe haven anymore. My home was invaded; what's to say my office hasn't been broken into as well?

Kneading my temple with my index finger, I dump my bag beside the desk and scan the room for anything out of the ordinary. At first glance everything seems in place. My desk is tidy and orderly, notebook neatly placed on the top right corner, laptop shut, a film of dust coating its silver surface. The heart-shaped slate coaster Michael gave me in my stocking last year sits to the right of my computer ready for my morning cup of coffee. A bundle of paperwork remains where I left it; in the centre of my desk beside a handwritten 'To do' list, which has five items crossed off and three remaining.

I move away from the desk toward the centre of the room. Shrugging off my coat, I drape the heavy, damp material over my arm. The air is too warm - almost stifling - and I go to the window and push it open, inhaling gulps of cool, wet air tainted with sulphur-thick rain. For a while I stare out at the drizzly sky allowing my eyes to fill with tears and my throat to clog. The thought that someone wants me dead is hard to wrap my head around. It's hit me to my core. Yes, I did something bad, something unforgivable, but I'm not a murderer. I'm not without remorse. I know what I did was wrong and in one way or another I've been paying for that selfish mistake for the last ten years.

I look down, away from the dull sky. My fingers rest against the cool glass of the window. I stare at my nails, which are bitten to the quick. When did that happen? They haven't been this bad for a long time. My fingers look skeletal and lined. Old before their time. My stomach grumbles and I place my hand on it, remembering for some strange reason the first time I felt James kick. I was lying on the sofa in my mum's house watching television with Greg. I was only seventeen years old; practically a child - younger than both of my kids are now. That first kick terrified me because it made the whole disastrous thing feel real. Realer even than the twelve-week scan.

Turning away from the window, I lick my lips and squeeze the bridge of my nose. My appetite was gone this morning, replaced by a sour taste on my tongue, a demonic pounding in my temples and a sudden case of irritable bowel syndrome. Right now, the thought of eating makes me feel sick.

With languid movements, I move back to my desk, drop onto the swivel chair and rub my tummy, willing the painkillers to kick in to ease the ache in my stomach and the merciless throbbing in my head. Blinking away tears, I check my watch. I have two hours to kill until my second session with Polly George. I open my laptop and log in, telling myself to read through the notes I made after our last session. A week has passed since I saw Polly and I wonder how she's coped at school this week, whether she'll be able to open up to me this session.

A knock on the door pulls me out of a sentence about Polly's slight shift in behaviour following her mother's departure from my office. I look up as Eimear pokes her head into the room, her brow creased with concern.

"You okay, hun?"

I nod, worried that if I speak, tears will come.

She fingers the star-shaped pendant on her choker, eyeing me intently. "You sure?"

"Yep. I'm fine. Just tired."

She nods and gives me a worried smile before closing the door.

I swipe wetness from the corners of my eyes and log in to my emails, determined to get it together.

A message grabs my attention. The subject title is 'Great To Meet You The Other Day'. I hover the icon over delete but curiosity gets the better of me and I open the message, surprised to see it's from Mark Monroe. M.O.N.

My business card had my email address on – of course. Leaning forward, I read the message quickly, hungry to know more.

Chapter Eighteen

Diary,

I can't find her diary anywhere. It's bizarre. I looked under her pillow exactly where I'd left it, but it was gone. Has she taken it to school? God, I hope not. What if she leaves it somewhere and someone happens upon it and reads it. Or, God forbid, a nasty little sod snaps a picture of the very page I read and Instagrams it – isn't that what teenagers do nowadays? And what would a teacher do if they found it? Would they read it? They'd have to at least open it to see who it belonged to because her name's not on the front. In fact, I don't even know if she's written her name inside it anywhere. She might not have, in which case she'd remain anonymous – unless the teacher recognised her handwriting – although that would be difficult considering how messy it is.

Oh God. I think my head's going to burst. My mood's all over the place. I'm worried because I've always had a savage temper, and I can't lose it now, not like before. But Rich had it coming, he really did, and I've put an end to it now. It'll take Polly a long time to come to terms with it, but what she doesn't know won't hurt her. I'm protecting her by withholding the truth.

I need to start taking my medication again, but it makes me so foggy-headed and I need to think clearly. Did Polly move her diary because she realised I'd found it? No. She can't have. I positioned it back exactly where I found it. Unless she's got security cameras in her room (which of course she can't have), there's no way on earth she could know I read it, is there? Unless...unless she found it odd that I didn't put her clothes away. I left them in a pile on her bed, and I NEVER do that. No. I'm being silly. There's no way she'd work that out.

Ugh. I feel sick thinking this way about my own daughter. Trying to suss out whether she's sussed me out. Sussed out my betrayal. But it gets worse. I went one step further. When I couldn't find her diary, I hunted for it. Hunted high and low and everywhere in between. I was careful to put things back in their place. I searched everywhere, determined to find the damn thing and then I found something else. Something that scared the shit out of me. Something else I can't understand. Something that leads my thoughts to places they should never, ever go. Just thinking about what I found gives me the chills. Makes me think things about her I shouldn't be thinking, and yet...how can what I found be explained? It doesn't make any sense, and not knowing terrifies me because of the track of my thoughts. Untrustworthy, un-motherly thoughts. And so hypocritical given my past actions.

I left it there in its Tesco carrier bag buried beneath her shoes at the back-right corner of her wardrobe. And now I can feel its presence throbbing in the gloom, tempting me to go back and look at it again. But I can't. I can't bring myself to go back in her room, let alone look inside that bag.

If I ask Polly about it and she confirms my worst fears, I might need to do something terrible.

No. I need to forget I ever saw it.

H

Chapter Nineteen

Heather

Polly slides into the front passenger seat wearing her large pink headphones. She smells faintly of shea body butter and her lips shine with pearly gloss.

In the silence of my little Hyundai i10, I hear the muffled sound of Oasis, Richard's favourite band. My fingers tighten on the steering wheel as I pull away from the house. Polly's clearly trying to cling on to him in any way she can.

For a beat, I'm consumed by anger so wretched I think my brain's going to burst. Damn Richard and his fucking cheating. Damn him for abandoning my little girl when she needed him most.

I glance left to see Polly looking at me. She looks concerned. I wonder if now is the time to try to find out what, if anything, she's told Doctor England. Has she mentioned her scar? I know I should have broached the subject before her first session with the therapist but I was too worried about bringing it up. The thing is, now that I've met Jessie England, I can see how diligent see is, how observant. She could present a problem, but only if Polly tells.

Maybe I should also ask Polly about what I found in the bag. Be casual about it…but I'm afraid she'll retreat into her teenage shell. Either that or she'll scream blue murder at me for poking about in her room, and I don't think I can handle that right now. God forbid she ever finds out I've read her diary. It could break us forever. My daughter prizes trust above all else. And she's a very justice-oriented person, like me. I know, however, that if I ever find out who took

Benjamin from me, I wouldn't be content with legal justice. I'd find a way to dole out my own as soon as I got the chance, and it wouldn't be pretty. Countless times I've imagined hacking a strange man to pieces because of what he did to my son. Sometimes I wake in the night convinced I'm covered in someone else's blood.

Polly's still looking at me.

'What's wrong?' she murmurs, tapping pause on her phone and pulling off the headphones, giving me her full attention for once.

For some reason my daughter's full attention is unnerving. It's like she can see through me to my bitter, useless core.

'Just worried about you, darling. Hoping this woman can help you feel better. I love you so much.'

To my surprise, she says softly, 'I love you too, Mama.'

Tears well in my eyes. She hasn't called me Mama since she was five years old. Since Benjamin.

I steel myself. Flick the indicator. Check both ways. 'What, um, has Doctor England asked you anything that made you uncomfortable in any way?'

Polly cocks her head. I glance her way. Turn the wheel.

'Not really,' she says, looking out of her window.

It's an infuriatingly vague answer. I take a deep breath and try to stay calm and patient. One wrong word and she'll pull away from me and I won't get the reassurance I need. Or, God forbid, the opposite.

'Are you sure, darling? She hasn't asked you anything about, you know, your scar or anything like that?'

'Why would she ? It happened years ago. It has nothing to do with what I did a few weeks ago.'

She has a good point, but I saw Doctor England looking at Polly's scar, and I heard her loud and clear at the house; she's concerned Richard hurt my daughter, and she probably thinks he created that scar. If she thinks that, that's better than her knowing the truth, but I need to make sure.

'Mum?'

'Sorry. I just – it wouldn't be a good idea to talk about how it happened, that's all.'

I glance at her to see a quizzical expression squinching her beautiful face.

'Why not? I got scratched by a cat. What's wrong with that?'

Relief encompasses me like a fluffy, warm blanket after an ice-cold bath. She doesn't remember what really happened. Thank God. I can stop worrying she'll give us away.

I pat her leg and give her a brief smile. 'Nothing, darling. Sorry. I'm tired. Talking nonsense in my old age.'

I catch an eyeroll before she pulls her headphones back over her ears and stabs play. Once again Richard's favourite band makes it through the cheap device, making me wish I'd bought her a more expensive pair.

For the rest of the drive, I embrace the wonderful sensation of relief and try to forget about what I found in her bedroom, but it grinds away at my temples with the insistence of a pneumatic drill. At some point, there will come a time when I need to broach the subject with her, but not now. Not when I've just learned such a lifesaving gem of information.

Chapter Twenty

Mark Monroe has asked me out. His email doesn't beat around the bush; it gets straight to the point. I re-read the message, a slight flutter beginning in my sore tummy, heat rushing to my cheeks. A second later, I frown – is he being genuine or is he a sexual predator trying to get close to me so that he can manipulate me into believing he's innocent?

My first instinct is to ignore the message. He could be the person Polly mentioned. But there's no denying the excitement bubbling inside me at the thought of meeting up with this man under different circumstances. Yes, he's a whole decade younger than me, which will probably mean we won't have much in common, but he's extremely attractive. And Eimear's always saying I need to get out more. Try dating. This would be easier than the whole dating website thing. A heck of a lot easier. Also, if he is the one Polly's scared of, it makes sense to get closer to him and find out the truth.

I lean back and stare at the words on the screen, re-reading the message over and over again just to make sure I'm not misinterpreting his words, which is stupid given that he's literally asked me if I'd like to meet him for drinks tonight. I frown: is it presumptuous of him to think I'd be free at such short notice? As far as he's aware I have a fifteen-year-old daughter, though I suppose she'd be old enough to stay at home alone.

I consider going outside and telling Eimear about his message, then realise I haven't completely decided what to do about it yet, and Eimear will only have one answer: say yes.

The words on the screen blur and I close my eyes and focus on my racing heartbeat, thinking how funny it is that

I'm having such a strong physical reaction to such a simple request, and how wrong it is, given that I suspect him of being a sexual predator. Then, without warning, the voice I've been unable to shake for years whispers I don't deserve to be asked out, not by him, not by anyone. I listen to this voice for a few moments as it reminds me of the past, of the awful things I did, of the person I was. Doubt trickles into my mind like spilt wine, bloodying all thoughts of agreeing to meet up with Mark Monroe. My excitement fades replaced by black thoughts. I will meet with him, but only to find out whether he's Polly's dark secret. I'll message him back to agree to this 'date' later.

I re-focus on Polly's notes, quickly becoming engrossed in my description of our last session.

An hour later, a knock at the door brings me out of a trance of remembrance and I stand, slightly dazed, expecting Eimear to stick her head around it. A moment later she does so, an excited glint in her eye.

"Mark Monroe's on the phone askin' for you. Sexy voice. Says he's not a client. Says he's sent you a message askin' you out for drinks but you haven't replied yet. He wants your answer now."

"What?"

"Mark Monroe," she stretches out her arm and wiggles the phone at me.

"Uh…tell him I'm busy," I say.

Eimear shakes her head. "Tell him so yourself."

She strides into my office and thrusts the cordless into my hand, leaving quickly before I have a chance to do anything about it.

The door is pulled to – not closed properly – I notice, and I stare at the phone, heart pounding. Telling myself to grow up, I raise the phone to my ear.

"Hello?"

"Hi. So, Jessie, drinks, tonight, 8.30, Turtle Bay?"

The smile is clear in his voice. I find a smile coming to

my own mouth and before I know what I'm doing I say yes. Yes, that'd be lovely. Then I chastise myself silently for forgetting I'm suspicious of this man.

"Great!" he says, "See you later."

He hangs up quickly, perhaps thinking I'm about to change my mind.

I flop onto my chair and lean my head back, staring in wonder at the phone, listening to the drone of the dial tone. What have I just done? What am I going to wear? Is he a paedophile or am I nuts?

Eimear's face pops round the door. "So? Please tell me you said yes."

I nod slowly and she laughs and jumps up and down transformed for a split second into her youngest daughter. "Whoop! You go girl. What you going to wear? Where're you goin' tonight?"

I fill her in on the details then hand her back the phone, trying and failing to quell the nerves rising inside me. Eimear throws me a wink over her shoulder then practically skips out of the room, shutting the door properly this time, her good deed done for the day. I sit and stare at my gnawed fingernails, thinking how ghastly I looked this morning and how rough I felt, wondering how on earth I'm going to transform into someone even remotely attractive by tonight, and how I'm going to go about my interrogation in a subtle way.

Minutes skip by, my mind filled with discarded outfit after discarded outfit and before I know it, Eimear's knocking on the door again to tell me Polly and Heather George have arrived. I stand and smooth wrinkles out of my striped shirt. Eimear shows Polly George into my office and shuts the door behind her. The girl wears her school uniform which consists of a white, open-necked shirt beneath a navy blazer, a short navy skirt and navy tights. Today, her blonde hair hangs loose below her shoulders, the ends ratty and in desperate need of a trim. Her face is pale but the shadows under her eyes aren't too bad, whether that's due to cover-up or feeling better, it's hard to say from a distance. Her eyes avoid mine as she walks to the sofa and perches on the edge.

"It's good to see you again Polly. How are you feeling today?"

"Okay. You?" She looks up and meets my gaze.

"I'm fine, thank you. I thought we could talk about your childhood today. Would that be okay?"

"All right, but first you have to tell me why you came to my school."

My breath catches in my throat. She saw me.

"I wanted to see if I could see you in another environment. It's something I often do for my clients."

"Really? I've never heard of a therapist doing that before."

"Well, it's not a widely used technique. Not yet anyway, but it's something I've found to be very useful."

"Is that why you came to my house too?"

I nod, maintaining eye contact. She stares back at me, face serious, pensive. The air between us is tense, broken only by a bark of laughter that bursts from her mouth, almost making me jump.

"I'm only playing with you, Doctor. I don't care if you went to my school or my house."

She seems a lot more confident than last time we met. Not as shy or reserved. I'm a little taken aback. Is she as innocent and genuine as I thought? Or is this evidence of a psychological disorder?

I eye her closely. She's staring down at her hands now. Today her fingernails are painted white. It's hard to tell whether she's upset that I visited her school and home. I need her to trust me; the fact she knows I've been poking around her life without her knowledge isn't the best way to gain that trust.

Uneasily, I wonder if I can trust her.

"I'm sorry if you feel I've acted in a way you didn't expect Polly. I honestly just want to help you to the best of my ability, and seeing different parts of your life can be extremely useful."

She nods and casts her eyes at the arm of the sofa, which she begins to pick at.

"I was just curious," she says.

I exhale a sigh of relief and lean forward. "So, I know you and your family went through a terrible time ten years ago when you lost Benjamin. It seems to me that the way you're feeling now could be connected to the loss of your brother. Would it be okay if I ask you a bit about that time in your life?"

She shrugs as if she couldn't care less and yanks a loose thread out of the chair. "Yeah, okay. What do you want to know?"

"Good. That's good. Let's start with how old you were when your brother went missing."

"Five."

"Okay. Now, I know this is hard as you were so young, but what do you remember about Benjamin?"

She wraps the thread around her index finger. I watch as the strand digs into her flesh turning her skin yellow. It must hurt but she doesn't wince. Once the strand is wrapped, she leaves it there and stares down at her finger.

"I can't really remember him," she says, giving me a quick glance.

"Could it be that you don't want to remember him? Perhaps because it's too hard?"

She stares at me blankly. "No. I just don't remember him. I was only five when it happened."

"Okay. It seems to me that this must have been an incredibly difficult time for not just you, but your parents as well. Do you remember anything about the time he disappeared?"

She shrugs and begins to unwrap the thread. "A little. I

remember Mum crying, like, constantly. I remember these big ugly camera guys hanging around outside. They reminded me of hyenas."

"Hyenas?"

"Yeah," she tosses the thread onto the floor and meets my gaze, "Predators, you know. Always hanging around, waiting to attack. Wanting something that's someone else's."

"Someone else's?"

"I'm bored. Can we talk about something else?"

She gives me a smirk, almost challenging me with her pale eyes, pushing me to comment on her rudeness perhaps, which of course I'd never do. Again, I'm surprised by this new side to her, yet aware that this glibness is most likely a defence mechanism. Talking about Benjamin is clearly difficult for her, which isn't surprising at all.

"Okay. Tell me about your father," I say, intentionally keeping my statement obscure. Giving her the chance to start with anything, say anything about the relationship, will mean she's not trapped into a narrower response that she might not be able to give.

Her eyes betray something now. They flick to the left and tears well. "I don't want to talk about him."

"That's fine. What would you like to talk about?'

She shrugs, picks at the skin around her nails. Without looking up, she says, so quietly I can barely hear her, "What do you think about cheaters?'

"Cheetahs?" I say, momentarily confused after the hyena comment.

She looks up, angles her head. "People who cheat."

"Oh." I feel my face growing hot and wish I'd opened both windows. "Well, it's not important what I think. Why are you asking Polly?"

She drops her gaze, shrugs.

"Are you talking about anyone in particular?"

"Maybe."

I clear my throat and sip stale water from the glass

Eimear gave me yesterday. "Could it be your father you're talking about?

She says nothing and won't look at me.

"Has he ever hurt you?"

She stares at her knees and brings her thumb to her mouth. Her teeth start to tear at the already damaged skin. Blood rises to the surface. A blinding ray of sunlight abruptly bursts through the window and catches the open cut, turning the blood orange.

This is what happened last time, just before she…

The girl's narrow shoulders begin to shake, and she glances up at me with tear-filled eyes. "I, I, I can't. I'm sorry."

She covers her face with her hands, jerks to her feet and rushes from the room before I have a chance to respond. A ringing silence fills my ears and I stare at the door, too shocked to do anything else. This is the first time a client has ever fled my office.

Exhaling shakily, I hurry to the door. Out in the reception area, Heather George has her arms wrapped around her daughter's trembling shoulders. She gives me a sad, apologetic nod and guides Polly out of the room whispering in her ear. As the door shuts, Eimear and I exchange worried glances.

"Think she'll be back?" Eimear says.

I sigh and knead my temples. "I hope so. I really, really hope so."

Chapter Twenty-One

Makeup works miracles. Somehow, despite my usual ineptitude with the stuff, I don't look like something the cat dragged in. I lacquer my hair with smoothing serum prior to drying and spend a while straightening it – something I haven't bothered to do for years – and the result is incredible. My hair seems to have grown three inches and it looks glossy and thick, falling in silky chocolate-brown ribbons to my breasts.

I smile at my reflection, trying to mask the worries kneading mercilessly inside my head. Taking a small sip of merlot, I tug up the neckline of my black top and turn to check out my bum. Tension stiffens my shoulders, so I practice a few yoga stretches, breathing deeply, Birdie's melodious music helping to ease my jittery nerves. Going on a date seems like a ridiculous idea given my state of mind and inability to shut out thoughts of the message scratched into my coffee table, but it's too late to cancel. I remind myself it's not a date anyway; it's an interrogation.

I consider driving but Turtle Bay is such a short walk and it's early so the streets will be busy. There's no chance my harasser will do anything to me now and I can get a taxi home if I want to. Also, despite the nastiness of his actions, he's not tried to hurt me. If he really wanted to do me harm, he would have stayed in the house and attacked me when I got home rather than scratching out the message and leaving. Indeed, it seems like all he wanted to do was scare me; which he did. Hopefully, now that he's gotten his anger out of his system, he'll leave me alone. Especially now that I've made the police aware.

I slip my feet into black ankle boots, grab my handbag and leather jacket and hurry downstairs.

Polly's tearful face jumps into my mind as I shut the front door and hurry out into the brisk wind. I'm too cold, my leather jacket not thick enough to ward against the icy breeze, so I up my walk to a jog, my breath creating clouds in front of my face as I pant, unused to the exercise, knowing I need to do this sort of thing more often. When the boys were small Greg and I used to take them to play badminton at the local leisure centre, which kept me pretty fit. Michael became really good and played at county level, but hasn't carried on at university, preferring to focus on his rugby, which he also played at county level. James was never as athletic, being more like me in that department than Greg.

At the top of the hill, I turn left and slow to a walk, knowing I need to get my breath back before I reach the restaurant. Up here on High Street, lamps cast fuzzy yellow discs onto the pavement and a boy racer roars past blaring hip hop, windows down despite the bitter cold. The brutal wind swirls litter along the curb in a frenzied dance as if propelled by an invisible puppeteer. Being Friday night, the street is full of couples and groups heading out for the evening. A middle-aged pair hurries by, the woman snuggling into her partner whose hands are shoved deep into the pockets of his jacket. I catch a snippet of their conversation: something about their Tesco shop. Bland, everyday conversation that makes me smile - then frown. Sometimes I miss little things like that. It's funny how such commonplace conversations add up to a lot when you don't have anyone to share them with.

Trying not to dwell on these thoughts, I glance at eateries as I pass: Jade Garden Chinese, a kebab shop, The Old Bell – which I quickly glance away from - Tesco Express and finally, Turtle Bay, its jungle colours and vibrant music welcoming and bright against the darkness. The boys and I have eaten here a handful of times, and every time we've come, I've loved it.

Something touches my elbow and I jump and glance down to see a gloved hand resting there. I look up into Mark Monroe's beaming face and step back.

"Oh, hi! You scared me," I say.

He chuckles and rubs his nose. "Sorry. I just got here too; shall we go in? After you, my lady."

He holds the door open for me and I nip past him, aware of how little room he allows me. He stands partially blocking the doorway and I'm uncomfortable with his apparent inability to understand personal space. And touching me already – what's that about?

I shake myself internally, ordering this hyper-critical voice to back off. He's one of those tactile types, which might not be so bad once I get used to it.

He follows me in, laughing and swearing about the wind. As soon as the door closes, the warmth of the restaurant encases me, easing the stinging in my face and ankles. The place is buzzing and the air smells delicious. Rich jerk spices stir my taste buds to life, and I turn and give him a smile, beginning to shrug off my jacket, but he darts forward and helps me, standing close. Too close. I clear my throat, tell myself to relax, and turn to face a curvy waitress who takes our coats and leads us to a table at the back of the restaurant.

Large multi-coloured bulbs hang from the ceiling, creating warm glows amidst the wooden tables. Fairy lights twinkle in the windows and upbeat reggae enlivens the space with funky vibes. At the centrally placed driftwood bar, people drink long cocktails, throwing their heads back and laughing, already sozzled it would seem. Everyone is dressed smart-casual, many of the women in tight jeans and low-cut tops like me, and I feel relieved to know I gauged it right.

Mark pulls my chair out for me, which, though unnecessary, I find quite charming and a tad creepy.

Creepy-charming – that's a new one.

I murmur thank you then watch as he strides to his chair and sits down opposite, leaning forward with a grin on his handsome face. He appears totally relaxed and his pale green eyes sparkle in the glowing light. He's wearing a tight black T-shirt and blue jeans. He looks good. Very good. He's the most attractive man I've ever met, and I feel a blush warming my cheeks. I look down, partly to hide my face and partly because his gaze is a little too intimate. Polly's face flashes in my mind and I meet his eyes, determined to do what I came here to do.

"So, Jessie, how was your day?"

"Not great, to be honest. How was yours?"

"Hey, hey, hey. Tell me. What happened?" he says, reaching out and touching my hand.

I automatically move my hand away, laughing awkwardly. "Troubled client. I can't really talk about it. That's the problem with my job."

"Come on, sure you can. Just give me a general gist."

I hesitate, not wanting to seem rude. "All right. She's very young and depressed. She ran crying from our session. Not exactly the effect I was aiming for!"

He smiles. "No, I guess not. But I'm sure you're doing your best. Poor thing. There're so many teenage girls struggling these days. Seven girls in my school are self-harmers – and that's only the ones I know about. It's terrible."

"Seven? Gosh. That is a lot." I'm genuinely shocked but intrigued that he brought that up. Could he be referencing Polly? Does he know about her suicide attempt?

"Let's change the subject, shall we?" he says brightly, "This is a bit morbid for first-date conversation, isn't it?"

We laugh and I begin to relax, though I keep my hands on my lap, out of his reach.

The waitress comes over to take our drinks order and I go for a Pina Colada. Mark orders the same, and I wonder whether he's doing it because he genuinely loves the same cocktail as me, or because he wants to make it seem like we have something in common, however slight.

I give him a smile and ask him about his day. He fills me in on the most interesting parts – skipping what I expect are the boring, normal bits. There's something so self-assured about this man that it borders on cockiness. He's a big gesticulator too, using his hands, head, arms and shoulders to tell his stories, and as he does so, he seems to take up the space between us and around us, his voice loud and confident, his aftershave drifting around me in intoxicating circles. A few people shoot glances our way and I resist the urge to smile apologetically at them, but all the same, I'm enjoying his exuberance. It's infectious but disquieting. In one moment, I find myself wishing he would quieten down, and in the next, I find myself wishing I was more like him. He's clearly used to being the life and soul of every party but, interestingly, he doesn't forget to steer the conversation toward me every now and then. Not often, but just enough to remind me that he wants me here. He is, I decide, a very charismatic man. Someone who could easily charm a teenage girl.

I tell him I'm divorced and fleetingly mention my invented fifteen-year-old daughter before moving on to tell him a little about Michael and James. I pause, interested to see his reaction, then reveal that James is only seven years younger than him. He laughs at this then raises an eyebrow and leans forward.

"And how, exactly, Ms England, do you know my precise age?"

Cheeks tingling, I begin to work out an inane lie about the receptionist at his school telling me, but he laughs and pats my hand, which has found itself back on the table. This time, I don't jerk away and, despite my embarrassment, the sensation of his warm, smooth palm on the back of my hand isn't entirely unwelcome. Then I remember why I agreed to come and pull my hand back.

"Don't worry, Jess, I Googled you too. I know you're thirty-eight and I don't mind the age gap one bit," he says with a grin that brings cute dimples to his cheeks that I hadn't noticed until now.

I flush more deeply at his use of 'Jess', wondering whether I like his shortening of my name. After a second's reflection, I decide that yes, I do like it. My father, who died when I was only nine from a heart attack, used to call me Jess. No one else has ever used the nickname and I've always stuck with Jessie because that was my mother's preference.

Knowing I'm wasting time, I switch to detective mode. I can't breach client confidentiality but I can take a different angle and skirt around the truth. Watching him closely, I say, "So how do you find teaching teenage girls?"

A frown pinches his eyebrows together. "That's a strange question."

"I'm just curious. It's just this teenage girl client of mine. She's playing on my mind." I don't elaborate and wait for him to speak.

"Oh…anyone I know?"

I'm surprised and alarmed by his directness. "I don't think so."

"Is that really why you came to the school today?"

Heat rushes to my face. "Of course not. I have a daughter who I'm thinking of sending there." I say the words crossly, folding my arms for good measure.

"Hey, hey. Relax. I'm just pulling your leg!"

It would seem weird now to ask him the same question again, so I try a different tactic. "Sorry – of course you are. I'm just worried about this girl. She says she has this dark secret. Have you ever had one of your students tell you there's something bad going on in their life but not say exactly what it is?"

He looks thoughtful for a moment, then shakes his head. "Nope. Students are more likely to go to female teachers, I think. They have that motherly touch, you know?"

"Yeah. That makes sense. It's just – and I know I shouldn't be telling you this, but I feel like I can talk to you already – it's just that she said that if she told me her secret, someone would hurt her."

There's a short pause before he speaks but his expression doesn't change.

"Really?" He doesn't look shifty or in any way cagey. He seems genuinely curious.

I frown inwardly, wondering what I expected would happen. Without being able to ask him point-blank if he's sleeping with a student, I'm clearly not going to be able to ruffle his feathers enough to get him to give anything away. He's either completely innocent or a great actor. Even if I asked him outright, he'd lie anyway. I give myself a mental slap and acknowledge shamefully that the real reason I accepted his request was because I fancy him.

"That's kind of scary," he says, "I can understand why you'd be so worried about her, especially if she's young."

I nod and change the subject. It's obvious that this isn't the way to find out if Mark Monroe is involved in this. I gulp my drink and tell myself to try to enjoy the rest of the evening. It seems as though I'll have to do this the normal way and hope that Polly confides in me soon.

*

I've drunk too much, so I'm sloshed and giggling like a teenager when we finally leave Turtle Bay. I can tell Mark's drunk too as he's weaving around all over the place and singing a Phil Collins song very badly as we meander away from the restaurant, the last customers to leave by far.

Though the roaring wind whips around us tornado-like pulling my hair into my eyes and mouth, I don't feel the cold. Giggling, I lose my balance and bump into Mark who laughs and wraps his arm around my waist, pulling me in tight against his hard body, and I don't mind the contact. I don't mind it at all. In fact, my belly flutters in response to his touch and I grin up at his shadowy face.

"This's been really fun," I slur, "Most fun I've had in yonks!"

"Yonks?" Mark says, laughing.

"Yeah, yonks. Ages. Years. God, tha's sad, isn't it?"

"Very sad."

"Hey!"

"Joking. Only joking!"

He turns at the top of my street, steering me home. It occurs to me to ask how he knows the way, but the thought is fleeting, dashed by a sudden overwhelming urge to pee.

"Run!" I shout, pulling away from him, "I'm going to wet myself!"

Laughing, footsteps pounding the pavement, I half-run, half-stumble down my street. I can hear him laughing, his feet thundering behind me, calling to me to be careful, but I carry on running, not caring, feeling like I'm flying. I jerk to a halt outside my front door, breathless and panting, and grin back at him, rummaging around inside my handbag as the urge to wee grows stronger.

"Damn key – where the hell is it?"

He grabs my bag from me, "Let me look," and finds it after only a second or two of rifling around.

I watch, swaying slightly, as he unlocks my door and holds it open for me. Giggling, I run past, kick off my boots and sprint through the house to the downstairs bathroom.

The relief is immense. I wash my hands and run my fingers through my hair. Leaning close to the mirror, I'm shocked by how bloodshot my eyes look and how pink my cheeks are. I give my head a little shake and decide I'll offer him one drink then send him home. No more for me though. I'm done. I'm going to feel horrendous in the morning. I gulp ice-cold water from the tap then flick some on my hot face. Feeling a little sobered up, I unlock the bathroom door and gasp: Mark Monroe stands two metres away in my kitchen wearing only his boxers.

"Uh – what are you doing?" I say.

He winks and waves two empty champagne glasses at me. "Fancy one more drink before we…get down to business?"

Business.

I laugh and shake my head. "Sorry Mark, but there's not going to be any 'business' tonight. I'm knackered, and while it's been really fun, the night's over. I'm going to bed."

His smile vanishes. He turns and yanks on his clothes, losing his balance when he pulls on his shoes.

I watch from afar, feeling the colour drain from my face. The atmosphere is tense now, so different from a few minutes ago.

His face is serious, his shoulders stiff as he turns and mutters goodnight. I don't reply, too shocked to say anything.

He leaves me standing in the kitchen gaping at him as he strides back through the house, opens the door, steps out and slams it shut. The sound reverberates around my now-aching skull. Unsteadily, feeling cold and hollow, I drift to the front door and pick up my keys from the carpet. Dismayed to find my fingers trembling, I lock the door then stare at the floor wondering how such a wonderful night could suddenly turn so sour and feeling angry at myself for enjoying my time with him when there's still a small chance he's the one posing a threat to Polly George.

A moment later, the need to vomit thrusts itself on me, and I dash back through the house, making it the kitchen sink in the nick of time.

Chapter Twenty-Two

Saturday is one of those written-off days. I check my phone a few times wondering if Mark has contacted me to apologise but there's nothing. No text, no missed call. Nothing. Part of me is looking forward to telling Eimear what happened when I see her on Monday, but another part feels very low. After I dropped my interrogation, our date was fantastic; I really thought we'd see each other again. But the tiny glimmer of hope that sparked in my chest last night is long gone now, replaced by a killer headache and the knowledge that continues to haunt me despite my best efforts: I don't deserve to meet someone and fall in love. I don't deserve that kind of happiness, not anymore. And I should never have allowed myself to like this man because I can't completely cancel out his involvement with Polly.

*

My hangover lasts two days. I trudge around the house feeling too rough to do anything much, counting down the hours until I can call my lovely youngest.

Eventually, seven o' clock ticks round and I dial Michael's number.

"Mum. Hi. Oh my God – you rang thirty seconds past the hour – shame on you – you're late!"

"Ha ha," I say, tucking my leg under myself and sipping ice water.

"So, how're you? Good week?" he says.

"Goodish. Horrid cold but work was okay. You?"

"Awesome. Saw Kiera again yesterday and she's even

more perfect than I remember."

"Perfect? That's high praise for a girl you've only just met," I say, hearing the scepticism in my voice and immediately regretting it.

Michael seems oblivious. "Yeah. She's cute and funny and all my mates are well jealous."

"Wow. She does sound amazing. What's she look like?"

"Fit. Fittest girl I've ever seen in real life."

I laugh. "Details Michael. Give me a few details. Or better yet, can you send me a piccy of her?"

"I haven't got one yet. I tried but she's, well, I guess she's camera-shy."

"That's a bit unusual in this day and age…"

I can picture him shrugging. "I like it. Means she's not one of those losers who has to take a picture of everything they do and post it on social media to prove they're having fun."

"That's true. So, describe her for me. Just give me the basics: hair, eyes, height, that sort of thing."

The line goes quiet for a few seconds. Is he scratching his head? Tipping his face to the side like he used to when he was little? I long to hold him then, and smell him, and just have him with me. My heart aches for him - and James. My gorgeous boys. I wish I had the courage to drive to Sheffield next weekend and surprise him. Take him out to dinner, but the nagging fear that I'll ruin his day will prevent me from doing it as it has before.

"She's a redhead. I'm not sure what colour her eyes are but they're pretty. And she's about your height."

"She sounds lovely," I say, tempted to wind him up about the fact that he can't remember her eye colour.

"She's from Oxford. Her dad's dead – died in a car crash when she was five, but her mum's still alive."

"That's awful," I murmur.

"Yeah, but it was a long time ago. She says she can barely remember him."

"Any brothers or sisters?"

"Nope."

"And how did she do in her A Levels?"

"Better than me – three As."

"Wow. She sounds like a bright cookie."

He laughs. "Yeah, Mum. Like I said, she's perfect, but she's not up herself at all."

I smile at the expression and hesitate, longing to press for more details but sensing he's no more to give at the moment. This girl may be 'perfect' but it's very early days and he barely knows her. Fingers crossed she'll turn out to be a keeper and as perfect as he believes. I find myself smiling as he excitedly fills me in on this morning's rugby game.

After our call, I decide to walk to Tesco Express to grab a tub of Ben n Jerry's. Within moments of leaving the house, I regret my decision and wish I'd driven as thoughts of the stabbed butterfly grizzle, twisting my gut and making me glance behind.

You're taking a stupid risk. Go back and get the car. When you walked to Turtle Bay, it was earlier and Friday night. There won't be anyone around now because it's Sunday evening.

But nothing's happened for ages. You can't live in constant fear. Anyway, the intruder left a nasty message, they didn't hurt you.

That's true, but what if they're waiting for the perfect opportunity – this would be it, wouldn't it?

I stop and look back. Scan the other side of the road. The street is perfectly empty.

I charge on, hands shoved deep, chin tucked in, determined not to let Little Miss Coward win, but night crawls through the streets bringing inky blackness and a thousand unseen eyes. Drizzle spits at my cheeks and the wind gnaws into my bones and begins to chew and grind. The sycamores lining my road sway and buck and the air whistles and wails, reminding me of Jack Skellington. I think about turning back for home, imagine snuggling up on the sofa under a blanket, a cup of tea warming my palms, crappy TV blaring, but the lure of sweet, creamy Salted Caramel is too great.

I cringe against a gust of viciousness and walk faster. Only about two minutes now until I reach the shop.

The sense of being watched pulls my eyes to the right. A person is matching me stride for stride on the other side of the road. They're wearing a long dark coat and – what? I look harder as I pound the pavement, hands fisting inside my pockets.

He or she is wearing a witch's hat.

But it's not Halloween. It's November.

The witch person stops in their tracks, turns and stares directly at me. Between us, the road is black and empty, save for snarling wind and a handful of dead-eyed cars. Lamplit, the person appears larger, but indecipherable; blackly amorphous, their face masked by the tilted tip of the witch hat.

My heart jolts. I think about screaming, but don't, worried I'm overreacting.

Why are they staring at me? And why on earth are they wearing that hat?

I keep walking, faster now, praying they simply caught me looking at them and wanted to make me stop, praying it's not the person who broke into my house, praying I'd listened to Little Miss Coward and driven to the shop to get my ice cream. Praying this isn't the person who, according to their recent message, despises me with every ounce, scrap and fibre of their being.

LYING BITCH DIE

What possessed me to walk, I'll never know.

You've fallen into that age-old trap of thinking it'll

never happen to you, that's why.

In the corner of my eye, I see the witch carry on walking, matching me step for step once more, and my blood calms to a simmer.

It's okay, Jessie. Everything's going to be fine. Lit, as Michael would put it.

I can see the shop lights bobbing in the gloom like a lifeboat at sea. Not long now until I scrabble onto the boat and escape the shark.

My muscles unclamp.

It's then that the witch bulls across the road straight at me shrieking as loudly as a banshee. And not in a way that anyone in their right mind would find funny.

I yank my hands out of my pockets and run like my life depends on it, because I have a feeling it does.

He's five paces behind me. I can hear his ragged breathing and slamming footsteps. I'm sure now that it's a man. A man in a witch's hat in November chasing me.

What are the odds? If I wasn't so terrified, I'd find it funny.

My lungs are ripping open, each inhalation a ragged tear down my throat.

The witch cackles again, - a breathless, shrill sound that screeches along my spine like claws.

I reach the shop, yank open the door, scream for help. Turning back, terrified he's following me inside, I see nothing and no-one except for the magazine rack and the gloom beyond the shop door.

A hand touches my elbow and I jump and spin around, but it's just a scruffy girl in Tesco uniform.

I'm trembling all over as I tell her what happened, digging into my pocket for my mobile.

'Do you want me to call someone for you?' she says, producing her own phone.

'No. No, it's okay. I'm just going to call the police.'

She nods and backs away. A couple of customers poke

their heads around the aisles and eye me curiously, looking away when they know they've been caught.

With shaking fingers, gaze settling on Psychology Today, I call the police.

Chapter Twenty-Three

Benjamin glanced over his shoulder. The stairs were a pool of gloom. The house was cold and quiet; so quiet that he could hear the tick of the big wall clock coming from the kitchen. He swallowed. He reached for the front door handle and pushed down. The door wouldn't budge. He tried again, putting all of his strength into the movement, but the handle remained fixed in one place. Stubborn like Polly, he thought.

He stared at the fuzzy, dark carpet. Tears filled his eyes. His chest felt tight. Claire was counting on him to come and see her secret. He had to find a way to get out of the house.

With a sniff, he stepped forward and jumped up and down stretching his arm up as far as he could to grab the front door key. His fingers brushed the metal but only just; he was too short to reach them. Sighing, he rubbed his arm where it had begun to ache and looked in the direction of the kitchen. The idea popped into his head as if by magic. The back door! He could leave the house by the back door. The one in the kitchen. The one that Mummy and Daddy always left the key in.

Benjamin tiptoed along the hallway. The kitchen was a spooky, greyish-yellow colour. The clock on the wall sounded louder in here, almost like it was trying to talk to him. Tick tock tick tock tick tock. Bad boy. Bad boy. Bad boy. The dishwasher light blinked at him like an evil red eye. The room smelt of washing up liquid.

Benjamin hurried over the slippery kitchen tiles to the back door. There it was, snug in its little black hole: the back-door key.

He reached for the key then froze. A creak. Coming from the stairs – he was sure of it.

He listened, using his puppy ears, hoping he'd imagined the horrible sound. A second passed. Then another and another…and a creak came again. Benjamin's heart pounded in his throat. He got on all fours and crawled toward the kitchen table. He crawled underneath the table and froze, eyes wide, as the soft scuff of footsteps sounded from the hallway. He watched, heart banging, hand over his mouth, as Mummy's legs walked into the kitchen. They carried her to the kitchen counter. He heard her open the fridge door. Light poured into the room. If she looked his way now, she would see him. She let the fridge door shut and the light vanished. Her legs carried her out of the room. He listened. The stairs creaked twice then there was nothing. No sound except for the tick-tock of the clock and the banging of his heart.

Wiping imaginary sweat from his brow, Benjamin grinned. He was so good at hiding. He always won hide and seek. That was one of the things that made Polly cross.

He crawled out of his hiding place, pushed himself to his feet and tiptoed to the back door. He didn't hesitate. He twisted the cold metal key and heard a satisfying click. Smiling, he carefully opened the door, stepped out into the back garden, and closed the door softly behind him.

Chapter Twenty-Four

I arrive early on Monday morning, shaken to my core after last night's ordeal. Two police officers reached Tesco Express ten minutes after my call, took my statement and drove me home. There was no sight of the man who'd chased me. The police said it was most likely a prank, some idiotic teenager getting his kicks off by scaring random strangers. I hope to God they're right.

My office is freezing so I turn the radiator right up then make myself a coffee and slip behind my desk. Without Eimear in the building my two-room business feels dead. Feeling vulnerable and nervy, I go on Youtube and select a relaxing playlist before checking my emails. Having resisted the urge to check my mail over the weekend, my mouth drops open in surprise to see I've received three emails from Mark Monroe. Not one, not two, three. The first was sent Saturday, the second yesterday and the third this morning at 6am. Fleetingly, I wonder why he didn't text or call me then I remember – I never gave him my mobile number. I don't have his either. He rang the office to ask me out last week and emailed me, having gained those contact details from the business card I gave him when I visited Polly's school.

The subject for all three emails is the same: SORRY! I open the first message and feel hope rise in my chest quickly followed by suspicion; the email is a long, detailed apology admitting how unacceptable his behaviour was, how badly he judged things, how he overreacted, how too much alcohol combined with a horrible day at work contributed to his temper tantrum, how embarrassed and ashamed he was of himself, and how he hopes I'll give him the chance to make it up to me. He describes our date as 'the best date I've ever been on' and ends by practically begging me to let him take me out again.

I lean back and twist my lips; he's apologised and wants to see me again. My stomach flutters at the thought of being wined and dined by this sexy man a second time – but then the ugly voice of reason hits: should I give him another chance and what if he has anything to do with Polly George? I flash back to Friday night, to the shock it gave me when he stormed out. His behaviour was so unexpected, and irrational. But then most people behave irrationally when they've had too much to drink. I shouldn't have let him into the house. I should have been clearer about my intentions, which is to say that I didn't intend to have sex with him on the first date. Definitely not. I'm still trying to suss him out, work out if he's a friend or a foe. But I can't deny I find him attractive and intriguing. Seeing him again could give me the certainty that he's innocent.

I open his second email to find another long apology. The same message but reiterated. The third message sent only two hours ago is the same again, but a little more desperate sounding. I slump back in my chair and frown at the screen. We only went out once…would I send three apology messages if I'd cocked up on a first date? Maybe. No. I don't know. Would it depend on how much I liked the guy? Yes. Probably.

Eimear's noisy arrival breaks my reverie. I push myself up and rush out of the office, desperate for her advice. She blusters into the room muttering about the weather. Her nose is pink, hair wild, pink padded coat zipped up to her chin. Huffing, she glances up and tosses her hair out of her eyes, jumping when she sees me.

"You're in early!"

"Fancy a cuppa?"

"Does the Pope poo in the woods?" Eimear says moving to her chair behind the reception desk and shrugging off her coat, "You look chipper today, hun. Do tell."

"Let me grab us some coffee first then I need your advice, big time."

"Ooh, sounds exciting. Anything to do with your hot date by any chance?" she calls as I move to the tiny kitchen area behind her office.

"Yep! Hang on a sec."

I heap a loaded teaspoon of instant coffee into the biggest mug I can find and make Eimear a regular-sized wake-me-up in her Little Miss Sunshine mug then hurry back into reception perching on one of the red waiting sofas.

"So?" Eimear says, cupping her face in her hands and leaning over her desk.

I exhale the full story – boxers and all. Eimear listens, head cocked to one side, finely plucked eyebrows rising now and then in response to my description of events. I try to keep things as factual as possible but every now and then I can hear excitement creeping into my voice. By the end of the story I feel a little breathless and slump back on the sofa, taking a gulp of now-tepid coffee.

"Whoa," she says, flapping her hands in front of her face, "before I give you my pearls of wisdom, I have to know one 'ting."

"What?"

"How sizeable was his package?"

I laugh. "Honestly, I didn't look. I was too shocked to check it out."

"Seriously? That's the first 'ting I'd have done – before chucking him out of course."

I roll my eyes and drain my coffee. "What do you think I should do? I mean, he's apologised and I did really like him, before…"

"Before he behaved like a five-year-old who got his ice cream taken away?"

I wrinkle my nose. "Yeah. But everyone acts like an arse

when they're drunk, don't they?"

"Yeah, but…I don't know," Eimear says, surprising me, "the 'ting that gets me is that he sent 'tree messages. That's a bit full on. Bit strange considering he's only been out with you once. I mean, I know you're hot as hell and all that, but…I don't know."

I feel myself hollowing out. I'd expected Eimear to tell me to forgive him and go out with him again. Give him a second chance. The chances he has anything to do with Polly are so slim and I like him. A lot.

She seems to notice my mood and comes around from behind her desk to perch on the table in front of me, which creaks under her weight.

"You clearly like him though, so why don't you give him another shot, only this time, don't let him walk you home. And make sure you play hard-to-get. Make him work for it."

"Yeah, okay. I mean, I know what you're saying about the three messages thing, but our date was amazing – before you-know-what happened, and he made me laugh. A lot. Made me feel better than I have in ages. But if he screws up again, that's it."

Eimear smiles and wraps me in a big bear hug. I'm surrounded by her perfume and fight the urge to sneeze. It's been so long since someone's hugged me that I stiffen a little.

"You deserve to be happy, you know," she whispers before pulling away, taking my empty mug from me and moving to the kitchenette.

At the small counter, she glances over her shoulder. Her eyes lock with mine. In an unusually serious tone, she says, "And make sure you find out if he's ever been a fuckin' cheater like my ex, hun."

As I watch her curvy figure sashay away, I feel a deep throb of sadness and a whiplash of shame. She's still hurting from her ex-husband's betrayal, more than I knew.

I push up from the sofa and embrace the small hope re-emerging in my breast. Perhaps it's time I forgive my younger self and give my current self the chance to move on. Mark Monroe may be exactly what I need in my life, my ticket back to happiness. As long as he's innocent, that is.

Before I can change my mind, I go back into my office and write a message back.

Chapter Twenty-Five

Mark replies immediately asking me if we can meet for lunch today. My first thought is: eager beaver or what? Then I tell myself to stop trying to find fault with his behaviour. I should be pleased that he wants to see me so soon; he's probably keen to apologise face-to-face to clear the air and start anew. Excited, I rush out to tell Eimear, but she's on her mobile, her face creased with concern. I hover in the doorway and she catches my eye. Her eyes are bloodshot. She ends the call and grabs her coat and bag.

"It's Pippa. She's had a fit. Sorry."

"Go," I say, "Let me know how she is."

She hurries out of the room, brow furrowed, face deathly pale. Poor Eimear. Poor little Pippa. Epilepsy. Eimear told me a couple of years back.

Guilt suddenly spears my heart as I remember my neighbour, Charlie. I need to visit him. I ring the hospital to find out visiting times. Promising myself I'll pay him a visit after work, I go back into my office and reply to Mark, suggesting we meet at Caffé Nero. Something low-key, not too fancy. He replies instantly again asking if we can meet at 12.30pm, but saying he'll have to be back at work for 1.30pm. Perfect, I think. A short, sober, day date. He ends his message by saying he can't wait to see me again and asking for my mobile number, in case something comes up at work and he's delayed or can't meet for any reason. I give him my number, tummy burbling like a brook, cold, dark voice whispering M.O.N., then check my reflection in my pocket mirror – thank God the worst of my cold has passed. I look decent enough.

Feeling selfish for so easily focussing on my appearance rather than Eimear and her daughter, I text my friend telling her I'm thinking of her and to make sure she takes as much time off with Pippa as she needs. I also tell her I'm happy to watch Rosie this evening.

I find Polly George's notes and read through. So much seems to have happened since she ran out of my office crying her little heart out. I need to analyse our last session, try to work out how best to help her. The scar beneath her ear flashes into my mind's eye and I wonder…was it self-inflicted? Was it an accident? Was it her father? Self-harmers rarely harm in such a noticeable place, and besides, the scar looked old. Years old. It's possible it could have been an accident – perhaps a child at school was mucking about with a pair of scissors? That's certainly something that could happen. I remember an incident back when I was in Year 4 at primary school when the naughtiest boy in our class intentionally stabbed a pair of scissors into another boy's back.

The thought that Polly's father might have inflicted the wound on her delicate neck sends a chill down my spine. Could he have been targeting her mother, but Polly got in the way? Scenarios whizz around my mind, each more distressing than the last, and I realise something important: I need to find out more about this man. I need to know how violent he really was. A frightening idea comes: has he returned yet? Is he back in the house with Polly and Heather? Polly is clearly so fragile. Her father's return could make her snap again.

Feeling cold and sick, I call Heather George and suggest she bring Polly in to see me earlier than Friday. She agrees and I arrange to see Polly tomorrow morning. I don't ask Heather about her husband.

When I see Polly, I'll ask her about him again, see how closely linked her problems are to him, because my feeling is that he might be the key to unlocking her trauma. Last time I tried to ask her about her father, she ran, so I'll have to tread with care.

Chapter Twenty-Six

I glance behind for the fifth time since leaving my car, unable to shake the feeling that I'm being followed. Outside Caffé Nero I take a few deep breaths and tell myself I'm being paranoid. No one's following me. I'm imagining things. It's the middle of the day. Everything will be fine.

Still, I'm shaking as I hurry into the café. I spot Mark's broad back straight away. He's standing next to a tall young man looking at the small selection of sandwiches in the refrigerator next to the till. Dressed in his sports kit, he looks more casual than Friday night but just as attractive. My stomach tightens and flutters. The dark voice chastises, warning me he might not be who he claims to be.

"Hi stranger," he says, looking relaxed, his smile wide.

"Hi. What're you going for? I'm thinking chicken flatbread," I say, deciding not to mention Friday night.

"Good choice. Me too."

He grabs two flatbreads and a Coke, querying if I want the same. I nod and we join the short queue. Realising he's going to pay for mine, I begin to protest but he shakes his head firmly.

"No way. This is just one of the bazillion ways I'm going to try to make it up to you."

I laugh and roll my eyes. "What other ways have you got in mind?"

"You'll see," he grins and his dimples return, making my tummy do weird flips.

I let him lead the way to a table for two at the back-left corner of the room. It's the only available table, so we're lucky. He helps me take off my coat and pulls out my chair for me again, but this time, instead of finding it chivalrous, I find it a little embarrassing. Too try-hard. Doing it in the evening is one thing, but in the day in a café…I catch sight of a middle-aged woman raising her eyebrows at Mark's behaviour and can't help but wonder what she's thinking. Is he being natural? Is he trying too hard? Is he genuinely a gentlemanly sort of man for whom this sort of behaviour is the norm? I try to think of any other man to ever pull out my chair for me, but come up emptyhanded. All I can see are snippets of television programmes set in the old days when treating a woman so gentlemanly was regular behaviour.

Still, I thank him and give him a smile. Instead of returning my smile, he launches into an apology as soon as his bum hits the chair.

Leaning forward, he stares deep into my eyes, puts his hands into a prayer position in front of his chest and pleads with me to forget Friday ever happened. Feeling uncomfortable - and aware he's not trying to lower his voice - I reach out and pat his hands, telling him it's fine.

"No, Jess," he says, "it's not fine. I really like you and I feel like I've screwed it up – us up – before we had a real chance to make a proper go of it."

I shake my head and make to pull my hand back, but he grabs it in both hands. His hands are warm and smooth.

"You're too good for me. That's why I'm making such a fool of myself right now – why I messed up on Friday."

I try to pull my hand gently out of his grasp but he holds on, his grip tightening. "Please tell me you'll try to pretend like Friday night never happened?"

I nod, feeling awkward.

He drops his gaze to the table and releases my hand.

"Please stop apologising. Everyone acts a bit stupid when they've had too much to drink. I've done it countless times. I'm just glad I didn't do it on Friday."

He nods, eyes on mine. "Thank you. Thank you so much. It really is great to see you. Can I see you again this week?"

Luckily, I've got a mouth full of bread, which gives me a few seconds to process his question. We've barely sat down and he's already asking to meet again. It's extreme, but then he seems like a pretty intense – no – passionate man.

Passionate? Try creepy.

I swallow my food. "Um, okay. How about Saturday?"

A shadow flickers across his face and he looks down at his unopened sandwich. "Oh. That far away? I was hoping we might be able to see each other again on Wednesday or Thursday. Catch a film maybe?"

"Er – okay. I'll have to check my diary first though."

He disguises his disappointment with a thumbs up then tears into his sandwich, devouring it like a starved wolf.

The rest of the date goes well, but there's something niggling me about him that I can't quite put my finger on, and I'm left feeling confused and lonely.

Chapter Twenty-Seven

I pop to Tesco for a card then head straight to the hospital.

The hospital is stuck in a 70s time warp. After paying the exorbitant parking fare, I'm greeted by a reception area the colour of jaundiced skin. I hate hospitals. Always have, always will. The smell of illness and disinfectant conjures up memories of Mum, especially of the final days of her life before the sickness finally won.

Everyone in the waiting area is old, pale and broken in one way or another. I only have to wait for a few seconds before the little old lady with swollen legs and thinning yellow-white hair in front of me hobbles away from the reception window.

"I'm here to visit Charlie Jenkins?"

Without looking up, the skeletally thin man behind the desk consults his laptop and mutters directions to Charlie's room. I take the lift to the third floor and make my way down the corridor, shivering at the sounds of someone's guttural groans.

The sooner I'm out of here, the better.

Don't be so selfish. Charlie will be desperate for a visitor. Stay as long as he wants you to.

The corridor is long and empty, lighting harsh, the sterile stench of hospital strong in my nose. I try to blank out memories of Mum here, her suffering palpable even though she never complained.

Finally, I reach Charlie's room and knock on the door, and he grunts, "Come in."

I enter his room and almost stop in my tracks when I see the state of him.

"It's not as bad as it looks," he croaks.

His entire right leg is in plaster and his eyes are black

and blue. A line of stitches about two inches long runs from his hairline to his eyebrow. Grey stubble lines his sagging jaw and his thick white hair looks greasy.

"I would ask how you're feeling, but…"

He chuckles then winces. "Turns out I broke a couple of ribs too. Whacked my head on the stairs, but I'll get over it. There's more life in the old dog yet!"

I hand him the card. He opens it and grins at the photograph of a golden retriever puppy with a bandage on its paw.

"They starve you in here, you know," he says.

"What happened? Was it your slippers? They say about fifteen hundred people are admitted to hospital every year from slipping on the stairs because of their slippers."

He snorts and pops another grape in his mouth. "I was pushed."

"What?" My stomach gives a giant lurch.

"Pushed. Someone pushed me."

"Have you told the police?"

He nods. "I didn't come around for a while so by the time I told them and they got to the house, the bastard had done a runner."

"Do you think it could have been him?"

"Who's him?"

"The man who was hurling abuse outside the other day. The one you scared off."

Charlie shakes his head. "Oh no. No, it wasn't him, love. I'm sure it was just some young scallywag trying to thieve something."

I don't say anything. What if it was the same man – the one who broke into my house and scrawled that message into my table? Cold sweat breaks out under my arms. I think about telling Charlie about what happened, then change my mind. Scaring him wouldn't be the best thing to do right now.

"How long until you can leave?" I say.

"Doc said he'll check on me tomorrow, see if I'm fit for dismissal."

"Are you going to stay with someone for a bit?"

He nods and chuckles. "Yep. My crazy sister's insisted I stay with her until my leg's fixed itself. I tried to fight it, but there's no saying no to Marge."

"Where does she live?" I say, relieved to know he won't be staying near me, just in case my harasser comes back.

"Not far. She still drives. Shouldn't be, mind. Bloody scary driver is Marge. No concept of right of way and half blind with cataracts."

Chapter Twenty-Eight

Diary,

Richard's been gone for ages and I hate myself for being this way, but I miss him. I miss the good times, which are all I think about at the moment. And I need him because I need to talk to him about Polly. But I've gotten rid of him now and there's nothing I can do to take it back.

I've been trying not to think about Polly's diary and what I found in that bag. Typically, the more I try to shove those things out of my head, the more they recur. I almost went back into her room yesterday to check that the bag was really there – that I hadn't imagined it. But fear stopped me. I wish I'd never found it. It doesn't bear thinking about…why does she have that stuff? Has she…

Just shut up! SHUT UP SHUT UP SHUT UP! I need to stop thinking this way about her, stop doubting my baby, stop thinking…just stop. But it's hard to stop. God, my head hurts. It's like there are a thousand drums and clashing symbols competing inside my skull. What the fuck is wrong with me? I've taken painkillers – too many – but they don't seem to work anymore. And I keep feeling tearful and anxious. Terribly anxious. And sometimes downright angry. Hateful. I know I ought to visit the GP, but I won't. What's the point?

I'm really starting to wonder what the point of anything is anymore…and then I remember my little girl, who's not so little and not so innocent anymore, and I remember I'm a bad mother and I need to be strong. Strong for Polly. Strong enough to help her get better. My problems can just go to hell. Polly might be acting fine, but I know she's not. She's hurting very badly. I need to pull myself together, stop doubting her, stop projecting my issues onto her. I wasn't that surprised when Doctor England rang to suggest an earlier appointment for Polly. I was relieved, glad that this woman can see that Polly needs more help. One visit a week isn't going to cut it.

When Polly came out crying at her last appointment, I thought: good. She's opening up, showing some emotion. I tried to talk to her in the car but she wouldn't answer any of my questions or tell me what she'd told Doctor England. It was so frustrating I nearly screamed. She stopped crying the second she shut the passenger door, turned her face to the window and ignored me. I nearly lost my temper. Nearly. Thankfully, I realised she was processing her breakdown, and I gave her time to think it over, instead of continuing to fire questions.

When we got home, she seemed happier and said she was going to Dana's all day on Saturday again to revise. She went up to her room – which is where she spends her time now when at home – and turned her music on full volume. I texted her to say dinner was ready but she didn't reply so I took it up and left it on the floor outside her bedroom. I hovered there for a moment, wondering whether to go in and she suddenly opened the door, which made me jump. She thanked me sweetly for dinner and apologised for being so moody in the car. For a split second, I thought she was going to bring her dinner downstairs and eat with me, but she said goodnight and shut the door. I almost burst into tears. Somehow, I held it together. I thought about ringing Sharon from work but didn't. Some things are just too private and personal to share. And there's that one thing I can never share with anyone, that secret I'm so thankful Polly's forgotten.

Thank God she's seeing Doctor England again soon. No matter what happens, I'll never stop loving my baby. I may be a terrible mother, but blood is thicker than water.

I'll do anything I have to in order to keep her safe.

H

Chapter Twenty-Nine

The wind has died down but my thoughts are turbulent as I drive to work on this dismal Tuesday morning. I see but don't see the road, houses, shops, cyclists, pedestrians, traffic lights, the cloud-clogged sky. I can't shift my mind from the fact that Charlie says he was pushed down the stairs. Someone broke into his home and attacked him. They could have killed him. Charlie's rather blasé assumption that it was a thief rather than the brute who has it in for me, doesn't pass muster. It's too much of a coincidence, considering only days earlier Charlie came to my defence in the face of a clearly unstable, aggressive individual. Not for the first time, but more like the twentieth, I try to work out who could have a problem with me, who could know what I did and still hold a grudge. Who could be so bent on revenge that they turn their anger on an innocent old man like Charlie? I can't think of anyone that might be. The only possible person would be female not male anyway. Unless…unless that female got a young man to do her bidding. But that seems so extraordinary.

A horn blares, yanking me into the present. I've not moved and the light has turned green. Raising a hand in apology, I drive on and pull into the car park outside my building.

Eimear won't be in today. I gave her the rest of the week off to be with Pippa, who cut her head when she fell from the fit. Apparently, Pippa's loving the attention; not to mention the time off school.

I had a text from Mark last night. He listed films we could see. I haven't even agreed to the date yet. I haven't messaged him back because I can't decide what to do. I like him but he's intense and there's still a dark voice in the back of my mind warning me he's not to be trusted.

In my office, I switch on my laptop, check my emails then go through Polly's notes in preparation for her arrival. Focusing on Polly's situation takes my mind off Charlie and I feel almost okay when the office bell rings.

Mrs George enters the building ahead of her daughter. The poor woman looks terrible; dowdy and lined and hopeless. In contrast, Polly is the image of youthful vitality and gives me a bright smile when I greet them. She really is a beautiful girl. For a moment I have a horrible vision of her and Mark having sex. Feeling sick and angry at myself, I force a smile.

Leaving Heather George with a cup of tea and a magazine, I lead Polly into my office and shut the door.

"How're you?" she says.

"Good, thank you. And you?"

"Not too bad. I've met a boy and he's asked me out."

"Really? That's wonderful," I say, wanting to broach the subject of Polly's father, but not keen to divert from a subject she wants to discuss.

"Yeah. His name's Dylan and he's really fit."

"Does he go to your school?"

"Oh no. He's not at school anymore."

"Oh? Is he older then?"

She grins. "Yes. But don't worry. He's only sixteen."

I smile, instantly reassured.

That means Mark's out of the picture then.

You sure about that? She could be lying. Maybe Mark's on to you and is pressuring her to make up a story about a young boyfriend.

Stop being ridiculous. There's absolutely no reason to think Polly would lie.

"The thing is," she says, crossing her legs and leaning forward, "he's already seeing someone else. He says he's going to break up with her so we can be together properly, but he hasn't done it yet. What do you think I should do? We've been meeting in secret and we've kissed and stuff…"

I try not to dwell on the 'and stuff' part of her admission and say, "What do you feel you should do?"

She shrugs and picks at her nail. Today's shade is baby pink. "I dunno. That's why I'm asking you. I mean, what would you do if you really, really fancied a guy but he was with someone else?"

I avert my gaze from hers. "I think I'd try to move on. Find someone single and available. There are plenty more fish in the sea, as they say. But I know it must be hard to do that when you like someone so much. I suppose if they truly like you, they will end the relationship with this other person so that they can be with you properly."

After a beat of silence, she whispers, "My dad cheats on my mum."

"And how does that make you feel?" I say, surprised and relieved she's brought up the subject of her father on her own.

She shrugs, looks towards the window and the grey sky beyond.

"Has your father been in touch at all?"

She shakes her head. A tear snakes down her pale cheek.

"Have you tried to contact him?"

"No. He doesn't care about me."

I decide to try again. "Polly, I know this is hard to talk about but has your father ever hurt you?"

"Physically?"

I nod.

She stands. I watch her waif-like figure drift to the window where she places her forehead against the glass.

"I'd rather not talk about it…yet," she murmurs, glances back at me, "if that's okay with you?"

"Of course. That's fine."

I'm disappointed but unwilling to push the topic. She

shifts her weight. My eyes find the scar on her neck.

"How would you describe your state of mind at the moment, Polly?"

She keeps her back to me and brings her fingertips up to the glass to draw or write something in the condensation from her breath. I can't see from this distance and wish I could. I wait for her reply. She remains silent and I begin to wonder if she heard me.

"My state of mind…um…not too bad, given that I tried to kill myself six weeks ago."

"Okay. Do you want to talk about why you did that?"

She glances around and stares at me, eyes narrowed. "Isn't it your job to work that out?"

Her tone is almost accusatory, as is the sharpness in her gaze.

I sip my water, stalling for thought. "Yes, I suppose it is. But I need a little help from you. The mind is a hugely complex thing."

"I know. I'm doing A level psychology next year. I've already read every book on the syllabus."

"Wow. I'm impressed."

She comes back to sit on the sofa and yawns.

"How would you say you feel about what happened?"

"You mean about hurting myself?"

I nod.

She frowns heavily. "Not good. Bad for my mum. She can't help me. She just makes things worse. But I'm pleased I got to see you."

"You needed help and by doing that, you ended up seeing a therapist and getting the help you wanted?"

She nods.

I smile, pleased to know she's viewing our sessions positively.

For the rest of the hour, I let Polly talk about her new 'boyfriend', and I begin to think that she's turning a small corner. I almost ask her about the word she began to write on the mirror. What 'MON' meant, but decide to save that for Friday's session, if I feel it's appropriate. It could trigger her, and I don't want to delve into that halfway through a session.

"He likes to call me Pretty Polly," she says.

"That's sweet – and true." I smile indulgingly, enjoying her happiness.

"Of course, he has no idea about the murder ballad called that."

I frown. "I must admit neither do I."

"Yes. It's really creepy. I came across it when I was googling my name once. It's from the olden days but is supposed to be based on real events. Basically, a young carpenter murders his pregnant girlfriend and buries her in a grave he's dug – he even shows it to her first - then the bastard hops back onto his ship to carry on with his voyage like nothing's happened."

I nod, unsurprised by the note of morbid glee in her voice. At that age, the brain often manufactures a flippant, surface-level appreciation of violence and death to soften its harshness.

I'm feeling happier when Polly and her mother leave. Polly exits my office smiling; a complete contrast to her departure at our last session, and I can't help feeling I'm doing a good job. I'm really helping this girl. Perhaps simply by being a non-judgemental but caring listener, I'm giving Polly something she's craved for a while: an adult confidante who she trusts. It seems she's lost faith in her mother's ability to be a parent. She's been abandoned and, I fear, abused by her father, and I'm beginning to realise it's no wonder she snapped six weeks ago. She's probably always wanted to talk about Benjamin, but that too has been denied.

With a cruel jolt, I remember that Polly's father might still be gone, but he could return any day, any time, and there's nothing I can do about it.

*

I'm typing up the session notes when the bell rings. My next appointment isn't until midday, so I jump at the sound.

At the door, I see a young man holding a bouquet of red roses.

"Ms England?" he says.

"That's me."

"Here you go," he says handing me the flowers.

I close the door, puzzled and curious, and pluck the pale pink card from the midst of the roses. The message reads: 'Beautiful roses for a beautiful rose. Yours, Mark xxx'

I chew my lip and re-read the message. The roses are gorgeous and they smell lovely but…is it weird? I exhale heavily and carry the bouquet into the tiny box kitchen where I arrange them in a crystal vase. My hand moves to my pocket, towards my phone. I want to ring Eimear, ask her what she thinks, but then my phone beeps. It's a text from Mark asking me if I like the flowers. I reply saying thank you – I love them. And I do, but I can't shake the feeling that Mark might be taking things too seriously, too quickly. He sends a selfie of himself grinning goofily, which makes me smile and I tell myself to stop being so boring and wary. He has nothing to do with MON. He's just a nice guy who likes me. After my session with Polly, I'm certain he has nothing to do with her. She's seeing someone who's only one year older than her. I need to embrace the moment and stop ruining things. I need to, as Eimear would say, wake up and smell the roses.

Chapter Thirty

I'm craving a bath by the time I get home. Icy drizzle has dampened my hair and chilled my bones, and I'm dog-tired and craving a gin and tonic, which I know I can't let myself have. Not on a Tuesday night. Not this week. I slipped last week. I won't do it again.

Slipping into drinking during the week is a habit I developed after Greg left, which only added to my guilt, as I'd wake up feeling sludgy and rough, unable to listen to the boys properly, barely able to get them to school on time. It was only when I messed up in a big way that I put a stop to it.

I cringe as I unlock the front door, remembering one morning when I was so hungover that I literally couldn't go to work. I'd had to ask Michael's best friend's mother to drive the boys to school, and had lied to her, saying I was too ill to get out of bed. But I wasn't. I was still drunk. I realise now that I was on the verge of becoming an alcoholic. Thank God I was able to pull myself out of it.

Relieved to get home, I kick off my shoes and lock the front door behind me. A second later, I freeze. A peculiar rushing sound meets my ears. I frown, trying to work out what it is. It sounds like running water. Did I leave the kitchen tap on this morning after I poured myself a glass of water? Surely not. I've never done that before.

I drop my bag and the bouquet of roses on the sofa, walk through the living room into the dining room-kitchen and stare in dismay and horror at the mess before me. Both kitchen taps are on, the sink is overflowing, water has flooded the kitchen and flowed into the dining room turning the carpet sodden. The kitchen bin lies on its side, contents spilled and floating like dead bodies. The space stinks of damp and mouldy fruit. It's a complete state. Tears fill my eyes and I dart forward, slop through the litter-swamped water and twist both taps closed. As expected, the plug is in the sink. Someone has done this to me on purpose. This was intentional.

Another sound – the same, but further away – comes from upstairs. And water is dripping from the ceiling.

I sprint upwards. The landing carpet is soaked. The bathroom door is ajar and the rushing of water floods my brain. I run into the bathroom; both sink taps and the bath tap are on full, plugs in. The bath has flooded as has the sink, and the bathroom bin has been emptied too. I twist off all four taps, yank out the plugs and stare at the destruction. I'm cold and trembling and everything suddenly seems too much. My feet and ankles are wet-through. I catch sight of my face in the mirror above the sink and don't recognise the frightened, mouse-like woman who stares back, her face sheet-white, lips shrivelled, chin trembling. I run to the airing cupboard, grab as many towels as I can hold and throw them on the bathroom floor. Grabbing the remaining towels from the cupboard, I run downstairs and throw those on the kitchen floor, watching as they absorb what seems like tiny amounts of water before turning into useless, wet lumps. Trying not to cry, I fumble inside my coat pocket for my phone, withdraw it and dial the police.

I explain what I've found, and get put through to the female police officer who came to my house before. She asks me to explain again. I do, aware my voice is shaky and alien and almost childlike. She tells me to stay at a friend's house for the night and deal with it tomorrow morning when I'm over the shock. Says I need to change my locks first thing tomorrow and that there's nothing more she can do at present. Almost as an afterthought, she suggests I get home security cameras installed in and outside my house. She says she's sorry this has happened to me. I barely say anything. Before I know what's happening, she's hung up and I'm alone, crying. I need to sort myself out, but I don't know what to do, so I go into my bedroom, take off my tights and curl up in bed. I lie there staring at nothing for how long I don't know. After a while, I stop shivering and force myself to move.

The only person I can ring is Eimear. I call her and explain what happened, my voice robotic now, mind numb. I vaguely register her telling me that she's getting her neighbour to watch the girls. She's driving over to pick me up.

I throw a few things in a bag, change into joggers and a jumper, and wait for her in the living room.

The knock on the door startles me to my feet. I move hesitantly to the front door and ask who's there. It's Eimear. Her Irish lilt is so wonderful to hear that I burst into tears.

Chapter Thirty-One

"Geez. Why on God's green earth haven't you told me any of this?" Eimear says.

I sip at the rich hot chocolate she's made me, my feet tucked under my bottom on the squishy blue sofa. Her house is small but cosy and ever-so-warm. Flames flicker in the Victorian fireplace casting soft light into the small living room, onto the framed photographs of Pippa and Rosie and the fluffy rug which lies atop oak floorboards. The house feels lived in and well-loved, and smells of family, of little girls and clean sheets and chocolate. The gentle click of a turquoise, heart-shaped clock sitting on the mantlepiece is mellow and calming. My eyes feel heavy. I stifle a yawn.

"I didn't want to make a fuss. I hoped it would just stop. That whoever wrote that message on my coffee table would decide they'd gotten their message across and leave me alone."

Eimear sighs and shakes her finger at me. "Next time, tell me. Okay?"

"Yes, boss."

She smiles and slurps her own hot chocolate. She looks like a big cuddly pink teddy bear in her fluffy pink robe and slippers. The girls are sound asleep in bed, safely tucked up with their night-teddies. It's nine 'o clock. I yawn again and this time Eimear follows suit.

"So, are you going to do it?"

"Do what?"

"Get cameras installed?"

"I'm definitely going to change the locks, but -"

"Do it, Jess. Get the cameras. I know it'll be a pain having workmen all over the place, but you're going to have to get people in to sort out the mess anyway."

"I'm worried it's going to cost the earth."

"Yeah, but it'll be worth it. For peace of mind if nothin' else."

I know she's right, but paying for security cameras on top of everything else feels like I'm giving in. As if my tormentor has won. I begrudge having to fork out a load of money for something like this. But I keep these thoughts to myself, knowing Eimear will tell me off.

"Imagine if you caught the nasty little sod? How amazing would that be?"

"How long do you think he'd get?"

"I dunno, but he deserves to go down for this," she stops, looks me dead in the eye, "and you've absolutely no idea who he is? Why he's doing this?"

"Haven't a clue," I say, which is almost true.

"You're staying here tomorrow night as well. You're staying as long as it takes to fix your house."

"Thanks. Oh shit. I forgot – I need to let Mark know whether I want to see a film with him. I'm saying no. There's no way I'm going to feel up to it."

Eimear perks up and beams at me. "Oooh? Decided to give him another chance, have you?"

"Yeah. We met for lunch yesterday. He sent me flowers today."

"Really? God, he's keen." Eimear's tone betrays something critical, which I understand.

"Think I'm ready for bed," I say as another yawn attacks.

"Me too. Try to get some sleep, hun."

She plants a motherly kiss on my forehead and leaves the room, yawning all the way to the stairs.

I down the rest of my hot chocolate and text Mark to say I'm not feeling well and won't be up for the cinema.

After staring at nothing for a while, I go upstairs and have my wash then curl up in the single bed in Eimear's spare room. Before I turn out the bedside lamp, I check my phone expecting Mark's response to be speedy like always, but he hasn't replied. The thought that he might be annoyed floats through my mind, but I'm too tired and worried to care.

Chapter Thirty-Two

First thing in the morning before any of the Blithes wake up, I leave voicemails with today's clients saying an emergency has come up, so their appointments will have to be rescheduled for next week.

I sit in Eimear's living room, listening as the radiator clunks to life, hugging myself, my eyes on the heart-shaped clock, counting down the minutes until I can begin to make calls and restore order to my life. I need to get someone in to dry out the floors, replace the carpets, fix the damp in the ceiling, change the locks and install home security tech. I need to contact my insurance company as soon as possible. I need to take back control. Eimear's right: I can't live in fear, which is what I've been trying to do the last couple of weeks. I need to act, make it impossible for this person to get away with these attacks. So far, his assaults have been personal yes, but focused on harming my home, not my actual person, which makes me think that he doesn't intend to hurt me, but I could be wrong. His next move could be fire.

There's been no reply from Mark, but right now I care little about that. There's no way I'll be able to muster up a smile, let alone go out on a date.

Footsteps and voices emerge from upstairs and a moment later Pippa and Rosie come running. They stop in the doorway and smile shyly at me.

"Good morning girls."

Pippa giggles and Rosie says, "I like your pyjamas."

I look down at my Minnie Mouse pjs, which seem so stupid and frivolous all of a sudden. "Thank you. I love your onesie."

Rosie beams. "Mummy got it me for my birthday."

They skip out of the room towards the kitchen. I hear the kettle boiling and bowls clattering.

Eimear shuffles in holding a huge mug of coffee and a plate of buttered toast, which she gives to me with a yawn, "Morning, hun. How'd you sleep?"

"Surprisingly well," I lie.

"How did Mr Intense take your cancellation?"

"Not sure. Haven't checked." I know what she means by the nickname, but it rubs me the wrong way.

"Have you asked him yet?"

"Asked him what?"

"If he's ever cheated."

I lock eyes with Eimear, surprised by the sternness in her voice.

"Oh. No. I don't think I'm going to. I'm not even sure I'm going to see him again."

Her jaw hardens. She rubs her neck roughly. Heat flushes her cheeks and she speaks quickly, each word a barb that pierces my conscience with needle-like precision. "Ask or you might regret it. If he's cheated before, he'll do it again. Someone will catch his eye and he'll be off, just like that. You won't know what hit you, and the thought of him shaggin' some skanky, cheating bitch will eat at you forever."

I nod and tell her I'll ask him. I won't.

She strides out of the room, back stiff.

I look down at my hands, head spinning. Shame writhes in my stomach like a grumble of maggots. Eimear's been badly hurt. The wound she's suffered is still raw and oozing. I'm relieved she doesn't know what I did before, because if she did we'd no longer be friends.

Chapter Thirty-Three

I find myself gazing at houses in estate agents' windows, wishing I could abandon my too-big, soulless house and move into a quaint little cottage in the middle of nowhere. I've always wanted to write a book…I could downsize dramatically, buy somewhere that needs a bit of a makeover, try my hand at DIY, give up my job, craft a story, live a quiet, peaceful life in the countryside far away from here, away from this man who has it in for me.

Workmen are in my house right now fixing everything. They say it'll take about three days to salvage the property, which isn't as long as I'd expected. The security tech will be up and running within a week and will cost me a lot, but I suppose it's worth it. I haven't got the guts to up and leave, sack everything in and start anew. And besides, where would the boys sleep when they came home? When they're older and married with kids I'll need room to put them up. It'd be selfish of me to trade my huge, characterless house for a smaller model.

I plod up High Street staring in shop windows, hands shoved deep in my pockets to guard against the chill. Every shop window twinkles with tinsel. Christmas lights hang from the buildings, soulless and dark, ready to fill the street with festive cheer come December 1st.

The sun is bright and mocking in a clean blue sky but it's too cold to be strolling about outside for long, and I trudge into Caffé Nero and buy a cappuccino.

The smell of crushed coffee beans drifts through the cafe. There's a constant flow of customers opening the door meaning cold air slips inside and seeps into my exposed skin. Busy voices surround me. They fade into white noise as I sip the frothy drink and I allow myself to remember.

The mug warms my fingers but the chill on my cheeks and nose is harsh and lingering. Closing my eyes against the café with its smiling, carefree customers and colourful coats, I cast my mind back ten years to the blackest moment of my life when I failed myself and my family. To the time I let my boys and husband down: the period self-hatred grew claws and began its creeping, inevitable journey into my heart.

Shame sears deep, scalding as an iron rod, but I force myself to recall every wicked second. I try to go through chronologically, from the second I saw him to the second I saw sense. That person wasn't me; that individual was younger, wilder, selfish. At the same time, she was and is me and there's nothing I can ever do to change that. I can never undo my actions or delete that decision. But what I can do is work out who I hurt most in the process. Who it is that feels it's their life's purpose, now, a full ten years on, to make my life a misery. Because I need to protect myself, if not for me, then for James and Michael. I may have destroyed my relationship with their father and been a terrible mother for a while, but I'm a good mother now and the boys need me. And I am a good person now, most of the time, I think.

But I wasn't back then.

Back then I put my own needs first - sod the consequences. But they're coming back to bite me in the form of a man hellbent on scaring and possibly hurting me.

I need to think back. I need to work out who this person is. Somehow, I need to make things right.

*

The moment I saw Evan, I just knew. I was twenty-eight, mother to two boys aged eleven and eight, married to a man I cared about, but didn't love or find particularly attractive. A man I had never loved. A man who, despite being lovely, made me feel trapped in a life I didn't want and never had. My whole life felt like a horrid farce and I was the fool caught in the middle of it.

It was nine o'clock on a Thursday night and Greg was home with the boys. I'd popped out giving the excuse that I needed to get a few essentials for the next day, but I'd been lying. The reason I'd gone out was because Greg was annoying the hell out of me, and I needed space.

I was in Tesco of all places – nowhere glamorous or exciting – and I dropped a tin of beans.

The tin rolled away from me and I rushed after it, head down, hair in my face, muttering obscenities under my breath. I'd almost caught up with the pesky tin when a large brown boot landed on top of it, stopping it in its tracks. I glanced up through the tangled net of my hair and smiled, then stared – or rather gawped - at the insanely attractive man who'd stopped my tin of beans. My stomach somersaulted and heat flooded my cheeks. I said thank you and he said no problem. As I straightened up I noticed he was staring at me too. And smiling. And his smile was incredible. He was tall and well-built with thick, sandy hair and sexy stubble and my body reacted just looking at him. I could smell him too and he smelled amazing. He ran his hand through his hair and asked me if I fancied going for a drink. I said when and he said now and we went, just like that, to The Old Bell. I didn't even think twice.

We barely spoke; just stared and smiled at each other and sipped our drinks. He drank Guinness and I drank red wine. In some kind of unspoken agreement, we left the table and moved to the hotel part of The Old Bell. Evan bought a room and I followed him up the stairs.

My body ached for him; every part of me tingled, throbbed. So far all I knew was his first name and the fact he lived locally, and sordid as it was, that was enough. In a way, knowing only those few details made the whole thing that much more thrilling.

He shut the door and locked it and a shock of adrenaline rippled through me like ice water. Then he moved, swiftly, confidently, pushing me down on the bed. I was blown away by how unlike Greg he was;

where Greg was soft and gentle and delicate and nervous in his touch and manner, Evan was strong and almost aggressive. We didn't even kiss. It was just pure animal sex. Raw and mind-bending and absolutely incredible.

Afterwards, we exchanged numbers and he said he'd be in touch. I used the shower in the ensuite, still rapturously reliving every intoxicating moment of our exchange.

It was only when I got home and discovered that James had been throwing up and was burning with fever that the first wave of guilt hit. Sadly, that wasn't enough to stop me seeing Evan again. I was addicted to the rush, the thrill, the pleasure, the fact that he desired me so intensely.

We met again the following week in the same place, same room. Evan was already there when I opened the door and he grabbed me and shoved me on the floor – took me right there right then. It was a little scary, but such a rush. Again, we barely said anything, just silently agreed to do it again.

And we did. The Old Bell became our meeting point and I became the world's greatest liar. I told Greg I'd joined a writer's group, decided to pursue my desire to write a book at last. He was surprised but pleased for me; he saw the life return to my face, saw my expression light up with excitement every week before I left for my 'club'. I felt guilty every time a lie escaped my rotten lips, but it still wasn't enough to prevent me from meeting Evan.

We were nothing more than fuck buddies and we shared few details of our personal lives. One day he had to cancel our meeting. My stomach hollowed out. Doubt crept in – and fear. Was our tryst over already? It was too soon. I wasn't ready to lose it – not yet. In his text he briefly mentioned it was something to do with his son. I knew he was married like me, but I didn't know he had a child. For some reason, knowing he had a wife wasn't enough to make me reconsider what I was doing, but knowing he had a child needled its way into my conscience.

We met again the following week. I asked how his son was and he told me he was fine. He didn't tell me anything more other than the fact that his son was his pride and joy. I didn't pry. Didn't want to know; shame was already in my bones working its sour magic.

One night about four months into our affair, I was on my way to The Old Bell to meet him and he grabbed me just outside my house, dragged me round the side into the back garden, pushed me onto the ground. I panicked, desperately fearful Greg would see us, but the thrill of what was happening was too much, and I went with it. I let him take me right there in my own back garden with my family only metres away.

Evan helped me to my feet then ran off. I glanced up as a light switched on in one of the upstairs bedrooms. There, standing in the window waving at me with an innocent smile of delight on his lovely little face, stood Michael. I waved back, forcing a smile as stab after stab of guilt tore through my gut. A moment later he disappeared and the light went off.

I stood there in the moonlit garden shivering, hating myself. I knew I'd never see Evan again. I texted him that very second saying I couldn't do this anymore and he never texted back. Much to my relief, despite him being local, I never saw him again.

I confessed to Greg a week later.

Chapter Thirty-Four

I know Evan has a son. Could he be the man attacking my home? He'd be ten years older now, possibly in his twenties like the man Charlie saw off. Evan was about ten years older than me back then - about the age I am now, so he could easily have a twenty-year-old son. It's unlikely but not impossible and, try as I might, I can't think of any other man who might hold a grudge against me.

But how do I go about finding Evan's son when I don't even know Evan's last name or address? I deleted his number the second I decided to end our arrangement.

Stumped, I sip the tepid remains of my cappuccino and stare unseeingly at the window. I feel empty, drained. Lost and helpless. I remind myself that within a week, cameras will be set up around my home. I wonder how to explain it all to James and Michael when they come back; Michael will be home in two weeks' time for the Christmas holidays. James won't return from Thailand for a while yet, but I need to work out a story. I can't tell them the truth; that I suspect the son of the man I had an affair with wants to hurt me. As far as the boys know, Greg and I divorced because we'd grown apart. I can't destroy that lie now by telling them the truth about this. Greg would never forgive me. He made me promise not to tell the boys what I'd done. Said he didn't want them to be any more traumatised than they already would be, given that their parents were going their separate ways.

I feel like slamming my head against the table. Anger sloshes about in the pit of my stomach and I jerk up and leave the café, steps jerky, body stiff.

The day is still mockingly bright and bitter, but I walk and walk, not caring where I'm going or that my face is redraw, body chilled right through. Anger carries me up the incline away from the hustle and bustle of shops toward the edge of town and out into the countryside. Insubstantial wisps of cloud drift across the fading sky. The fields are brown and furrowed like an old man's forehead, the trees skeletal, bushes reduced to brown bones. Mulchy brown leaves line the pavement. The atmosphere is heavy with the scent of mud and car fumes. Cars whizz by, too close, too fast. I rage up the hill, the soles of my feet aching. My lungs burn from the icy air and exertion, and my mind churns with remorse.

Finally, out of breath and exhausted, I perch on a tree stump at the edge of some woods and stare at my knees. I'm shaking. With numb fingers I pull my phone out of my pocket and see ten missed calls and five texts. I hastily unlock the screen and see who they're from, expecting them to be from the workmen, but they're not. One text is from Eimear checking on me, asking me when I'll be back, and now, for the third time, demanding I find out whether 'Mr Intensity' has cheated before. The other four texts and all the missed calls are from Mark. My heartbeat falters and my nerves sizzle with alarm; ten missed calls? Four texts?

I read his texts. Every message reads the same: *Tried to call. I need to talk to you. Call me back. M xxx*

The time is 3.45pm and daylight is fading. He's texted me every hour on the hour since 11am. Most of his missed calls were at midday. He hasn't left any voicemails.

Fear and his nasty friends batter my brain like bullets – he's been in an accident – he's hurt – bleeding – doesn't have anyone else to call…but if it was that urgent, would he bother with three kisses? And why hasn't he left a voicemail telling me why he needs to speak to me so urgently?

My finger hovers over his number as I try to decide whether to call him back. I can't really be doing with this. I need to focus on how to safety-proof my life; not how to deal with an intense man I've only just started seeing, and who I might not see again.

But curiosity and compassion get the better of me and I text him asking what's wrong, apologising for not replying sooner. He texts back immediately: How are you feeling? Up to seeing a film next week instead? M xxxxx

I shake my head, bewildered. He is way too keen. Not simply passionate, but far too intense. I can't cope with this kind of pressure – this intensity. Not now, anyway. Not with everything else that's going on.

My fingers linger over the screen as I try to put into words the kindest and gentlest rejection possible. His handsome face and bright laugh enter my mind, but I don't dwell on what I could be losing. The time isn't right. There're far more pressing things for me to focus on right now. I need to concentrate on making myself safe and helping Polly.

Realising I've walked a fair distance from town, I arrange an Uber then text Mark back: *Not feeling good to be honest, thanks for asking. I'm really sorry but something bad's happened (family thing), so I can't see you anymore. It's a shame we didn't meet at a better time, but I must put my family first. It was great to meet you. Good luck with everything, Jessie x*

As soon as I press send, I'm hit by a swell of relief so strong it leaves me reeling. Though chilled to the bone, I feel better; warmed by the thought that I've made a decision that means I have one less thing to worry about.

As I wait for my lift, the day greys into dusk and I think about Eimear's cosy house, imagine snuggling up on her sofa next to the roaring fire. I feel a tad more positive. I can deal with this. I've already taken steps to fix up the house and soon I'll have secret eyes in and around my home that will protect me. If this man tries to do something else, I'll know – I'll catch him in the act – or before he even manages to strike. I'll show the footage to the police, they'll arrest him, and then, at last, I'll know who he is and why he hates me, and this nightmare will finally be over.

I climb into the warm car and receive a text from Mark that sends a shiver across my neck.

You're making a huge mistake. Where are you? We need to talk. Please call me.

Chapter Thirty-Five

I need to help Polly, so I must put all of my own problems and fears out of my mind, which is far easier said than done.

In the end, last night, after a lot of pestering from Eimear, I switched off my phone and threw it in my bag.

Since the text he sent me on Wednesday, Mark's sent another five texts, each expressing the same one-track mentality, an identical fixed need. He wants to meet up, talk things through. His texts aren't aggressive. If they were, the guilt I feel every time my phone bleeps would dwindle away and be replaced by anger – and probably a hint of fear. Part of me wants his messages to transgress so that I can work myself up into a rage and respond to him fiercely in a way that would kill his desire to continue his peculiar texting barrage. But it's not happening. His tone remains agreeable, if odd. Because isn't it odd to text someone this many times when you've only been on two dates?

Maybe I should have rung to explain more fully; taken the time to meet up for a quick coffee, explain face-to-face. Maybe that's all he needs.

Eimear says I should ignore him. Disregard the niggling wasp and it'll give up and buzz away, move on to something sweeter. But I'm not so sure. It feels like he needs to hear the words straight from my lips with me sitting opposite, but the thought of doing that is exhausting, especially when the cameras still aren't installed in my home. Tonight, I'll be back in my own house for the first time. Eimear thinks I should stay at hers until the cameras are in, but the locks will be changed soon, and I can't burden her anymore. Besides, I've barely slept a wink since staying at hers, and I need my sleep. Even now at the start of the day with two strong coffees streaming through my veins, I feel like I could curl up in the waiting room and sleep for twenty-four hours.

I stifle a yawn as Polly strides in with her skirt rolled up in a way that would set her teachers' heads rolling. I did the same thing when I was fifteen. Externally, she looks like any 'normal', well-adjusted girl. If anyone met her right now, they'd think she was fine. She's good at hiding her inner turmoil, but I know she's still unwell and battling to cope. It's up to me to work out how to unlock the secrets she guards.

She sits down, leans forward and gives me a warm smile – the first she's given me to date. I reciprocate and steeple my fingers under my chin.

"How are you feeling today, Polly?"

She rifles around inside her satchel, seeming not to hear me.

"Polly?"

"Huh? Oh. Sorry. I need to show you something. I think maybe it'll help you understand why I," she swallows, her smile gone, eyes misting over, "you know. Why I did what I did."

My heart begins to race at the unexpectedness of what she's saying. Something to show me? Could it be her diary?

She withdraws a small white envelope from her bag. She glances up at me, hesitates. A frown flickers across her beautiful face. I can see her struggling, questioning herself.

Fearful she's going to change her mind, I reach out for the envelope, give her a reassuring nod, a gentle smile.

"It's okay. You can show me anything."

But she doesn't hand me the envelope. She stands up and drifts away from the sofa toward the windows that look out onto the city streets. Not far away, traffic drones. A car horn beeps. Sullen clouds blanket the swollen sky, soon to break.

I watch Polly closely as she stands staring out of the

window, not down, but forward, head aloft, shoulders tense, back rigid.

"If I show you," she murmurs, "you have to promise not to tell anyone."

"Of course. Like I said at our first meeting, as long as you don't tell me that you're going to hurt or kill yourself or someone else or that you know of a child or elder who's being abused, everything you say remains confidential."

Her shoulders shake a little. "She won't like it."

"She?"

"You know. Her. The one who's really pulling the strings."

My heart thuds. Is she talking about herself in the third person? Her mother perhaps?

I decide not to pursue that line of questioning; I need her to show me whatever's in that envelope. If she feels it will illuminate her issue, I need to see it. I feel almost jittery with the suppressed urge to get up from behind my desk and rip the envelope from her hands. My legs jig under the table and I sip some water, tell myself she'll give me the envelope in her own time. If I push her, she might change her mind.

"Ugly, isn't it?" she murmurs.

"What's ugly?"

"That," she says, gesturing to the city below.

"Oh, yes, it is."

"I hate it here," she says.

I stay silent. She's feeling her way toward me, working herself up to showing me.

"I hate being here, where it happened."

She sighs again. It's a long, heartfelt sigh which makes my chest ache. She looks so young and fragile. At fifteen years old, I was loving life. Life revolved around friends and boys and house parties and hockey. Simple, fun things that life's supposed to be about at that age. I assume by 'where it happened' she means where she tried to take her own life, so I don't prompt her for more information; I wait and attempt, with difficulty, to still my jigging legs.

She looks down at the envelope in her hand. Looks up at me. "I can trust you, can't I?"

I nod, smile encouragingly.

Without further pause, she strides across the room and places the envelope in my hand. She perches on the edge of the sofa and begins to gnaw at the seeping skin around her thumb, eyes downcast, free hand plucking at a loose thread in her skirt.

"Open it," she whispers.

Chapter Thirty-Six

The black night air was a lot colder than Benjamin thought it would be. He tried to zip up his coat but couldn't do it, so he tugged it closed with one hand and trailed his other hand along the brick wall, turning right and shuffling across the back of the house toward the side path that led to the drive.

The brick wall felt hard and rough against his soft little fingers. He didn't like the feel of it but he did not want to lose his way.

Their back garden looked creepy in the shadows. Moonlight turned the trees into horrid, big giants with black arms that could swoop down on him at any moment. He was cold and scared but clamped his jaw shut and felt his way forward, determined not to turn back. Claire's secret was going to be so good. He was going to get to see something nobody else – apart from Claire – had ever seen. He was going to get to see magic, like Harry Potter. He might even become magic too. He pictured Claire's smiling face in his head and grinned.

The scrapey corner of the wall told him he had got to the end of the back part of the house. He turned right and took a small step forward, reaching out for the side gate. His fingers found the metal sliding lock and he lifted and slid it open, jumping a little at the squeak it made.

An owl hooted and he bolted through the gateway, not bothering to close it behind himself. He stopped and listened and took great gulps of cold air that made his teeth hurt. The owl hooted again and something small and quick darted across the sky – one, no, two of them. Benjamin knew they were bats. He shivered. Bats made him think of monsters. He hoped there were no monsters out tonight. In films and stories, monsters always came out when it got dark.

Turning on his puppy ears, he shuffled forward up the side of the house. His fingertips hurt now from the scratchy bricks. He told himself to be brave and think about Claire and her secret and what it would look like. Excitement bubbled up in his tummy and he stepped bravely away from the safety of the brick wall and shuffled forward. In the darkness, he could see the large, hulking shape of Daddy's car. It shone in the light from the big round moon. Benjamin shuffled past the car and stopped at the end of the driveway.

He stared out at the dark houses and the dark, dark road. He knew how to get to Claire's house because Mummy had walked him there a lot of times. He turned left and told himself to run to the first streetlamp. When he got to that one, he could have a rest and get his breath back and get ready to run to the next one. He didn't know how many streetlamps until Claire's house, but he was glad they were there. With the moon and the streetlamps, it was not as dark and scary and monsters would not go near the light. Monsters liked the dark. They liked to hide in shadowy places then jump out and grab children when they were walking past. But if he stayed close to the light, he would be okay.

Benjamin counted to three then ran away from his house. He used his arms to make him faster, like he'd been taught in school by Mrs Dewer. He was halfway to the streetlamp when he tripped and fell. His knees and hands slammed into the concrete pavement and he cried out in pain and shock. One of his teddy bear slippers had come off and his foot began to get very cold. He stayed there on his hands and knees for a moment, trying not to cry. Tears fell anyway. His knees were stinging. The palms of his hands hurt too. Sniffing, he made himself stop crying and told himself to be brave, like Daddy. Daddy wouldn't cry if he fell over. Harry Potter wouldn't cry either. If they wouldn't cry, he wouldn't cry.

He pushed himself to his feet and looked around for his lost slipper. There. It was back the way he'd come. He hopped back to it and slipped it on then walked quickly to the streetlamp. He wasn't going to risk running anymore. He would just walk really, really quickly.

When he reached the light, he rested his hand against the cold metal and waited for his breath to come back. One streetlamp down, not that many more to go. When Mummy walked him to Claire's house, it never took long to get there.

Benjamin took a deep breath then pushed himself off from the light and shuffled towards the next one.

He was almost there when he heard something behind him that made him stop mid-step. His heart banged harder and he whimpered.

Something was there. He could hear it. Something was following him.

He told himself to turn around and see what it was, but he couldn't move. Fear nailed his feet to the spot.

He began to shake all over and wee trickled down his legs.

The thing behind him was making strange moaning noises. It had to be a monster. One that wasn't scared of light. The monster had found him and it was going to eat him up.

Benjamin told himself to run, but his feet wouldn't move. He squeezed his eyes shut and covered his face with his hands.

Maybe if he stayed very still, the monster wouldn't see him.

Chapter Thirty-Seven

Silence bleeds into the room. Polly's eyes are closed, her head turned away from me and the white envelope in my hand. For a second or two, I stare at the piece of folded paper. Whatever's inside this small rectangle of paper has affected Polly deeply. I wonder if anyone else has seen the contents; has Heather? Has the girl shown her mother? My instinct is no. She hasn't shown her or anyone else for that matter.

Steeling myself with a deep breath, I untuck the envelope lip from its position, noting how Polly hasn't licked it closed. Maybe she couldn't bring herself to. Maybe the thought of putting her tongue to the paper was too close for comfort; contaminating.

I glance up. The girl's cheeks are stained with silent tears. Her eyes remain closed, her chest rising and falling too fast.

Not wanting her to change her mind, I slip my fingers inside the envelope and withdraw its contents: four photographs. Polaroids. They've been inserted facing down toward the back of the envelope. I lay them face-down on my desk in front of my laptop. Polly sniffs. I stare at the backs of the photographs. Each glossy, white backing bears a name handwritten in black ink. Women's names. Jennifer Browne. Rachel Taylor. Katie Shrew. Samantha Newbury. Nothing else, just names. The handwriting is slanted to the right, scribed in long, elegant lines.

I turn over Jennifer Browne and stare, mesmerised by the face in the photograph. I swear I've seen this woman before but can't for the life of me pinpoint where or when, under which circumstances. She lies on white sheets, eyes closed, head resting on a white pillow, asleep by the looks of it. The person behind the lens must have stood over her, close, because the picture shows her face and bare breasts but nothing more. Jennifer's breasts are small and pert, her skin pale, complexion smooth revealing only a few shallow crow's feet which place her in her thirties, though lower or upper end, it's hard to say. She has shiny brown hair that stops just past her collarbone. She's slim and attractive with long eyelashes and barely-there make up. Gold studs dot her earlobes and a golden necklace with a heart-shaped locket lies on her chest bone. A gentle smile pulls at her sleeping mouth and a light sheen of sweat covers her forehead. She appears peaceful, content.

I look up. Polly has drifted back to the window, her fingers lightly tracing something on the misted glass.

I turn over the next photograph and stare at Rachel Taylor. I don't recognise this woman at all. She too lies on a bed, but is staring into the camera lens, a flirty, challenging glint in her hazel eyes. Like Jennifer, Rachel is naked to the waist. She too has small, pert breasts, pale, flawless skin and brown hair. She looks younger than Jennifer. Thirty at a push.

Katie Shrew is also a brunette and appears to be asleep, like Jennifer. Katie's nose is pierced with a tiny silver stud. A small tattoo of a butterfly graces her neck. I don't think I've ever seen Katie Shrew before either.

The last photograph is of Samantha Newbury who I don't recognise in the slightest. This woman is the oldest of the four, early forties perhaps. Her brown hair is greying at the temples and fine wrinkles line her brow and eyes. She too is very attractive, slim and pale-skinned.

Clearly Richard George's type.

These women must be Polly's father's conquests; the photographs: mementos he kept. Mementos Polly somehow found.

My stomach squirms with disgust. Poor, poor Polly. What must the girl be going through?

Guilt kicks in a second later as I remember the night in my back garden when Michael so nearly caught me. I was so selfish. Unhappy yes, but selfish to do what I did. I could – should have – told Greg we needed to go our separate ways, then given in to the desire to be with another man. But I didn't. I cheated and lied and almost got caught by my son having sex with some almost-stranger right outside my own house when my entire family was snuggled up inside completely innocent and unaware what I was up to. Maybe Richard George and I aren't so different after all.

I glance up and catch Polly watching me, gauging my reaction no doubt. Her expression is unreadable.

"I'm so sorry," I say, gathering the photographs and slipping them back into the envelope.

She rubs her eyes and moves back to sit on the sofa then stares toward the window and exhales.

I wait for her to speak, but she remains mute and frozen, reminding me again of a porcelain doll.

"When did you find these?" I say.

Eyes still on the window, she says, "Just before I…"

"Oh. I see."

Her head snaps around and then she's staring at me with those near-translucent blue eyes. "Do you?"

I sip my water and meet her gaze, careful to make mine bland. She sounds older than her years, and there's a sad sort of acceptance in her voice, as though she's not expecting me to understand – thinks no one can.

"Where did you find them? How did you find them?" I say gently.

"In his diary. It was gross. He'd written about them too. All of them. Every sleazy detail."

"Oh Polly. I'm so, so sorry."

"It started before Benjamin died. He was seeing one of them back then."

"Did he…did he express any guilt?"

"Nope. He doesn't even mention Benjamin's

disappearance. There's a break of about three years after Benjamin went, then he starts doing it again." She shakes her head hard and fat teardrops splash onto her legs.

I pass her a tissue which she takes, dabbing carefully under her eyes, clearly not wanting to mess up her mascara.

"How would you say finding this out has affected you?" I know it's a stupid question, but I need to get her to open up.

She glances up at me, a strange smile tugging up her mouth. "How would it affect you, if you found this out about your own dad?"

There's a nasty edge in her voice; she's lashing out at the closest person to her, someone she knows will forgive anything. I take a deep breath, answer her honestly.

"I'd feel betrayed. Confused. Angry."

"Who'd you be most angry at?" she says, scrunching the tissue into a ball so tightly that her knuckles push up against her skin.

I hesitate. Think about it. "Him. Followed closely by them. The women – only if they knew he was married though."

"They knew. They got off on it."

"How do you know that?"

She shrugs. "They must've known. All that sneaking around."

"Have you," I pause, suddenly not so sure this is a good question to ask, "have you thought about talking to him about it?"

She stares, eyes unblinking. I re-cross my legs but maintain eye contact. "It's too late for that," she says.

"Too late?"

"Yeah. He's gone hasn't he? Left us again."

"If he was here and you felt up to it, what would you say to him?"

She murmurs, "I don't know." She pushes herself up from the sofa, walks slowly towards my desk and picks up the photograph of my sons.

"What happened to their dad?" she asks, voice soft.

I fleetingly wonder how she knows my husband's not in the picture anymore. Then realise my ring finger is bare. She must have put two and two together.

"I'd rather talk about you, if that's okay?" I say.

She strokes the photograph. "Has Michael got a girlfriend?" she says, raising her eyebrows playfully and giving a little giggle.

Disturbed by her sudden change of tone and subject, I reach out for the photograph. She smiles sadly and passes it back.

"Oh, it's time," she says looking up at the wall clock.

"See you on Tuesday?" I ask.

She nods. "Thank you. It's been good to finally tell someone about what I found. I feel a little better, just for showing you. Sorry if I'm all over the place. Sometimes I can be a bit rude when I'm upset, you know?"

I nod and stand up, pleased to hear her say our session has helped.

As I see her out, I think about our next meeting. To move on, we need to address her feelings towards her father and the women he slept with. I also need to find out whether Richard George abused her. It will be a slow and painful process, but something she needs to go through if she's ever going to regain a healthy mental state.

Despite Eimear's words echoing in my head, I switch on my phone. No texts, but a voicemail. I listen, worried I'll hear Mark's voice, but it isn't him. I sigh with relief and listen to the message.

It's the locksmith saying he won't be able to change the locks on my doors because he's broken his leg. I immediately set to work googling more locksmiths, but everyone I call is booked up or unable to do the work for some reason or another. I finally manage to book a guy in, but the earliest he can come is a week on Monday. Michael will be here then, and he'll want to know why I'm changing the locks. To be fair, he'd need to know at some point in the future anyway, because he has a key and might turn up one day unannounced and try to get in…

I glance at the photo of my youngest son and nibble my lip, wondering what version of the truth I'll end up telling him. I hate lying to the boys, but I can't very well tell them that I think the man taunting me is the son of a man I cheated on their father with a decade ago.

I think about Polly and her mother, and for a while I'm steeped in stomach-curdling hatred for my former self. I used to be one of those women; the kind that take what they want, to hell with the consequences. The type that ruins people's lives by pursuing their own gratification.

But I'm not that person anymore. I'm good and kind and I deserve to be happy. Don't I?

Also, remember you're only human. Everyone makes mistakes. No one's flawless.

I think about Eimear. If someone so lovely can like me, that must mean I'm okay. But a nagging voice whispers that Eimear doesn't know about my past. She doesn't know what I did. How brazenly I fucked someone else's husband, someone else's father. How close I came to scarring my little boy for life.

Chapter Thirty-Eight

I feel him before I see him. Hand on the front door, about to step inside, I glance around. Mark's there, standing right behind me, an apologetic expression on his handsome face.

"Hi," he says taking a small step back.

My heart bangs.

"Can I come in?" he says.

I hesitate. Look at the empty street behind him, at his eyes, which are red-rimmed as if he's been crying. He sighs and goes to turn away. My pulse steadies. I reach out and touch his shoulder.

"Sure. Come in. You're right. We need to talk. I shouldn't have ended things the way I did."

He beams and strides in ahead of me, then holds the door open as if it's his own home, bowing to me and calling me 'my lady' as I hurry past him lugging my bag. I drop my bag in the hallway and go through to the kitchen, telling myself to relax. He needs closure and I can give him that now over a nice, calming cup of tea.

My house still smells of damp but if he notices it, Mark doesn't say. He follows me into the kitchen and leans against the counter watching as I flick on the kettle and grab two mugs.

"Feeling better?" he says.

"Yes thanks. I had a horrible head cold and then I came home and realised I'd left the plug in the sink and the tap running."

"Oh God, really? No wonder you couldn't meet up," he says, lunging forward and grabbing the two mugs of tea before I can.

He carries them into the living room and, as an afterthought, I chuck a few biscuits on a plate and take them into the room. He's hovering, looking around for somewhere to put the mugs so I gesture for him to hand me mine. I perch on the edge of the one-seater sofa, placing the plate of biscuits on the only coffee table left in the room. He grins and sits down on the two-seater opposite, placing his tea on the bookshelf to his right. With a sigh, he kicks off his trainers and extends his legs, crossing them at the ankles. Getting relaxed – too relaxed for my liking. A faint odour of vinegar rises from his dirty white socks.

I sigh internally. I want to get this over with as quickly as possible. Twenty, thirty minutes tops.

"I need to apologise," I begin.

Mark waves his hands in the air. "No need. Really. I totally understand. If I felt all snotty and gross then came home to find my place in a mess, I'd freak out too. Not sure I'd go all the way and tell you it was over, but…"

"Thanks – for understanding. I've still got a lot going on to be honest, and, though we get on well and we've had a bit of fun, I really don't think I'm ready to see anyone. I thought I was, but I'm not. I need to focus on work and -"

"Hang on, hang on," he says, frown furrowing and jerking upright, "so even though you're feeling better, and the house is fine now, you still don't want to see me anymore?"

He puts his hands in a prayer position and leans forward, looking into my eyes. I sip my tea and try to make eye contact with him. Despite the coolness of the room, he's perspiring, and his teeth are gritted behind his lips. Tension shoots into my body and I rack my brain for the right thing to say to calm him down.

He bows his head over his hands and mumbles something I can't make out.

"I'm sorry Mark. I really am, but I need some time to myself. I thought I was ready -"

His head snaps up. "Yeah, you said. But what is that?

Time? If you like someone, you make it work. And you like me. You like me just as much as I like you. I can tell."

Oh God. The message is not getting through.

"I do like you," I say in what I hope is a firm, no-nonsense voice, "but I'm not ready for a proper relationship, and you need to respect that."

He snorts and pushes himself to his feet. Planting his hands on his hips, he stalks over to me and leans down bringing his face close to mine. Removing the cup of tea from my hands, he places it on the table then grabs my shoulders and gives me a gentle shake.

"I really, really like you, Jess. I've fallen for you. I know it's early, but it's the truth. I can't get you out of my head, don't you get that? You've done something to me – something amazing." He releases me and throws his head back with a laugh, running his hands through his hair. I move to stand, needing to put some distance between us, but he drops to his haunches in front of me.

"Be honest, Jess. Don't shy away from this. You like me too, I know you do."

This close up I can smell him and for the first time, stale sweat leaks through his overpowering aftershave.

I open my mouth to speak but he puts a clammy finger to my lips and shakes his head gently, a tender smile on his face. "Hey, hey. Let's not speak for a while. Let's just enjoy being in each other's company."

The urge to cry abruptly attacks and my breath catches; I never, ever should've let him in.

I sit still and breathe slowly, fighting the fear rising in my heart and trying to think of a way to get him out of the house without escalating the situation.

Chapter Thirty-Nine

In Benjamin's head, the monster had red eyes and enormous, sharp, black teeth. It was even taller than Daddy and covered in black spikes that dripped green slime. Its claws were like a lion's claws. Its tongue was long and pink and funny-shaped, like a snake's, and its favourite food was little boys. The monster was very fast – a lot faster than Benjamin – but its ears weren't very good, so if he could stay very still and be very quiet and find a good place to hide, the monster might not find him.

But right now, Benjamin knew his chances of making it were small. He was out in the open and he was breathing too loudly.

He clamped his hand over his mouth and kept his eyes squeezed shut, using his puppy ears to listen. The monster had gone quiet. It was probably watching him from the shadows, waiting to pounce.

Benjamin opened one eye and looked around. Bats fluttered past the streetlamp, making him jump. He wished he could fly away, zoom to Claire's house on a broomstick like Harry Potter. The monster wouldn't be able to get him if he was high up in the sky. Up there he would be safe and sound and –

Something hit his ankle. He cried out and started running. He didn't think about where he was heading. He just ran and ran, pumping his little arms and legs hard. He ran straight across the road towards some other houses. It wasn't the way to Claire's house but he didn't care. Something hard hit the back of his leg and he tried to run faster, but his teddy bear slippers made running difficult. He kicked them off and ran along the pavement bare foot. His feet hurt. The skin of his feet scraped against tiny stones. Tears ran down his cheeks. Another small, hard object hit him, this time on his back. He cried out but made little sound. He was too breathless to scream. He could hardly see anything, but he could hear footsteps racing after him. The monster was coming. It was going to catch up with him and dig its long sharp claws in and eat him up.

Benjamin followed the pavement around a bend and headed past streetlamp after streetlamp. He didn't know where he was. He ran and ran and then he tripped and fell. His hands and knees smashed to the ground and a cry tore from his lungs. He stayed there, panting, trying not to think about the pain and how scared he was and how any second the monster would come up from behind, grab his legs and drag him back to its cave.

Another hard thing hit his back and he scrambled to his feet and ran on, heading up a hill where there weren't many houses at all.

There looked like there might be a field up ahead. Maybe he could hide behind a bush. Trick the monster into thinking he'd gone a different way.

Benjamin's lungs felt like they were about to burst and tears blurred his sight. He pushed on past the last house and headed for the field, which looked like a dark grey lake in the almost black night.

At the fence, he stopped and looked both ways. There. Over there was a kissing gate!

He ran to the gate, pushed it in, slipped around the edge and sprinted out the other side onto damp, grassy soil that felt lovely and soft on his feet after the hard concrete. He was in the field, but he wasn't safe yet. Something whizzed past his ear and he heard a low cackling sound. A witch! Was a witch following him? Was it a witch like the one from Hansel and Gretel? For a second, Benjamin was frozen to the spot. His imagination went wild with pictures of cauldrons and bones and child-sized cages.

The witch-monster cackled again, and he set off running across the field, the only light coming from the big gold moon. Footsteps chased him and the cackling grew louder and louder. She was going to catch him. She was going to take him back to her cottage in the woods and put him in a cage and when she was ready, she was going to throw him in a bubbling, hot cauldron then cook and eat him for her dinner!

Sweat dripped into Benjamin's eyes, making them sting. He blinked and carried on running until he ran into something so hard that he bounced off it and collapsed on the ground. He couldn't breathe. The wind had been knocked out of him. His stomach hurt and his heart pounded. He told himself to get up but he couldn't. He couldn't move because he couldn't breathe. He curled up into a ball and closed his eyes and listened.

The sound of the witch's heavy, fast breathing filled the air. She was standing right over him. She'd found him.

Benjamin coiled into an even tighter ball and began to sob.

The witch cackled. It was a high, cruel sound. One he would never forget.

Something hard jabbed at his ribs and he gasped and rolled away and pushed himself to his feet and ran. He climbed over the fence that he'd run into before and sped away. Maybe he'd taken her by surprise. Maybe she hadn't expected him to get up and run away like that…

Lungs burning, he pushed his little body as hard as it would go. Ahead there was a big, black object. A house! Somewhere he could hide.

With hope giving him one last surge of energy, he ran with all his might towards the building. His foot squelched through a pile of stinky stuff but he kept on running. She was still running after him, so he couldn't stop even for a second. If he stopped, she was bound to catch him.

The house was surrounded by a fence. Benjamin climbed up the fence and jumped down the other side, crying out as his ankle twisted on hard ground that rustled like straw when he limped forward.

The building was completely black and it looked like the sort of place ghosts might live, but Benjamin had no choice. He limped forward and slipped around the side of the building. The air smelt of cow poo. He sank to his knees and clamped both hands over his mouth and listened, hoping desperately that this was a good enough hiding place to keep him safe.

Chapter Forty

"Fancy a takeaway?" Mark says.

"Look, Mark, I think you should go. I don't feel very well."

I try to stand up again but he holds up his hands, a glint in his eyes. "Oh no you don't, missy. Let me look after you. You look cold. Look, you're shivering. It is pretty cold in here. Shall I light the fire?"

"Yes. Yes, that's a great idea," I say – anything to get him away from me.

He grins and walks over to the fireplace, arms swinging. Crouching, he picks up small logs and throws them into the grate. I glance towards the living room door; it's so close – all I have to do is run into the hallway, take a few long strides and I'll be at the front door.

Mark's whistling now and the flames are rising already. He glances over his shoulder and smiles at me. "Better?"

I nod, annoyed at myself for not making a move for the door.

Mark stands up and stretches, yawns and slips his hand into the pocket of his tracksuit bottoms.

"What you fancy? Pizza? Indian? Chinese?"

"Chinese," I say, thinking that might be the quickest.

"Great! Got a menu?"

"Yeah. It's in the kitchen. I'll go get it."

My heart drums as I push myself up and leave the room, walking quickly, though not too fast – I hope – to arouse suspicion.

As I leave, Mark sighs contentedly and flops onto the sofa. The sound of the television bursting to life gives another welcome sign that he's relaxing; not suspecting anything.

In the kitchen, I grab my phone. My palms are slippery with sweat. I turn and head straight back to the living room, stopping in the doorway, the mobile held up.

"Get out or I'm calling the police."

Mark's head snaps up and confusion flickers across his face. "What – Jess – what are you doing?"

"I want you to leave. Now," I say, taking a step into the room, "If you don't, I'll call the police."

Shaking his head, he pushes himself up from the sofa and steps closer, hands held up in surrender. A nervous smile creeps into his face as his eyes flick back and forth between me and the phone. "Is this a joke?"

"No, Mark, this is most definitely not a joke. I've told you I don't want to see you anymore but you're not getting the message. I'm going to say it one more time and then you're going to leave and never come back. I. Don't. Want. To. See. You. Again. Got it?"

Tears shine in his eyes and his smile disappears. He swipes the tears away with the back of his hand. His shoulders slump. At last, he seems to be taking in my words.

"Okay, okay. I guess I've done it again, haven't I? I'm so sorry, Jess. If you let me explain, I -"

"No." I take a step closer, jab the mobile towards him and flick my head in the direction of the hallway.

He sighs again and leaves the room. I follow close behind, heart racing. Mark opens the front door, stops and looks round, expression sombre. "I wasn't going to say anything, but I know you lied."

I frown. "What are you talking about?"

"You lied about having a daughter. You have two sons but no daughter. I googled you. I thought you lied because you found me on Match.com, discovered where I worked and wanted to check me out in person. The idea excited me, made me think you were super-keen, but, you know, playing hard to get."

I shake my head, mind buzzing. "I lied because I was investigating a client, one of your students. Something she did led me to you. To be brutally frank, when you flirted with me at the school, I thought you couldn't have anything to do with her, but now, after this, I'm not so sure."

He frowns and barks out a laugh. "Really? God."

"Please leave, Mark."

"No – wait a second."

He's in the doorway, not making any move to leave. Clicks and crunches pierce the silence as he rolls his neck, once, twice.

I swipe my phone, but he doesn't seem to notice. His thoughts are elsewhere, brow furrowed with concentration. He scratches his head, clearly thinking. His jaw clenches and unclenches.

"Please Mark. Please go." I raise my voice. "Mark, I need you to go."

He nods, eyes wet. His larynx bobs up and down. He nods and backs out of the door, eyes locked on mine. "Okay. I get it. I'm sorry I scared you, Jess. I know I can be intense sometimes. Take care of yourself."

The second the front door closes, I lunge forward and lock it, my phone clutched so tightly in my right hand that it hurts.

Chapter Forty-One

Saturday is a dead day. I can't face going into town for my weekly shop. I can barely even drag myself out of bed. My mind spins with thoughts of Mark. Fear he still hasn't got the message has lodged itself in my chest like a knife. It's hard to breathe let alone move, so I sit on the sofa huddled up in a blanket with the fire roaring, the television on though I don't really hear what people are saying. I want to ring Eimear and ask her to come round, but don't want to intrude on her proper day off. She's already helped me out this week – sooner or later she's bound to get sick of me being so needy. She'll be back at work on Monday anyway, so I can confide in her then, when I've had some time to put things into perspective and calm down.

I check my phone regularly throughout the day. There's nothing from Mark, which ought to help, but it doesn't. I keep hearing noises outside and jumping up, thinking he's outside my door. At least security cameras will be installed on Monday morning, so if he decides to continue to harass me, he'll get caught and I can take the footage to the police and get him restrained. I've not deleted any of the texts he sent before; that ought to stand up as evidence of harassment adding to my case against him.

Several times I pick up my mobile to call the police and tell them what happened last night, but something stops me. Deep down I know they'd not have much to go on; I invited Mark into my house – he didn't force his way in. I even made him a cup of tea. He didn't hurt me, didn't resist at all, not physically anyway, when I told him to leave. I can't shake the niggling thought that the police will think I over-reacted. On paper, he's clean. He's a well-respected teacher at a good school. He has no record as far as I'm aware anyway – although his words ring in my ears, making me wonder. I've done it again. Done what again? Not realised when someone said they didn't want to see him anymore? Pestered someone until they lost the plot? Stalked an ex-girlfriend?

My stomach feels like it's been hollowed out with a spoon, but I can't eat. Instead, I sip lukewarm tea and wait for today to be over. At least tomorrow I can speak to Michael and be reminded of something and someone good in my life. Someone who doesn't want to hurt me.

Chapter Forty-Two

Following a nightmare-wracked night and a horribly lonely day, I call Michael half an hour early, fingers crossed on my lap in the hope that he'll pick up.

He does and the second I hear his cheery voice, it's like I can breathe again.

"Mum! Hi. I'm glad you called earlier than normal – everything okay?"

"Yeah," I begin to lie, then decide to opt for the truth for once, "kind of. I starting seeing this guy and when I decided he wasn't right for me, he wouldn't let it go and, well, I stupidly let him in last night so I could explain and make him realise I really didn't want to see him again and he still didn't get the message. It was a little scary to be honest."

"Oh God. He didn't hurt you, did he?"

"No, no. I managed to get him to leave, told him I'd call the police if he ever contacted me again. I'm just a bit shaken up."

"Thank God you're okay. That's what you get for being so awesome," he says, and I adore him for trying to lighten the mood.

I manage a laugh. "Anyway, enough about me. How's your week been? You're still coming down next Saturday, aren't you?"

"Yep. And I've got a favour to ask."

"Oh?"

"I know I said it'd be weird for you to meet Kiera so soon, but she's dying to meet you so I thought I'd bring her with me, if that's all right?"

Disappointment floods me. I was so looking forward to it just being the two of us. To catching up properly and cooking him his favourite meal and having him to myself, no distractions. But I'm being selfish again. I clear my throat and force lightness into my voice. "Course you can bring her! I'd love to meet her too. Is she a fussy eater or a veggie or anything?"

"Nope. She'll eat anything – and she eats like a horse!"

"Like you then?"

He laughs.

I hesitate, not sure whether to ask, but knowing on a practical level I need to. "So…shall I make up James' bed or will you two be in your room?"

"My room, if that's okay?" Now it's his turn to sound awkward.

I smile and remind myself he is eighteen and so is this girl, Kiera. They're adults and it's not surprising that they're already sleeping together. I'm hardly one to judge, anyway, having got pregnant with James when I was seventeen.

Still, my boy's growing up and it makes me ache. It only feels like yesterday that I held him in front of me, his head in my palm, the length of his body spanning my forearm – a perfect fit - and admired his beautiful baby-blue eyes. God, how time flies.

"Mum? Mum – you still there?"

"Yes - sorry – I was just remembering when you were a baby."

"Are you getting all sentimental on me?"

"I can't help it. My baby boy's all grown up."

"I'll always be your baby," he says, and though it's a cheesy thing to say, it's what I need to hear most in the world right now.

Chapter Forty-Three

Cameras are installed, I haven't heard from Mark for four days, James sent me a long email describing all the fun he's been having and Michael's coming home on Saturday. Things are looking up – finally. Even the sun is shining into my office, huge and beaming in a glassy blue sky, the weather fresh and cool, more spring-like than wintry. Christmas is only two weeks away and I need to get shopping. Michael has a wish list on Amazon, so I spend more than I should on gifts for him, then wonder whether to get something for Kiera. Deciding that yes, a small gift would be a nice idea, I order her a set of cupcake-shaped bath bombs then order Disney onesies for Pippa and Rosie and the new Jamie Oliver in hardback for Eimear.

Knowing I need to get on with work, I bury myself in Polly's notes, preparing for her arrival. Time whizzes by and before I know it, Polly strides into the room like she owns it and flops down on the sofa. She looks relaxed and healthy; hair in a high ponytail, make up perfect, eyes bright and clear. It's as if a totally different person has entered the room from the one who showed me those pictures on Friday. But I'm growing used to Polly's moods, and beginning to think there can be only one explanation. Dissociative Personality Disorder, also known as DID. Someone with DID has multiple, distinct personalities. The various identities control a person's behavior at different times, and the condition can cause memory loss, delusions or depression. DID is usually caused by past trauma, which would make sense given Polly's history.

"Morning. Want to know why I'm in such a good mood?"

"Yes, please tell. I must say, it's great to see you with a

spring in your step."

She smiles and leans forward. "My boyfriend's asked me to be his girlfriend, like, for real! How cool is that?"

"Oh, so he's your proper boyfriend now, is he?"

She nods and cracks her neck. "Yep. I love him. He's perfect. He makes all this other stuff seem like nothing, you know?"

"It's wonderful you feel like this now, but it's still important to deal with what happened. With your feelings about your father, don't you think?"

Polly shrugs as if she couldn't care less. "He's gone. He's a liar and a cheat. What more is there to say?"

I watch her, trying to detect the real Polly under the bravado. She glances up and tilts her head.

"What's wrong?"

I sigh and straighten my blouse. For a moment, I'm stumped. I don't know how to proceed. Then I remember what I wanted to ask her about, and this seems like the right time to ask her.

"Your mother told me that when she found you in the bathroom, after you'd hurt yourself, there was something written on the mirror. Three letters: M.O.N. Can you tell me what these letters mean?"

Polly's eyes fix on mine. A small frown creases the space between her fair eyebrows and her eyes narrow. She licks her lips. Her jaw clenches. I can see her mind racing, wonder if she's trying to conjure up a lie, or if her emotions are getting the better of her.

"Polly, you needn't tell me if you don't feel ready to."

Her mouth twists into a strange smile that doesn't meet her eyes and she looks away, toward the window. Silent tears wet her cheeks, but she doesn't move to wipe them away. It's like she doesn't feel them there. She rises from the sofa and begins to pace back and forth in front of my desk, eyes straight ahead, almost zombie-like in their flatness.

"Polly, really, if you're not ready, you don't need to -"

"Monster. I was writing the word monster."

"Can you tell me why? Why that word?"

I hold my breath, hoping she won't pull back now – this is clearly something she needs to express.

She stops pacing, stands directly in front of me, stares down into my eyes. There's something absent about her gaze that makes me feel cold. I tell myself to stop being stupid and try to offer her a small smile of encouragement.

"Everyone's got a monster inside them, haven't they?" she says, "Everyone's guilty of something."

"And what do you feel guilty of, Polly?" I say, unable to look away from her dead, dead eyes.

"Nothing. I've got nothing to feel guilty about."

"Good. That's very good," I say, though I doubt her words; depression often comes with self-hatred and guilt. As I know too well.

"I don't think I need to come to our sessions anymore," she says softly, moving to the door.

Shocked, I stand up and move around to the front of my desk. "It's good that you're feeling better, but maybe you ought to talk to your mother about it before making any snap decisions?"

She gives me a small wave and opens the door.

I'm too shocked to respond and watch open-mouthed as she leaves the room.

I feel like the wind's been knocked out of me by a train – what just happened? Did Polly just end our sessions?

Moving back to my chair, I stare at the closed door and try to work out what to do next. Polly's definitely not 'fixed' for want of a better word. I haven't even worked out a full diagnosis for her yet.

Suddenly, the day doesn't seem so rosy. If Polly doesn't come back, I will have failed her. Not only that, but I'll have failed her poor mother too. Just like I did with Roman and his mother.

For a long time, I stare sightlessly at my photograph of

James and Michael, willing it to buoy me up, but it doesn't. Visions of Heather George finding Polly bleeding or dead consume me. Try as I might, there's nothing I can do to block them out.

Chapter Forty-Four

Polly's decided she doesn't want to see Doctor England anymore. Says it's a waste of time, that she doesn't have suicidal thoughts anymore. I asked her if she thinks seeing Doctor England helped and she shrugged. She seems upbeat, but there's something a bit forced about it, like she's putting it on.

Last night, Polly actually came downstairs and watched MasterChef with me. She laughed at something Greg Wallace said! Her eyes were bright and present – it was as if I was seeing her for the first time in years. And her laugh – such a beautiful sound - it made me want to cry with joy.

She even told me she's decided to apply for Cambridge University and wants to read Psychology, which seems a bit close to home, but anything that gets her lit up like she was last night, gets a big fat tick in my book.

Of course, she needs to get excellent GCSE grades first, then ace her A levels. I mentioned this as lightly as I could – really, I was trying to snoop and find out how her revision's going. She knew what I was getting at – bright spark that she is – and reassured me that she and Dana have been working their socks off and her teachers are still predicting 8s and 9s. Even in Religious Studies, which she makes no secret of the fact she hates.

After a glass of wine, I relaxed and came close to asking her about her love life, but I'm glad now that I didn't. Knowing Polly, she'd probably see right through me and work out that I read her diary. I still feel guilty for doing it. I'm glad that when I went to find it that second time, I couldn't. Still, I can't help worrying that this older boy's going to take advantage of her or get her pregnant. And with Rich gone, if something like that happened, I don't know how I'd cope. Not that I'm saying I'm gutted he's gone – I'm not. Also, I don't think Polly misses him now; she hasn't questioned his absence once, which is hardly surprising given the way he's behaved over the years. I only wish I'd seen sense and gotten rid of him years ago. But I thought we needed each other after Benjamin. I told myself his countless affairs were his way of coping with our loss. What a load of crap. He was a selfish monster, unfit to be a husband or a father.

Just thinking about it is making me want to tear my hair out. Christ, I need a drink.

I also need to find out why she's hiding that bag in her bedroom, but I have to find the right time to ask her.

H

Chapter Forty-Five

I've become obsessed with watching the small screens that show me live footage of the front and back of my house. Last night, I sat and watched it almost without a break. Tonight, while I wrap presents, I glance up at the screen every few minutes, almost hoping Evan's son – if indeed that's who the culprit is – turns up and does something.

It's midnight. I go around turning off all the lights then sit and stare at the screen for another few minutes. With a sigh, I go to close my laptop and a movement in the video window that shows the front of my house catches my eye.

Heart in my mouth, I lean forward and stare at the film. Both doors are locked, though the locks are unchanged. I reach for my mobile and grip it tightly, ready to call the police if need be.

A man wearing a black balaclava stands outside my house staring at my front door. My fingers hover over the number 9 on my phone, but I don't call, not yet. Curiosity has me in its grips. Leaning closer to the screen, I watch with baited breath as the man continues to stand and stare. He has a bag hooked over one shoulder. He looks tall and thin and he wears jeans and a dark jumper. No coat. His hands are gloved.

Trembling, telling myself I'm being stupid and need to call the police now, I stab 999 into the phone and raise it to my ear. I'm connected immediately and a husky female voice asks me to state my emergency.

"A strange man's standing outside my house. He's done stuff before. He's wearing a balaclava and gloves. Please send someone quickly."

I rattle off my address and listen as the woman tells me someone's on their way, make sure the doors are locked, lock yourself in the bathroom or another room with a lock and wait for the police to arrive.

Sweating and shaking, I grab my laptop, rip out the cable and sprint upstairs, taking them two at a time, eyes never leaving the screen where the man continues to stand and stare at my front door. It's hard to believe he's only a matter of metres away.

I run into the bathroom, lock the door and perch on the toilet seat, laptop on my trembling knees. To think I was wishing this would actually happen…what an idiot.

The man shrugs his bag off his shoulder, unzips it and pulls something out. My heart beats harder, but I continue to watch as he shakes the thing he's holding. After giving it a few vigorous shakes, he walks up to the side of my house, raises the object and begins to wave it up and down. Then I realise what's happening – what he's doing. He's graffitiing my house. Relief crashes through me like broken glass as visions of him hurling petrol onto my front door then lighting the fumes fade away to be replaced by a horrible message that will hurt my heart but won't kill me.

Police sirens sound in the distance, getting louder and closer by the split second. The man's head whips in the direction of the sound. He chucks the spray can on my driveway, turns and runs out of view.

I drop my laptop, race to the bathroom door, unlock it and run through into my bedroom just in time to see blue lights whizzing past. I look for my tormentor, but darkness has swallowed him whole; I can only wait, and hope the police catch him.

Chapter Forty-Six

Diary, I think I'm in shock. I feel...I don't know what I feel. I can't believe it. I need to ring someone, speak to somebody, but I don't know what I'd say. I don't think I can bring myself to say the words out loud. Maybe they've got the wrong person. Made a mistake. Maybe the body is disfigured beyond identification, because they want me to go down to the station now, to identify it. They don't want me to be up here in my room writing this. They'd think I was crazy if they knew what I'm doing right now. Writing in my diary. People don't do that when they find out a loved one's dead, do they? Who goes and writes about it in their diary? No-one. No-one except a crazy person, that's who. Right now, I feel kind of crazy. I mean, I ought to feel something, but I don't. My heart's not even beating faster than normal. It's like I'm sedated or something. I feel spaced out. Like I'm not really in my body, like the bed and my dressing table and my shelves are there, but I'm not. I need to go though. I need to go and identify the body. That's what they said, so that's what I need to do. There's nothing else to do, is there? No. That's right. Get up and go. Stop being stupid and just go.

H

Chapter Forty-Seven

They caught him. The police actually caught him!

I yank on jeans, jumper, coat and trainers and hurry outside into the chilly night, tempted for a beat to use the light on my phone to see what he scrawled on my house, but I don't; I need to get to the station quickly. I don't know why I feel the urge to hurry so much – it's not like he's going to escape or anything. Maybe the need to see his face, finally have answers and put an end to this madness is what's making me drive like a madwoman through the dead streets.

I'm breathing hard when I pull into the carpark but force myself to drive slowly in case I get caught speeding by some officer outside having a vape. The carpark is filled with police cars. It's a big station – the city's biggest. I've never stepped foot in it before and feel nervous and self-conscious as I enter a harshly lit reception area that smells faintly of male body odour.

The waiting area consists of about twenty red plastic chairs, a coffee table topped with magazines and a dead fern in a chipped white ceramic plant pot. Several tired-looking people dressed in scruffy clothes sit on the chairs, some staring at their phones, others staring into space. An electric hum buzzes in the air and the space is cold, the walls white and covered with dog-eared posters.

I approach the reception desk and wait while an obese man with a bushy beard taps away at his computer, pretending he doesn't know I'm there. I grit my teeth and stare at his gleaming bald head, removing my hands from the counter which feels gritty beneath my fingers. Blinking out tiredness, I stifle a yawn and give the man a smile when he finally looks up.

"How can I help?" he says in a bored drawl.

"I've been asked to come in to report a crime. They've just caught the man who did it and -"

"Name?"

"Sorry?"

"Your name?"

"Jessica England."

"Take a seat. Someone'll come get you in a bit."

Irritated by his rudeness, I turn away sharply and perch on the closest seat.

Now that my adrenaline's receded, tiredness hits hard. I buy a can of Coke from the vending machine and sip it while I wait. I think about texting Eimear to tell her the good news but don't for fear of waking her up. The large plastic clock on the wall opposite me reads 1.30am. I rub my face and finish the rest of my Coke then fold my arms over my chest and let my eyes rest.

A few seconds later, I feel a presence standing over me and jerk up. It's the female officer who came to my house before, Officer Black. She nods hello and gestures for me to follow her, explaining that they've questioned the man and have a photograph of him to show me.

Officer Black leads me into a small meeting room with beige walls. She sits one side of a small table and gestures for me to take the chair on the other side. I sit down, nervous and alert again with adrenaline.

"This is him," she says, sliding a photograph toward me.

I stare at a close up of a young man. He looks unhealthily thin, almost skeletal, with greasy blonde hair and dull brown eyes. I try to find a hint of Evan in him but there's nothing similar about the two men.

"Who is he? Why was he doing this to me?" I say, looking up.

"His name's Tyler Mason. Local kid. Twenty-two years old. Says someone blackmailed him to do it. Won't give a name."

She shrugs and slides the photograph back across the table. "I take it you've never laid eyes on him before?"

I shake my head. "Is there any way of getting him to say who blackmailed him? They might blackmail someone else to carry on harassing me, now that this Tyler guy's been caught, mightn't they?"

Officer Black shakes her head. "I think that's highly unlikely. Now we've caught Tyler, word'll get out how we caught him and whoever's behind this will know you've got cameras. I doubt they'll risk pursuing you anymore," she pauses, leans in a little closer, and I notice a fine white scar on her chin, "are you sure you can't think of anyone who might have it in for you?"

I sigh and rub my eyes. "It's a long shot, so I didn't mention it before, but I did think that maybe it could be the son of someone I had a fling with ten years ago."

Doubt creases the officer's face.

"I know," I say, "unlikely isn't it?"

"I'd say so, yes. Given it's been ten years as well…"

"So - what's the plan now?" I say, suddenly desperate to go home and get in bed.

"That depends on whether you want to press charges or not."

"I do, yes."

"Good. Right. Stay here. I'll go get the paperwork. Want a cup of tea or anything?"

"I'd love a strong coffee. Thanks."

I watch her leave the room and knead my temples. A tension headache has me in its teeth. For the hundredth time, I dig deep, desperate to work out who hates me enough to do this. Once again, I come up empty. All I can hope is that my tormentor feels they've hurt me enough to let it go.

Chapter Forty-Eight

I drag myself to work relieved it's Thursday but wishing it was Friday. Every year I take two weeks off at Christmas, so there's only today and tomorrow to go until I can put my feet up and get a much-needed rest. With Michael around the house I'll feel safer, even if someone with a grudge against me is still roaming free. I try to forget the fact that my lovely boy will be gone after three weeks, leaving me on my own again.

Eimear's already here. She squeals like a child when I hand over gifts for her and the girls then says she's bringing mine tomorrow.

I fill her in on my night and she gives me one of her huge bear hugs, which turns out to be what I needed.

"I guess you'll never know who was behind it then?" she says, munching her way through a bag of crisps. She offers me one and I decline, too nauseous with exhaustion to stomach anything yet.

"The only way I stand a chance of finding out is if they try something again, and the officer who dealt with my case doesn't think that's likely, but I don't know…this person must either be incredibly angry at me or psychotic – or both, and people like that don't just give up. If this person believes I need to pay for what I did, will anything stop them from making it happen?"

"And what precisely, hun, did you do? I know there's something locked away in you. Something you need off your chest. Come on, spill. We've known each other long enough now, don't ya 'tink?"

I look up from my bitten nails and meet my friend's gaze. I know she can keep a secret. But I also know she despises – and rightly so – cheating. Her ex betrayed her the same way I betrayed Greg. Sometimes, withholding the truth is the kinder choice. If she learns what I did, she'll feel as though I've betrayed her too; and I don't want to add to her hurt.

I swallow with difficulty.

"One day, when I'm feeling braver," I say, pushing myself up from the sofa.

"Promise? You know comin' clean'll do you the world 'o good," she says, turning her attention to her laptop.

"I know, I know. Mr Greer at ten, is it?"

"Yeah. Oh – I forgot to say – Mrs George rang on Tuesday evening and cancelled her daughter's appointment for tomorrow. Says thanks but Polly won't be needing to come anymore."

I nod, trudge into my office and close the door.

Instead of sitting at my desk, I lie down on the cream sofa, close my eyes and think about Polly George. My heart aches. I've failed in my mission to make her better. She's still not anywhere near to being in a good state of mind. She needs help. I only wish she'd let me be the one to help her. But, as is always the way in my line of work, when a client says they no longer require my services, that's it.

Telling myself I did my best, I try to think positively. Perhaps Polly will see sense after Christmas and book in to see me again. Perhaps Heather George will ring me for some advice and I can suggest that Polly continues seeing me. Perhaps Richard George will re-enter Polly's life and trigger a realisation in the girl's mind that she still needs help. Or perhaps Polly has got what she needed from me. Perhaps she really is ready to stop our sessions, and she'll go on to live a full and happy life.

Perhaps, perhaps, perhaps…

Perhaps not.

Perhaps Heather will walk into her daughter's bedroom on Christmas Day and find Polly lying dead in a pool of her own blood.

*

I'm about to get ready to leave work when Eimear rings through saying she's got a young woman on the phone, desperate to talk to me. I tell Eimear to put her through, hoping it's Polly ringing to say she wants to continue to see me, but the second I hear the voice on the other end of the line, I know it's not Polly George. This is a voice I've never heard before and one laced with fear.

"Is that Doctor England?" the girl says quietly.

"Yes. Who's this?"

"Dana. Dana Whiting. Polly George's friend."

"What's wrong? What's happened? Is Polly okay?"

"I shouldn't be calling you. Polly'd kill me if she found out…"

"Is she okay?" I repeat, trying to stay calm.

"I, I don't know. I don't think so."

"What d'you mean? Is she hurt? Has she hurt herself?"

"No – not that I know of anyway. I don't know where she is. I think she's at home. At least, I hope she is. It's just that Polly's mum rang and told us something awful and I'm worried Polly's going to totally freak out when she finds out. I don't know if she knows yet, but she's been acting really weird these past few months and -"

"Hang on, slow down a sec. What did Heather tell your mum?"

"It's Polly's dad. He's dead."

What? Richard George is dead?

"Hello? Doctor England?"

"I'm here. Sorry. It's just such a shock. Polly thought..."

"Yeah, I know. Polly thought he was off doing the dirty on them again. It's just – this is so mad – I don't know how Polly's going to handle this. She's been through so much and I'm worried this's gonna be one thing too much. And her mum's pretty crap. I can't picture her being able to get Polly through this, you know? And I knew she was seeing you so I thought I'd let you know. Thought maybe you could check up on her or something?"

"I can try. Although she decided she didn't want to continue our sessions, but maybe now that this has happened, she'll want to carry on with them."

"There's something else," Dana says, her voice taking on an extra tinge of fear.

"What?"

"She's been lying to her mum."

"About what?"

The girl goes quiet for a few seconds and I give her time, fearing she'll have a change of heart and not tell me whatever it is Polly's been lying about.

Dana sighs. "Shit. I've got to tell someone, just in case."

"Given everything Polly's been through, it's hardly surprising she's hiding things, but you need to tell me, Dana. If I'm going to help Polly, the more I know the better."

"Shit. Okay. Every Saturday Polly's been telling her mum she's coming to mine to revise, but she doesn't come to mine. She goes to see this guy. She's dead secretive about him, only says he's older and incredible. It's weird 'cos she used to tell me everything, but, like I said, she's changed so much in the last few months. Sometimes she acts really weird, like, kind of crazy-weird. Says stuff I know she can't mean. And I feel like a shit saying this 'cos she's my friend, but sometimes she can be a bit scary. Like she's not completely right in the head anymore. I don't know. I've said too much. I'm probably imagining it anyway, you know?"

I almost exhale with relief; Polly's been going to see her boyfriend, that's all. He might be older but at least nothing more sinister than that's been going on. And the fact that this man is older than her explains the need to keep her visits secret, from Heather at any rate. Though why she'd keep the details away from her best friend is hard to work out.

"Thank you so much for telling me this, Dana. You've done the right thing. You're right – Polly's not in a great mindset and finding out her father's dead will hurt her a great deal."

"Thanks, Doctor, for saying that."

"One more thing – do you know the circumstances of her father's death?"

The line goes quiet – has she hung up?

"Dana? You still there?"

"Yeah. It's just, it's pretty gross. I don't know if I should say. It's gonna give me nightmares as it is."

"That's alright," I say, burning with curiosity but not wanting to scar the poor girl, "don't tell me. I'm sure it'll be on the news soon anyway. I can find out then."

"You don't want to know. Believe me," she sniffs and begins to cry, "Sorry. It's just…poor Polly. I'm sorry. I've got to go."

The dial tone drills in my ear. The girl's gone.

Feeling shaky, I look up when Eimear pokes her head round the door to say night. Her face drops when she sees me.

"Christ, hun. What's happened?"

I shake my head and drag my hands down my face. "It's not me. It's Polly George. I'll tell you tomorrow. Go on, get home to your lovely girls."

"You sure?"

"Yeah. See you tomorrow."

Eimear closes the door and I stare out of the window at the greying sky. The drizzle abruptly turns to hard bullets, slashing against the window like it's mad at the world.

A bit like how I feel right now.

The unfairness of it all scorches me from the inside out; first the girl loses her twin brother then she discovers her father's betrayal, develops depression and attempts to take her own life - and now this.

I want to break something, hurl my desk at the window and hear it shatter, let the vicious rain flood the room. But I don't do any of that. Of course I don't.

Instead, I sit and think – or at least try to. I glance at my phone: to ring or not to ring? Heather George's grey face fills my mind. I'm worried about her too. What will she do in response to this news? Her husband was a cheat and a bully but she was still clinging to the part of him she loved, that much was obvious. She too will be devastated by the news. The very least I can do is try to reach out. Ring. See if she wants to talk. I got the impression she didn't have many people to turn to.

Taking a swig of water to wet my parched throat, I find Heather George's house number in my phone and press dial.

Chapter Forty-Nine

Benjamin cowered behind the wall of the large, abandoned farmhouse. Plops of rain fell on his head and back and he began to shiver. Now that he was staying as still as a stone, he was cold. His feet were the worst because he'd lost his teddy bear slippers. He wanted to rub them to warm them up and blow hot breath onto his icy hands, but he didn't dare move. The witch was still here. He could hear her stomping around, her feet squelching through the mud. Every now and then, she cackled, and every time she cackled he jumped and hugged his legs tighter to his chest. He was sinking into the mud now and worrying he would get sucked into the ground. But if that happened, he wouldn't be caught by the witch and cooked in a cauldron and eaten up, so he thought that was a better thing to happen in a funny sort of way.

Thunder rumbled in the sky, making Benjamin jump. Wind whipped at his clothes and found a way in, nipping at his skin. He wrapped his coat around his little body and tried to close the gaps. His coat rustled and he froze, hoping and hoping the witch hadn't heard him move.

She was close now. Very close. She cackled again, her high voice screeching in his ears. Thunder boomed and the rain beat down harder and faster, pouring into his eyes and making it hard to see. He could hardly see anything now anyway, what with the thick rain and the dark. He blinked out the rain but it came back into his eyes. He wondered how the witch could see, then remembered she had magic powers. She could whisper a spell and make a thing that stopped the rain getting in her eyes.

So far, he hadn't heard her say any spells. That was one thing to be glad about. If she knew a spell to show her where he was hiding, she would have used it, wouldn't she? Yes, he told himself, yes, she would. Witches were normally very clever. They knew how to find little kids like him, but this witch hadn't found him yet. Benjamin thought maybe this witch was a stupid one. He'd never heard of a stupid witch, but that didn't mean there weren't any around. If this witch was stupid, maybe she would never find him and she would give up and go. Then he could run back across the fields and try to get to Claire's house in time to see her secret.

The witch cackled again. This time, she sounded like she was quite a long way away. Maybe she was leaving.

Crossing his fingers, Benjamin used his puppy ears to listen. Yes. Another cackle, but quiet. Very quiet. She was moving away. She was going to give up and go home back to her cottage in the woods!

Thunder roared again, closer and louder, but this time Benjamin didn't jump. Instead, he smiled. The witch was leaving. He was going to be fine.

He would wait a little bit longer – just to be sure - then he would get up out of his hiding place and carry on with his journey to Claire's house.

Chapter Fifty

I give up trying to get through to Heather George after the third attempt. I picture her curled up in the foetal position on the floor, the lights off, her eyes wet and wide and staring as she tries and fails to work out what happened to her husband and what on earth she's going to do about Polly.

To distract myself from these morbid thoughts, when I get home, I pour all of my remaining energy into cleaning the house from top to toe. Enya's calming voice keeps me company, soothing my nerves and easing the guilt weighing down my shoulders, but no matter how much I focus on polishing and wiping and hoovering, nothing can free me of the idea that I've failed Polly George and her mother. That very soon I'll hear about the girl ending her own life.

At nine 'o clock, I settle down on the sofa with a much-needed glass of wine, telling myself it's nearly the weekend and after what I've found out today, I deserve something to take the edge off.

After a while, I drift off into a welcome snooze, only to be jerked out of sleep by frantic pounding on the front door. Shaking myself into a state of alertness, I untuck my legs, now consumed by pins and needles, and stand up, fear knocking against my rib cage like a thing possessed.

Mark. It's Mark again and this time he's not taking no for an answer.

I back away from the hammering and edge out of the room, glancing every which way for my phone. I can't remember where I put it when I got in. All I know is that I haven't looked at it since I left the office.

"Doctor England! Jessie? It's Heather, Heather George!"

Relief rushes at me. It's not Mark - it's Polly's mother. I freeze for a second then dart into the hallway and hurry to unlock the front door. The poor woman is drenched. I stand aside and gesture for her to come in and she hurries past me, smelling distinctly unwashed.

"Please, come into the living room. Take a seat by the fire. I'll grab you a towel."

She does as I say and I hurry upstairs, grab a couple of warm towels from the airing cupboard, carry them down and wrap them around the woman's scrawny frame.

"I'm sorry," she says, voice raw, "I tried to call you back but there was no answer. In the end, I called your office. Your colleague wouldn't give me your address at first but when I explained who I was, she did."

Eimear must have popped back in – maybe she forgot something – that's lucky.

"It's fine. Honestly. I was trying to ring you to find out how Polly's doing. I was – am – concerned. I'm so sorry about your husband. Does…have you told Polly yet?"

"How do you know about Rich?" she says, glancing up at me through red, swollen eyes.

"Dana called me. She's worried about Polly too."

Heather nods and looks down at her hands, which are shaking. "I told Polly. I thought I should, you know, before she finds out from someone else or sees it on the news. But I made a mistake. I shouldn't have told her. Not yet. Not the way I did, and now she's gone. That's why I had to speak to you."

She looks up, eyes beseeching. "She left, just like that, without saying a word, and now I don't have a clue where she is. She's not at home, she's not at Dana's, she's not at any of her other friends' houses…I just, I thought you might know. That she might've told you something. That you might be able to work out where she's gone?"

I hesitate. Client confidentiality dictates that I not reveal anything to anyone but, given the news Polly's just received and what she tried to do to herself less than two months ago, I think I'm justified in telling the girl's own mother what I'm about to tell her.

Inhaling deeply, I tell her what Dana told me. I wait, expecting the woman to be shocked, but to my surprise she shakes her head sadly.

"I knew she was seeing an older boy. I did a terrible thing. I read her diary. I don't have a clue about this boy's whereabouts though, do you?"

"No. I'm pretty sure Dana doesn't know where he lives either. She said Polly was very secretive about the whole thing. But if she has gone to be with him, that's probably not a bad place for her to be right now, is it? In our sessions, she spoke about him and clearly feels very close to him. If she's with him, I expect he's looking after her as best he can."

Heather looks at me. "If. If she's with him. We don't know she's with this…man, do we?"

"No. We don't."

"You think I should call the police? Say she's missing?"

"I don't think it would do any harm."

Heather nods. Taking a shaky breath, she pushes herself to her feet, peels the damp towels off her body and folds them up then hands them to me.

"Thank you, Jessie. If anything occurs to you about where she might be, please ring me straight away."

I nod and give her what I hope is an encouraging smile. "I'm sure she'll be home soon. She probably just needed to see her boyfriend, tell him what's happened. Make sure you keep trying her phone. She's bound to get back to you soon."

Heather nods weakly and I show her out into the cold, wet night, wishing there was more I could do as she drives away. If I was Heather, I'd drive straight to the police station and report Polly missing, and can only hope that's what she decides to do.

Chapter Fifty-One

"You seen the news?" Eimear blurts the moment I walk into the waiting room.

"No. What is it? What's happened?"

"Come here, take a look," she says, gesturing with her long pink nails for me to join her at her laptop.

Shrugging off my sodden coat, I lay it over my arm and cross the room. My limbs are achy with anxiety, my head pounding from dehydration and too much alcohol. After Heather left my house last night, I finished the entire bottle of wine and went to bed without drinking any water. It was a stupid, stupid thing to do. At the time it was the only thing I could think of that would ease the pain and anguish I felt every time my thoughts veered to Polly and her mother and my failure to help them.

But I tried. I really did.

"You okay, hun? You look awful," Eimear says wrinkling her nose, "And – ugh – did you have one too many drinks last night by any chance?"

I massage my temples and groan. "Yeah. Thanks for giving Heather George my address by the way. It was really important she talk to me."

"Phew. I was a bit worried I'd done the wrong 'ting, but the poor woman sounded on the verge of a full-blown breakdown. Everything okay now?"

"No, not really. Polly George has gone missing."

"Oh lord. Really?"

I nod grimly and drag my hands down my face.

"And she's no idea where she might be?"

"No. I suggested she might be with her boyfriend, but I don't have a clue where he lives, so I was pretty useless. But it gets worse."

Eimear raises an eyebrow. "Can't see how it can get much worse than that."

"Polly's friend rang me, told me Polly's dad's dead, which explains why she's run off. I only hope she hasn't gone and done something to herself. I'd never forgive myself if -"

"Don't," Eimear says, holding up her hand, "don't you dare try to pin the blame on yourself. You're a bloody good therapist. You'll have done everything humanly possible to help this girl. Just look at what your other clients have said. You don't do that enough, you really don't."

I sigh and shake my head, try to brighten my voice. "What's this news story then?"

I glance down at the laptop and Eimear turns up the volume.

"Seems like death's a craze around here at the moment. But seriously, you'll never believe it. Scary how something so awful can happen right on your doorstep. It's crazy stuff. Crazy," she says, backing away to let me see the screen.

A newsreader wearing a scarlet dress begins to speak, her tone grave: "A murder investigation has been launched after the bodies of one woman and one man were found in Somerset in an abandoned farmhouse in Eastbury on Thursday. A member of the public discovered the bodies and paramedics pronounced both dead at the scene. The woman has not yet been formally identified. Investigators have not confirmed the cause of death, with a post-mortem due to take place later today. Detective Chief Inspector Nicholas Bridgewater, from the Police's Homicide and Major Crime Command, said: 'We believe that these individuals were attacked in other locations and moved here after death. We are trying to establish the motive for these attacks and would like to hear from anyone who has seen anything suspicious in this part of Somerset in the last few months.' A police cordon is in place and the area around where the bodies were found is out of use."

"God. How horrible. That's only minutes from here…" I murmur.

"I know. Scary stuff. Serial killer on the loose in Somerset – just doesn't sound right, does it?"

"No. But you can get psychopaths anywhere."

Eimear shudders and closes her laptop. "Yeah. Like I said. Scary stuff."

Chapter Fifty-Two

Benjamin felt like he had hidden for long enough. He hadn't heard a peep from the witch for a long time. She must have gone. She probably didn't like all this rain and thunder either. She probably wanted to get back to her cottage in the woods where it was cosy-warm.

Even though his skin hurt from being so wet and cold, he smiled as he came out from behind the wall. He had beaten the wicked witch! He had found the best hiding place ever and been too clever for her. Polly always found him so quickly when they played hide and seek and she was it. When it was the other way around, he could never find her. One time, Polly hid so well that Mummy and Daddy couldn't find her either and they started to get worried. Daddy was just about to go searching in the street for her when she jumped out from an old bag under Mummy and Daddy's bed, scaring him very much. She went on and on about how much better she was at hiding than him. She went on and on until he got upset and Mummy had to tell her to stop. When Mummy turned away, Polly gave him a really nasty look then ran upstairs crying. Mummy had gone to make her feel better. Mummy always did that, even when Polly was bad.

Benjamin told himself to think about what he was doing. He needed to work out how to get to Claire's house, but it was dark and wet and windy and loud and he was so tired that thinking was hard.

He walked across the squelchy mud, hoping he was going back the way he came. He had run across a field to get here. He had climbed over a fence to get here too.

He wiped water out of his eyes and looked around for the fence. There! There it was. He could just make it out. It wasn't very far away at all.

Benjamin moved faster, slipping and sliding on the sloshy mud, thinking how much fun it would be to play in the mud if he wasn't in such a hurry to get to Claire's house.

Thunder boomed and lightning ripped through the sky, lighting up the farmyard and the big building – and another building he hadn't noticed before. He stopped and blinked, terrified. Lightning was dangerous. It could hurt you. Daddy said it was hot, like fire. If he got hit by it, it would hurt a lot. He didn't know how much it would hurt, but he thought it would hurt more than the bruises on his knees. If he was going to be okay, he needed to get away from the lightning.

Benjamin forced himself to hurry towards the fence. He slipped a few times and pushed himself back up. Thunder roared and lightning flashed again, closer than before. He squealed and began to clamber up the fence then screamed as a high-pitched cackle came from nearby. The witch was back!

He fell off the fence, pushed himself up and ran back the way he'd come. Slipping and sliding, terrified tears blended with the rain, making him blind. He reached out with both hands and blinked to clear his vision but he couldn't see the wall where he'd hidden before.

Thunder growled and lightning lit up the sky and he saw the other building – the one he had not noticed until the lightning came. It didn't have any doors, just a big black mouth. He ran inside that black mouth. The ground changed from squelchy mud to scratchy straw. Inside it was so dark he could not even see his hands. He stumbled forward, feeling for a wall – something he could hide behind. He bumped into something hard and curved, dropped to his knees and crawled around it. Trying to hold his breath, he hugged his knees and listened, eyes wide in the pitch-black barn.

He heard a rustling sound and gasped. The wicked witch was here. She had followed him into the building. She was looking for him.

Benjamin squeezed his eyes closed and covered his face with his hands. Fear made him shake and his knee hit the thing he was hiding behind, making a small bumping sound. He frowned, heart slamming so hard it hurt. If the witch was in here with him, she might have heard that sound. She might be standing right next to him right this second, but it was so dark he would never know.

Outside, the wind wailed and thunder rumbled. Lightning flashed – he could see it behind his closed eyes. He held his breath, hoping the witch was gone.

Some time passed. He didn't know how long. His shoulders began to relax and he peeled his hands away from his eyes.

A split second later, a deep voice shouted, "BOO!" in his ear.

Benjamin shrieked and scrambled to his feet. Lightning flashed again showing him the way out and he ran toward the opening, but the witch was hot on his heels cackling so wildly he knew for sure she was mad.

Chapter Fifty-Three

There are a few bits I need to get for tomorrow evening's meal, but I can't face food shopping, so I drive straight home after work, determined to put Polly and Heather George out of my head.

When I get in, I run a bath, shake the rest of my Epsom salts into the tub and lower my weary body into the water. Feeling my mind take a downward spiral, I practice deep yoga-style breathing and visualise Michael's smiling face. Just one more sleep and he'll be here, and everything will be better. I'll not mention work; I'll focus on him and Kiera. I'll spoil them rotten with tasty snacks and home-cooked meals and treat them to a fancy meal out.

Now that I've wrapped my head around the fact that it won't just be Michael and me, I feel quite excited about meeting Kiera. If she's as lovely as Michael says she is – and I'm sure she is – it sounds like we'll have a great time together. I try to picture an attractive eighteen-year-old girl at Michael's side, but my mind keeps conjuring up Polly. Annoyed at myself, I grab my razor and shave my legs, forgetting to put shaving foam on first. I wince as the blade slices through my skin. Raising my calf out of the water, I stare at the long, bloody line running up my shin bone. It reminds me of the scar on Officer Black's chin – then the scar on Polly's neck. I never found out how she got it. It could have just been a silly accident. Probably was.

The more I think about it, the more I think I was wrong about Richard George; that Heather was telling the truth about her husband and he did only hit her the one time. Given the fact that Polly was brave enough to show me the photographs of the women her father slept with, I'd have thought she would've told me if he'd also hit her – or her mother. Then again, the girl is very hard to read. Possibly the most complex client I've ever dealt with. Perhaps it's no wonder she ended our sessions. She probably would have ended her sessions with any therapist trying to treat her. Maybe it wasn't just me.

The thought is reassuring. It means I did the best I could; I didn't screw up, not really. I didn't fail her.

I roll my eyes at my inability to think about anything else and dunk my head under the hot water. A drink would help, but I still feel rough from drinking so much last night.

Exhaling a hot breath, I lift myself out of the tub and wrap up in a fluffy white towel. In my bedroom, I look at the clock and calculate how long it is until Michael arrives. He's due to come at midday tomorrow – only seventeen hours until I see my boy. A warm bubble of excitement enters my tummy as I picture his lovely, happy face. I'm dying to listen to him talk about his first term at university; about his course, friends he's made, his highs - and lows, which, knowing Michael's upbeat nature, will be few and far between.

It feels so long since I've seen him, and I suppose it is. He hasn't been home since I dropped him off at the end of September. It's the longest I've ever gone without seeing him in the flesh. I remember how hard it was to put on a brave face when he waved goodbye outside his halls of residence; how I burst into tears the second he disappeared; how I loved seeing the excitement on his face but hated it at the same time, then chastised myself for being so selfish.

I towel dry my hair then pull on my dressing gown and make my way downstairs. Dinner is a low-calorie spaghetti bolognese for one – quick and easy.

I eat in the living room flicking mindlessly through the channels until I land on a nineties romcom. I half-watch the film, half-flick through a magazine, nibbling on toffee popcorn and knowing I'll regret it tomorrow when I get on the scales. At least I'm staying off the booze tonight.

At ten o'clock, I can barely keep my eyes open but when the news comes on, I watch.

The news is, of course, dominated by the murders of that man and woman. But there's something new. Another body has been found.

God. When is this horror going to end?

The newsreader, a handsome grey-haired man in a silver suit, says: "Earlier today, sniffer dogs found a third body at the scene. Unlike the bodies of the man and woman found yesterday, this body is believed to belong to a child. Detective Chief Inspector Nicholas Bridgewater, from the Police's Homicide and Major Crime Command, said: 'We believe the body we discovered today has been at this location for several years. At this stage we're unable to say whether these murders are connected.'

The newsreader clears his throat, adds, "The body of the man has been identified as that of fifty-two-year-old, Richard George, local resident and construction worker. The body of the woman is yet to be formally identified."

I lean forward, heart pounding. Richard George is the man they found? I shake my head, unable to believe my stupidity; how I didn't put two and two together and work this out before, I don't know.

A picture of Richard George appears on the screen. My heart feels like it's stopped. Bile rises in my throat and I try to swallow, but I can't.

I know the man in that photograph. I know those steel-blue eyes. I'll know them until the day I die.

He's the man I had an affair with ten years ago. The man I cheated on Greg with. The man I had sex with in my back garden while my family was just metres away.

Richard George *is* Evan.

I slept with Polly's father. Heather's husband.

Fuck.

*

I make it to the bathroom just in time. Sinking to my knees on the cold tiles I vomit again and again until there's nothing left to give.

For a long time, I remain hunched over the toilet bowl, fingers clasping the white seat, trying not to inhale the stench of my own sick. I feel too weak to move, so I just sit on the floor and rest my sweaty head on my hands. Tears attack, and soon I'm sobbing, bemoaning my past and my present. To think that Polly's father is the man I had an affair with is unthinkable and yet it's true. And he's dead.

I smear my tears away, angry at myself for crying. It's Polly who should be sobbing her heart out; Polly who I've hurt. I'm just as bad as those other women, the women in the photographs. I tore Richard George away from his family just like they did. I took him and made him mine when he wasn't mine to take. I took something that didn't belong to me. I helped to destroy Polly's family. I contributed to Polly's depression, to her suicide attempt. The reason she's so messed up is partly because of me. Me and her father and our cruel, selfish lust.

A fresh swell of tears rises. I crush them, frowning hard, squeezing my eyes shut. My temples pound and I embrace the sensation, the pain. I deserve to be hit this way.

I heave myself to my feet, flush the toilet and close the lid. I sit down and try to think back over my sessions with Polly. I need to work out if she's known all along that I slept with her father or if she chose me to be her therapist out of pure coincidence. I know of five other therapists in the area, three of whom are women. Assuming a teenage girl would rather be treated by someone of the same sex, that means there was a one in four chance of Polly choosing me. My website is very good; I spent a lot of money making it clear, attractive, professional, easy-to-navigate; and Eimear updates it regularly with positive reviews from clients. But I know two out of my three female competitors also have excellent websites. So, again working on assumption, that means there was a one in three chance of Polly choosing me. Heather George mentioned that Polly chose me, but that doesn't necessarily mean she chose me because she knew I slept with her father. It could mean Polly did some research and decided I sounded like the best person to treat her.

But hot, itchy doubt is needling its way into my mind like an army of fire ants and I can't ignore it. Rubbing my aching stomach, I move away from the toilet and walk on wobbly legs to the sink. I swill out my mouth with cold water and brush my teeth, thinking constantly. The thought that Polly chose me because she knew makes my blood run hot and cold in my veins. Feeling lightheaded, I perch on the edge of the bath and stare sightlessly, seeing not my bathroom, but my sessions with Polly, from our first session to our last.

In session one, she struck me as a little odd. Her moods swung. She showed signs of distress. She cried, scratched at her injured wrist, fainted. Surely all of this couldn't have been an act? I remember her face went pale – how could someone possibly fake that? Then again, I also remember something that made me feel uncomfortable at the time. What was it she said exactly? Something about secrets.

What if it was all a game? A trick? What if she only pretended to pass out?

No. That's crazy. That would mean…

I can't complete the idea: it's too chilling. And I know this girl – or at least I think I'm beginning to. Polly is vulnerable and hurting. She's harmless to everyone but herself.

Only a psychopath would go to such extremes and Polly George isn't a psychopath.

I turn off the TV, not wanting to hear any more.

Chapter Fifty-Four

Diary,

Rich is dead. Polly's missing. My life's falling apart. And Benjamin's dead; I've known it for years but haven't been able to say it out loud.

I realise I've become an expert at lying to myself. And to others it would seem. It makes me hate myself all the more. But I can't give in. Not yet. Not while Polly's out there somewhere. She's the only thing keeping me going right now.

I know she's not dead. I'd feel it in my bones if she was. No – she's gone into flight mode. I never should've told her about Rich. Not so soon anyway. She's too fragile, and I should've known better. But, like normal, I've screwed up again. Doctor England thinks she's run off to be with her boyfriend and that's what I want to think too. I need to believe she's gone to someone she feels she can trust and confide in. It's pointless wishing that person was me. She's closed herself off to me for a long time now, longer than I wanted to admit. I put it down to her moving into her teenage years, but, really, she shut herself down a long, long time ago. And I bet Doctor England's right: it had a lot to do with Benjamin, which was all my fault, but I can't go there. I won't go there. It hurts too much.

And now Rich. Rich's dead, lifeless body lying on a bed in a morgue. Eyes closed, skin grey. He didn't really look human. Didn't look like he'd ever been a living, breathing being. He looked more plastic than skin.

I asked the grief counsellor how long he'd been dead. He said he didn't know, but the policeman thought he was murdered around October time. When he used the word 'murder' I went dizzy. Had to rest my hands on the bed. I didn't want to know, not really, but the words came out. How was he killed? The grief counsellor looked awkward. Even through my tears, I noticed that. He looked at the floor, wouldn't look at me. Said the police thought he'd been drugged first then moved to the location they found him, where he'd been – shit, someone's at the door.

H

Chapter Fifty-Five

In the morning, I try to rouse myself with a couple of expressos, but the bitter coffee only makes me feel more nauseous.

I rush about tidying up last night's debris, telling myself to focus on Michael and Kiera's arrival; trying to convince myself that my worries will float away like dirty water down a drain the moment I see my boy.

I down a pint of water along with four painkillers hoping the extra dosage will be enough to rid me of the pains attacking my skull, then I get dressed, choosing a pair of black leggings and a long white shirt, over which I throw a grey cashmere cardigan because, despite the throbbing heat in my head, the rest of me cannot warm up. I pull on black ankle boots, glance at the time, realise I need to hurry.

Grabbing my keys off the kitchen counter, I hurry out of the front door through the icy drizzle and unlock the garage. Inside, it's freezing and an awful stench permeates the stale air. Pinching my nose, I step further into the large, cluttered space and pull the garage door shut behind me to keep out the cold. I yank the pull light and it buzzes to life like a hoard of angry flies, shedding light on a ton of cardboard boxes piled high with bits and bobs, a broken freezer, an ancient bookcase filled with dusty books and an old door. My boot heels clack and scrape against the concrete floor as I walk further into the space. I pull my shirt collar up over my nose and welcome the sweet, fruity scent of my perfume which goes some way to disguising the foul smell in the air. With a hard frown, I scan the floor trying to identify the source of the stench. I haven't been in here for a long time, three possibly four months. In that short period something has clearly crawled in here and died.

I make the mistake of glancing up at the rafters and shrink away at the sight of masses of dust-ridden cobwebs, one of which is hosted by a huge-bodied brown spider which seems to be staring down at me silently saying I'm the king of the castle and you're the dirty rascal - I can drop down on your head any second I choose, crawl onto your cheek and dig my fangs into your skin. Darting forward, I catch my arm on the splintered bookcase and my skin tears. Blood pricks the surface of my skin and I lick my finger and wipe it across the fine cut. I haven't got time to mess about so I decide to continue my search for the stinking thing another time.

The only object I can move on my own and that will go at least some way to obscuring the graffiti Tyler Mason sprayed onto my house is the old door. Gingerly picking my way through the boxes, I make my way to the door, recalling when Greg removed it from the porch to open up the entrance to the house. Not given to swearing, I remember finding it hilarious how Greg's frustration turned him potty-mouthed for the hour or so it took him to remove the door. An ache in my chest takes me by surprise and I let myself dwell on Greg for a moment, wondering how he is. He was – is – a good man.

Wary of splinters, I tug my cardigan sleeves down over my palms and pull the door away from the wall. It's heavy. I manage to move it a few steps backwards before needing a break. I rest, holding the door upright and my eyes fall on the space where the door was. I jump and almost cry out when I see the dead, mangled creature.

A rat. Eyes gone.

Bloody holes stare sightlessly up at me. The poor thing lies on its back, its stomach ripped open, insides writhing with maggots.

I look away. A cat must have attacked it then left it here for the maggots to feast on.

Feeling sick, I shuffle backward and drag the door along

as quickly as I can. My shoulder and back muscles whine but I push on, desperate to get out of the stench. I'll clean it up later.

I drag the door out of the garage and lean it against the wall to hide the red 'W' and 'H' that Tyler Mason managed to graffiti on my house before the police sirens scared him off. Mason made the letters as big as he could, clearly aiming to write the word 'WHORE' as instructed to by the person blackmailing him.

Standing back with my hands on my hips, I sigh; part of the H remains visible, but I can't paint over it because my house is made of bricks, and besides, I haven't got time to pop to the shop then come back here and give the house a paint job. At least the door obscures most of the vile red marks. Michael will ask about the door and I'll tell him the truth. I've no other choice.

*

When I reach Tesco, the carpark's at a standstill, customers hovering in between the rows of cars as they wait for others to get in their vehicles and leave. Tapping my fingers on the steering wheel, I glance at the time. Michael and Kiera are due to arrive in half an hour. I really want to be there when they do, but it doesn't look like I'm going to make it.

After a ten-minute wait, I nab a parking space. Yanking up my hood, I jog through the blinding rain into the shop. Once inside, I rush around grabbing a few last-minute essentials then speed to the shortest queue which still holds five other customers. My phone bleeps and I pull it out, expecting it to be a text from Michael saying he's nearly at the house, but it's a message from Mark Monroe. My stomach churns as I read the text. He wants to bring me a letter of apology and two new Champagne glasses – can he pop round later? Anger makes me clench my teeth. I shove my phone back in my coat pocket, not bothering to text back. If he texts me one more time, I will call the police. I've given him enough chances to leave me the hell alone.

Time ticks on, the queue unbearably slow. My watch tells me I'm definitely going to be late, so I pull my mobile back out of my pocket and text Michael to apologise. He's pretty used to my time management, so won't be too surprised. I only hope Kiera doesn't find my absence rude.

A slow Christmas song plays, mocking my need for speed. I sigh and tap my foot as the old lady in front of me struggles to find her purse. To distract myself, I glance at the conveyor belt to check I haven't forgotten anything. With a groan, I realise I've forgotten to get beer for Michael. The old woman's still trying to find her purse, so I leave the queue, muttering to the next person that I just need to grab something. I hurry along the alcohol section, grab four cans of Stella and dash back to the queue just in time to see the elderly lady hobble away.

Giving the female cashier a quick smile, I add the beer to the conveyor belt and try to be patient as she scans my items with the urgency of a sloth.

Chapter Fifty-Six

Diary,

I look and feel like death. There's nothing left in me to throw up. I didn't get to the bathroom in time. Threw up on the carpet on the landing, practically crawled back here. I keep having dark thoughts. Keep thinking about the role I've played in all of this. How I could have stopped it. Keep thinking about how many paracetamol and anti-deps I've got. How many I would need to take to end everything. Then I think about Polly. How she needs my help. How she's always needed my help and I've never really given it and now is the time for me to finally step up and do it. Do it properly. Be there for her when no-one else will or can. Doctor England's tried, but it clearly hasn't worked. Maybe the only cure for Polly is the one I've been dreading all along. The one I would not let myself consider because to consider it was to admit the most horrific thing in the world. It would have broken me completely. Of course, Rich was oblivious. Always has been. So many times, I came close to telling him what I thought happened and so many times I lost courage. I turned inward. I hated him for his blindness. For his betrayal. And that hatred's led to this, for which I can only blame myself.

I should've left Rich a long time ago. But I was too weak. I was – am – pathetic. A pathetic mother. The worst. Unforgivable.

At first, I felt so pleased with, so proud of myself. Twins. I produced not one, but two lovely, perfectly healthy babies. I felt like a hero. Everywhere I went people admired them. Polly and Benjamin, the blue-eyed, blonde-haired babies. Prettiest babies ever. The most beautiful, precious things in the world. And then I found out about Rich's secret life and I suppose I sort of imploded. If I'd tackled the subject head on, spoken to him, tried to wrap my head around the why of it all, maybe Benjamin would still be alive. Because it all started then. And I blamed Rich. I still do. But I blame myself most of all, and when I think of the hands that ended his life, I know they're mine, and I can't bear to think of how those hands acted. How, of their own volition, they took his life in such a brutal, inhumane way. I can't write it down. I can't say it out loud and yet the words that counsellor said ring in my ears, and the worst thing of all is that they ring true.

I can't stay here. I need to go and find her. Now.

H

Chapter Fifty-Seven

Benjamin ran out of the barn into the wild, wet weather. Rain lashed down hard, thunder rumbled, lightning flashed and cracked. Benjamin stumbled forward blindly. Straw snaked around his ankles and mud splashed up his legs and clung in huge clods to his feet, making him slow.

He glanced around. He couldn't see the witch, but he couldn't stop. Last time she'd tricked him. She could be playing another trick. Any second now she might swoop down on him from the booming sky on her broomstick.

He turned right and ran around the back of the barn. Lightning hit the ground only a few metres in front of him and he cried and stared at the spot where it hit. The air smelt burnt but it was too wet for fire, which was one good thing.

He ran forward and saw a curved block rising out of the ground. It was the perfect hiding place. He ran over to it, slipped, fell, pushed himself back up using the rough side of the curved thing. The big object was made out of bricks, but he couldn't tell what it was. He crept round to the other side of it, crouched down and peeped out from behind the wall. He could just see the back of the large barn. The witch was not there. He pulled his head back behind the wall.

The curved wall only came up out of the ground to the height of his tummy button, so he had to make sure he was very small. He knelt. His feet and legs sank into the thick, gloopy mud, but they didn't go in very deep. He stayed as still as possible, scared that if he moved he would make a loud squelchy sound that would tell the witch where he was hiding. Luckily, the rain still fell hard and fast, so Benjamin thought that if he did make a sound, she still might not hear him.

His heartbeat began to slow and his little chest stopped rising and falling so quickly. He licked his lips and tasted salty water that was quite nice. He thought about leaving his hiding spot and trying to make his way back to Claire's house to see her secret then he remembered what had happened before and stayed put. He would hide for a lot longer this time, just to be extra sure she had gone.

A high cackle suddenly burst through the sound of the rain and he whipped his head around. Not that far away, but far away enough so he could not see her face, stood the witch. A big cape flapped around her, making her look like a giant bat.

Benjamin scrambled to his feet and pushed his back against the curved wall.

"Leave me alone!" he screamed.

Tears poured from his eyes and he blinked and sniffed. His body shook. He glanced both ways, wondering which way to run.

But it was too late. The witch let out another high, wicked cackle then ran straight towards him. Benjamin was too scared to move. He held his hands up in front of his chest and pressed his back into the wall and closed his eyes. Two hands slammed into his shoulders and then he was falling backwards, falling over the top of the wall. Lightning flashed lighting up the whole sky and he opened his eyes and stared into the smiling face of the witch – but it wasn't a witch.

It wasn't a witch who had pushed him.

It wasn't a witch at all.

Before his head hit the bottom of the well, Benjamin's last thought was of Claire's secret.

Maybe he would get a chance to meet Claire's baby dragon another time.

Chapter Fifty-Eight

Juggling my handbag and food shopping, I dash through the bullet-like rain. I don't look in the direction of the old door leaning up against the wall, but I do run through how mine and Michael's conversation about it will go. It's such a shame that one of the first things I'll have to talk to him about is this. I'll need to tell him about the other incidents too. About Tyler Mason's attacks. Tyler Mason must have also been the one who pushed poor Charlie down the stairs. Thank God Charlie didn't get killed. He could have broken his neck falling down those steep steps. I decide not to mention that to Michael. He doesn't need to know that too; it'll only upset him more, and now that Tyler's been caught, I'm not in danger any more. At least that's what the officer said, and the words of a police officer are good enough for me.

With ice-cold fingers I try the front door. It's open. Michael's already here. My baby boy's home!

A smile pulls at my cheeks, making them ache. It must be ages since I've smiled properly.

Grinning like a maniac, I open the door, drop my handbag on the floor in the hallway, kick off my boots and call out, "Michael! I'm home!"

I wait for his voice but the house is quiet. Dropping the soaked carrier bags, I shrug off my waterproof and hang it up next to the door. Maybe they're up in his bedroom. Maybe they're up to no good. I wrinkle my nose. The thought makes me feel icky. I shut the front door and don't bother locking it, reminding myself that I'm safe now Michael's home. No one can hurt me anymore.

Straightening my shirt so that I look presentable, I raise my voice and try again.

"Michael? You here?"

There's still no response. I think about going upstairs, then think better of it; if they are in the middle of something, I'm sure they'll come down when they're ready.

I pick up the shopping bags and head up the hallway. The lights are all off. With difficulty, I open the kitchen door and walk in, then stop in surprise. The bags fall from my hands. A tin thwacks the floor tiles and rolls out of one of the bags. I reach down, pick up the tin and frown at Michael, pleased to see him but confused. He's sitting on one of the dining room chairs – which wasn't in here when I left - the chair ought to be in the dining room around the table, which I've already laid for lunch – and his eyes are closed. For a moment I wonder if he's pretending to be asleep and brace myself for a sudden explosion of movement and laughter, but he remains where he is, fast asleep, face peaceful, lips slack. He's wearing a stripy blue and white jumper and dark jeans. Dark brown stubble dusts his jaw.

"Michael? Michael, honey – wake up," I say softly, walking towards him, wondering where Kiera is. Has she not come after all? Will it just be the two of us? My heart warms at the thought.

A sound behind me makes me whirl around and I see someone dash across the hallway into the living room – a flash of fair hair. It must be Kiera. Perhaps she's shy.

"Kiera? Is that you? It's Jessie, Michael's mum."

There's no answer, so I leave the kitchen, cross into the dining room and approach the connecting door that leads to the living room. As I reach out to open the door, it opens towards me and I step back, a welcoming smile on my face.

"Hi, Ki -"

"Hi," Polly George says. She's wearing a bright red wig that flows in luscious curls down to her waist.

I look down. In her hand, she holds a knife and she's

wearing black leather gloves.

Chapter Fifty-Nine

"Polly – what – what the hell are you doing?" I say stumbling backwards into the dining room table.

"I'm not Polly. I'm Kiera. I'm Michael's girlfriend. It's lovely to finally meet you, Mrs England." She speaks in a falsely perky voice. Her smile doesn't reach her eyes, which are as cold and glassy as shattered crystals.

Polly tears off the wig and tosses it on the floor. I stare at the red wig, heart clattering, mind playing catch-up. "You're the one who Michael's been dating?"

"Got it in one."

"But why?"

But I already know. She's been playing me all along. Pretending to be the innocent victim, when really she's the one who's been pulling the strings, wreaking havoc with my life.

Everything she's orchestrated, if this is true, whistles through my mind at breakneck speed: the man screaming at me – the message scored into my table – the decimated butterflies – the list feels endless. Act after act of chaos and cruelty.

I take her in. The cold, empty stare in her eyes, the eerie steadiness of her hand as she raises the knife and runs her finger along the razor-sharp edge. I try to work out her plan. Get inside her head. But I don't recognize this Polly. This version of the girl is front of me is either the real one – whom hitherto she has hidden - or one of her personalities. My gut told me she could be suffering from Dissociative Identity Disorder. This Polly could be one of those selves, a dark manifestation of trauma designed to give her back control she has lost. If this is the case, a fraction of hope remains, because it may be that one of her other selves will take the reins and stop whatever horror this Polly has planned.

However, the fact that she has deceived Michael and tricked me for this long screams of extreme self-control and a manipulative, devious personality. It shrieks of psychosis. And that, of course, is terrifying. If Polly is a psychopath, nothing and no one will derail her plan.

I have to hope and pray she reverts to a more rational, moral Polly. If she doesn't…

With a smirk, she flicks the knife toward the kitchen. "When you're doing piecing the puzzle together, join Michael in there."

Michael.

I stand my ground, and will my body to stop shaking. "Polly, what's all this about?"

"Move. Now."

Her eyes narrow and the smile on her face wavers. I stay as I am, determined not to show my fear and reinforce her belief that she holds the power.

"What are you doing?" I say, keeping my eyes on hers.

"A little thing called payback."

"What?"

"Come on now, Jessie. Don't play the dumb card. You know what you did. Ooh, I know. Let me jog your memory." She pulls her mobile out of her dungarees, flicks through, holds the screen to my face. "Recognise this guy?"

Chapter Sixty

There's a picture of Evan on her phone. He's standing with Polly grinning at the camera, one muscular arm wrapped around her shoulders. A few inches away stands Heather George.

"Evan's your father?" I act dumb.

She pockets her phone, does a slow, mocking clap. Her fingernails gleam gold. "Penny dropped has it, Jessie?"

Gold, the colour of victory. This is what it's all been about. My affair with her father.

My heart thuds horribly. "I'm sorry, Polly. I really am. I -"

She angles her head, gives me a pitying look. "It's too late to say sorry."

The vacuousness in her eyes is frightening. How did I not see this before? This real Polly.

"What's wrong with Michael?"

"Nothing – not yet anyway. But there will be if you don't do what I say." She flicks the knife in the direction of the kitchen, smirking.

I hesitate, not wanting to obey her; I must try to maintain some control here.

"Get in there or I'll go in and slit his wrists," she says calmly.

Fear for Michael slices through my gut like a machete. I inch into the kitchen determined not to turn my back on her. Glancing at the knife block on the counter, I can see one's missing - she's taken it. It's the smallest, sharpest knife I own. I sharpened that very knife a few weeks ago.

"Stand next to your beloved son," she says.

I do as she asks. "What have you done to him? Why's he asleep?"

"Sedatives," she says simply, as if bored. "Don't worry. If you do what I tell you to, Michael'll be fine. When he wakes up, he'll find you dead and me gone. He'll carry on thinking I'm Kiera from Nottingham University, but he'll never see me again. I've already destroyed my burner phone. I really do like him, you know."

"Have you…slept together?" I say, partly because she's only fifteen and if anyone found out Michael would be accused of rape; partly to keep her talking.

She laughs. "We've done stuff. Everything really, apart from that. Michael's a proper gentleman. I've told him I'm ready countless times over the last few weeks, but he wants it to be special, whatever that means."

"Where did you get the sedative from?"

Polly rolls her eyes and steps closer, wiggling the knife around like a magic wand. "Aren't there more important things you want to know before we get on with it? Like… hm…I know! Why I slit my wrist in the first place?"

Heart racing, I nod and place a gentle hand on Michael's shoulder, hoping the contact might wake him up. If he wakes up, maybe he'll stand a chance of reasoning with her, especially if she really likes him, like she says she does. A dark voice whispers in my ear that no one can reason with her because she's a psychopath.

"Isn't that what you've been trying to figure out all this time, Doc? Why I cut myself? Who'd hurt me if I told you my big, bad secret?"

I swallow a lump in my throat. "Yes. Why did you hurt yourself?"

"Surely you know the answer to that by now, don't you? Go on. Have a guess."

I hesitate, opt for what I now believe to be true but could never in a million years have worked out before. "Did you do it to make yourself more believable? To trick me?"

"Bingo!" Polly smacks her hand on the wall three times, eyes locked on mine, "Wow, Doc. You're not as dense as I thought. And why do you think I'm here now?"

"Because you want to punish me, like you punished your father." Everything's clicking into place. The truth is horrifying. She killed her own father.

Her eyes shine and she nods appreciatively. "And the last whore he went with. She's been punished too. She was a local, like you. Sadly, one died in a car crash and the other two are too far away. One's moved to Australia of all places and the other bitch lives in Scotland. I might track them down one day."

"Why kill them?" I say, glancing around for something – anything – I can use as a weapon.

Polly shrugs and glances at the window. "Why not? As soon as I found Dad's diary and saw what he'd been up to, there was only one way to fix it. And besides, it was fun. Especially winding you up. Bet you thought I had Dissociative Identity Disorder, didn't you, Doc? Exciting wasn't it – to think you had a client with such a rare condition? Bet it was the highlight of your sad little life, apart from shagging my father in your own back garden the night my brother Benjamin died."

Her eyes dart back to mine. She takes a step towards me and jabs the knife at my stomach.

"I'm so, so sorry, Polly. I was young and selfish and -"

"Fuck off! You loved it. You all fucking loved it. All the sneaking around and lying and cheating and taking other people's lives for granted. You got off on it. Don't give me bullshit excuses. I don't give a fuck that you were unhappy in your own marriage. Nothing gives you the right to do what you did. Nothing gives you the right to live after what you've done. If my father'd been home that evening, he wouldn't have been so tired, he'd have heard Benjamin leave the house, he'd have caught him, brought him back and…" she trails off and stabs the knife into the fleshiest part of my stomach.

I gasp as the blade pierces my skin just enough to draw

a trickle of blood. Looking down, I see a tiny rosebud bloom in the wool of my jumper.

"Please, Polly, please don't. You don't want to do this. You've already killed two people. In a short time, you'll look back on what you've done and you'll regret it. You'll never forgive yourself. And think about your mum. She loves you so much. If you leave now, I promise I won't say a word to anyone. Client confidentiality is something I always abide by. I won't betray your trust. You can even carry on seeing Michael if that's what you want." I immediately regret my last lie. Polly's highly intelligent. She's no fool. But I'm desperate. Clutching at every lifeline I can.

The knife digs a touch deeper. I look up into the girl's face and it's twisted. Her eyes are glazed over with madness, and that's when I know for certain that nothing I say will save me. The absence of remorse in her expression and voice at the mention of those she's killed alongside her confession of committing premeditated serial murder tells me one terrifying, undeniable truth: Polly George is a psychopath.

"Three," she says.

"Sorry? I don't understand."

I've killed three people. Soon it'll be four. When I get the chance, Tyler will pay for being so incompetent."

She states this in such a matter-of-fact tone that cold sweat breaks out under my arms.

"Who was the third?" I say, not sure I want to know but searching for anything that will prolong our conversation and stop her pushing the knife all the way in.

She yanks the knife away from me. I release a shuddering breath and place my hand over the small wound. It stings, but could be a lot worse.

I watch as she runs her finger along the blade, letting it rest on the blood at the tip. She raises her hand and looks at her fingertip which is stained with a tiny bit of my blood. Without looking at me, in a bored voice, she says,

"Benjamin. I killed him too. When I was five. I was playing a game and pushed him into a well." She shrugs, glances at me. "I didn't mean to kill him, but it was fun."

Horror makes my pulse judder.

"Cadaver dogs never found him because the well was over twenty metres deep. Five metres less and they might have done. Wasn't I lucky?" She tilts her head and smiles. "Anyway. I'm bored now, so let's get on with it, shall we, Doc?"

"Get on with what?" I say, staring at the knife in her slim hand. A hand that I once thought so helpless.

In her other hand, she raises a pair of needle-sharp nail scissors.

Chapter Sixty-One

Polly opens her mouth to speak, excitement bright in her eyes; but I open my mouth and scream as loudly as possible. She's too shocked to react instantly, so I dive at her, grabbing her wrist and squeezing as hard as I can, digging my nails – short as they are – deep into her flesh. She screams through gritted teeth, and the knife slips from her grasp and hits the floor, spinning under Michael's chair.

I'm a lot heavier than Polly and use that to my advantage, throwing my full weight onto her so that she falls on her back. I land on her chest and try to grab her other wrist but she's too quick and stabs the nail scissors into my right side, once, twice, thrice. I gasp and roll off her onto my back. She pushes herself to her feet and glares down at me.

"Don't move," she says, stabbing the bloodied nail scissors at me. She backs up towards Michael's chair, eyes never leaving mine, and sinks to a crouch. With her free hand, she feels around under the chair for the knife.

I make to push myself up but she shouts, "Stay the fuck there!"

Her hand touches the knife handle; she smiles and slides it out, and I push myself up and run out of the kitchen along the hallway. She screams like a witch, so close, too close already. I'm yanked back by my hair, my fingertips brushing the door handle. On instinct I thrust back my elbow and it makes contact with some part of her – her face, I think. She cries out and loosens her grip on my hair and I dart forward again for the front door, but she's too quick. The knife rips through the skin of my lower back and I stagger forward, the pain intense, disorienting. I reach for the door handle but she's there, shoving me sideways. I stumble, glance around at her as she swipes the knife at my face. I lurch backward and grab the banister, using it to propel myself onto the stairs which I sprint up, two at a time.

Her footsteps thunder after me. I reach the landing, grapple with the bathroom door handle, yank open the door and run into the room. Her feet hit the landing and I turn and lock the door, standing back as the handle jerks up and down. She's trying to get in but she can't. She doesn't say anything. I wait, panting, the pain in my back coming alive, expecting her to rant and rave, try to kick the door down, but the house is silent and still. I can't even hear her breathing, though I know she must be as breathless as me.

I creep up to the door and put my ear to the wood to see if I can hear her. As long as she stays up here Michael will be safe. She can't have gone downstairs yet; I would've heard her footsteps – a creak or something.

I stay close to the door, listening. Seconds pass, then minutes. I begin to fear she's managed to retreat downstairs without me hearing her – that she's gone back into the kitchen – that she's doing something awful to Michael. I glance at the lock on the bathroom door, consider sliding it back, opening the door a crack. The thought that she's hurting Michael builds in my head. Visions bombard: she's cutting his wrists, slicing open his jugular, stabbing him multiple times. All to get back at me. And he's defenceless. Knocked out by the drugs she's injected into him. Helpless. Bleeding. Dying.

I pull my face away from the door and open my mouth to call out to her, not sure what to say but willing to say anything to stop her hurting my baby. I close my mouth, tortured by sudden doubt. She wanted me, not Michael. She said she liked Michael. She wants to punish me. I try to make sense of her mind, of the way she's thinking, what she wants. If I can work her out, maybe I can save us both. It may be that she doesn't want to hurt Michael at all. Or, that she'll do anything to make me suffer, to see me punished for what I've done – in which case, surely she'd want to watch me watch my son die, for that would be the ultimate torture. She must know that. She's a clever girl. She's been planning this for a while. She'll have slaved over the details, imagined the moment she inflicts the most pain on me. But she's only sedated Michael, which suggests she doesn't want him hurt, let alone dead. Of course, there's no way of predicting how she'll behave, especially now that I'm locked in here and she's out there.

No. I'll wait. Listen and wait. She'll crack eventually. She'll want to let me know what she's about to do to Michael. She'll want to give me a chance to come out and try to save him.

I lean forward and rest my cheek lightly against the door, heart pounding.

Time passes and I begin to waver again. A floorboard creaks outside the door. Eyes wide, I listen, pushing my cheek into the wood. She's still upstairs, out there.

I swallow dryly, lick my lips. Listen.

Another creak and then an ear-splitting crack, centimetres from my ear as she slams something into the door. I lurch away as she continues to hammer an object into the same spot, over and over. The wood splinters under the attack. It's weakening. Abruptly, she stops. Everything goes silent. My heart is on fire, as is my back. I stare at the damaged door, hoping she's given up, but then something slams into the weakened wood, something heavy, capable of breaking through. Between each slam I hear her grunts of exertion. I glance around the bathroom for something to use as a weapon. My nail scissors aren't here. My shaver will be of little use.

Wood and dust falls away from the door and a long thin gash appears. The smashing continues. I need to hurry.

My eyes find the stone toothbrush holder. I tip out my toothbrush and seize the object. It's quite heavy. If I manage to land a blow, it will hurt her, give me a chance to get away before she can react.

With a roar, Polly delivers her final blow and a hole the size of my head appears in the door. Her arm reaches through the hole and I see what she's trying to do and dart forward. Using the toothbrush holder, I smash at her hand as she reaches for the lock. I catch her fingertips and she screams and withdraws her arm. My weapon slips from my hand and rolls away.

"Fucking bitch. Open the fucking door!"

I stand still, eyes trained on the hole, hands fisted. Her face appears in the space. A red mark which is beginning to purple discolours her forehead. Her pale face is flushed and blue veins throb in her temples. Her hair looks tangled, the neckline of her grey top dishevelled. She yanks her face back and stabs the knife through the hole, narrowly missing my stomach.

"Do you want to hear a story, Jessie?"

I distance myself from her, taking refuge near the toilet, wracking my brain for a plan.

"Jessie? A story? Yes?"

I exhale, say nothing. Her face appears again, and she nods as if I've given her permission to go ahead. She smiles wide and for one alien moment, she is extraordinarily beautiful. Her eyes fix on mine and the smile drops, replaced by an ugly pout.

"Yes," she says, "I'll start with this. Take a pew, Doc. This is quite a long story and you don't want to be uncomfortable."

I ignore her and stand my ground. The searing pain in my back and side seems to be intensifying but there's no way I'm sitting down or lowering my guard. The minute I do, she's bound to attack.

"Fine. I'll sit though, if you don't mind."

Her face disappears from the hole in the door and I imagine her sitting cross-legged on the carpet outside the bathroom, like a schoolgirl getting ready for story time.

"The first one was fun but not as fun as you. Remember the photos I showed you? Well she was the one staring back at the camera. The bitch with the nose piercing and chavvy tattoos. My father was clearly deranged when he fell for her. She worked in a bloody tattoo parlour in Trowbridge of all places. He met her just like he met you actually, in a fucking supermarket. Propositioned her right then right there. Didn't even offer to buy her a drink by the sounds of it. Isn't it funny how the three of us all keep a diary? Or, should I say kept, in my father's case."

In spite of myself her words paint a picture in my mind, and I find I can clearly visualise 'Evan' chatting up the young attractive woman then whisking her off to the nearest hotel. With a sickening jolt, I realise he must have written every sordid detail down – from the moment he met each of us, to the moment each fling ended. How else would Polly know that he and I had sex in my back garden? Did he write about the intimate details? About what he did to us and what we, in return, did to him? Shame burns and bubbles like a boiling kettle in my chest.

As if privy to my thoughts, Polly laughs bitterly. "First he fucked her doggy style then she let him fuck her up the arse. How whorish is that? Worse than you, but not by much, is it, Doc?"

"What did you do to her?"

"Stalked her every Saturday for around a month. Found out her habits like the time she left for work, when she left work for home, where she lived, that sort of thing. I was only thirteen then. No way I'd pass for sixteen, no way she'd give me a tattoo without parental consent, so I had to get Tyler involved, and God was he easy prey. Caught him on my phone wanking off to child porn. Showed him the video. Threatened to show the cops. He was terrified. I had him then. I instructed him to get up to all sorts of mischief, a bit like I did with you. Also made him think I liked him a bit and played on his neediness. He was so easy to control, embarrassingly so."

"But why? Why go to all that hassle?" I'm stalling - wondering when the sedative in Michael's blood will work its way out.

"Entertainment. Revenge. Both. It was fun. It started small. First, I got him to get a tattoo off her then complain that it was crap, shout the place down, make a scene, humiliate her. He said she nearly broke down crying. I was gutted to miss it. Had to hang around outside and listen, which was okay, but I really wish I could've seen her face up close. But at least I got to see the best prank. Tyler filmed it for me on his phone – it was brilliant! Pure genius if I do say so myself. He waited until she was in from a heavy night out then broke into her flat, tied her to the bed and pissed on her, as instructed. It was priceless. Absolutely priceless. Stupid bitch didn't even report it – too embarrassed I reckon. A week after that, I crept around the back of her house – she always let her dog out just before she went to bed at night – waited until the dog was doing a piss, then let myself in through the back door. She was downing a pint of water at the kitchen sink. I ran at her and injected her with the same sedative I've injected Michael with. She didn't make a sound. It was so easy. She was out for the count almost immediately. Obviously, she turned into a dead weight, but I'd come prepared. Tyler and I squished her into my father's biggest suitcase and wheeled her out to her own car then drove her to the farmhouse, and -"

"Tyler helped?"

She laughs. "That simpleton will do anything for me. I've made sure of that, like I said."

I don't respond. The excitement in her voice makes my skin crawl. I don't want to know what happened when she got the tattoo artist to the farmhouse, but I know she's about to tell me. It's like she's being dying to tell me for two years.

"What did you do with her car?" I ask, wanting her to skip the part at the farmhouse, praying Michael will wake up.

She snorts. "What do you think? After we'd finished up at the farm, Tyler drove her car back to her house and parked it exactly where she usually parked. Then we walked for a couple of miles in the direction of Eastbury, called a taxi and got driven the rest of the way back to my house. I wore black leggings, a black hoody, black trainers, a black hat with my hair tucked up inside. Tyler wore black too, so we were basically invisible. It was midnight by the time we were done at the farmhouse. Mum was on a night shift. Easy peasy. No brainer."

"Polly, can I ask you a question?"

Her face appears in the hole. She's smiling but her smile doesn't meet her eyes, and I find myself wondering if it ever has. She plucks a hair out of her mouth. "Sure. Fire away, Doc."

"Does killing make the pain go away? When all's said and done, what difference does it actually make, to you? To your happiness?"

She glances to the right then looks straight at me and says, "When happiness isn't an option, killing is the next best thing. Killing makes me feel something. Death makes me feel alive. Ironic, isn't it? And you know what? I felt truly alive in the farmhouse that night."

"I don't want to know," I say quickly.

She ignores me and ploughs on, voice quick and breathy with excitement. "She let him fuck her up the arse so I thought her death should be equally fucked up."

"Please," I say. "Don't."

But she carries on, delight ringing in her voice like that of a five-year-old on Christmas Day morning. "She was unconscious, so I didn't get to hear her screams, but it was still such a rush, making her body suffer like that."

She stops, and I wait, hoping she's going to move on.

"If she'd been awake, she'd have passed out from the pain pretty quickly anyway…"

I clamp my hands over my ears, desperate to block her out, but I can still hear her gleeful voice.

"Ever heard of that torture method they used back in medieval times? Where they shoved a metal rod up someone's arse hole? Well, I didn't go that far – too gross – but I did beat her with a rod. Tons of blood. Of course, she stayed unconscious - better for her I suppose. Well, yeah, definitely better for her. I thought the pain might wake her up, but no. She just lay there like a corpse. And I got angrier and angrier about it. I think she stopped breathing after three, maybe four hits on the head. There was so much blood and gore…Tyler couldn't stop blubbering. He didn't want to help, but I didn't give him a choice. He can't stand the thought of going to prison and being away from his precious Minecraft. Anyway, we hid her body and the rod behind an ancient tractor then covered it as best we could with a ton of mud and straw. I was sweating like crazy by the time it was done, but God, did I feel good. Like, crazy high, like I was on E or something – not that I've ever taken E."

The casual tone of her voice stirs something I've not felt yet: extreme anger. Bitter, bilious fury.

"And you don't feel bad for what you did to that woman?"

"She deserved it. I feel *better* for doing it. You reap what you sow. Tyler's had a few sleepless nights though. You should have seen his face. Even he understands society's version of right and wrong. He really hates the sight of blood, bless his little cottons."

"She deserved to die because she slept with your father?"

I wait for her to respond, but she doesn't.

"Polly?"

"You're too simple to understand," she says lightly. I can almost see her rolling her eyes at me.

I crush the urge to say what I'm thinking. If I stay quiet, maybe she'll stop telling me such hideous things.

She yawns loudly. "I'm bored. Come out now or I'll go and slit Michael's wrist with these nail scissors. Poetic justice, don't you think?"

I'm too shocked and upset to speak.

She carries on. "I like Michael but I don't love him. I don't know if I've ever loved anyone or anything or if I even possess the ability to love something other than my own interests. Interesting, isn't it, how different minds work?"

"How can you even consider hurting someone you like?" I say, trying to think what to do, scanning my useless bathroom, desperate for some sort of weapon I can use to bash her head in.

"Liking someone is moot in the grand scheme of things." She yawns again. "Hurry up or I'll go downstairs, take this lovely knife and slice right through poor, naïve Michael's pretty little carotid arteries. I can't make up my mind – nail scissors to the wrists or knife to the neck? I'll have to do eenie meenie miny no."

For a few seconds, I'm overcome by a wave of dizziness so strong that my vision blurs. I sway and lean against the sink. The urge to throw up attacks. I breathe slowly, inhale, exhale, inhale, exhale.

"If you don't open the door in -"

"I'm coming."

Close to passing out, I walk forward and slide the lock back. I pull the door inward and stare at her. She stands in front of me smiling, the knife held at waist-height, directed at my stomach. She flicks it in the direction of the stairs. Silently, I obey. I don't have the presence of mind or the control to fight her right now. Standing upright and walking without passing out seems to be a challenge as it is.

I take the stairs slowly. I can sense her one step behind me, eyes boring a hole in the back of my head, the kitchen knife never wavering from its position. I picture it slicing through my spinal cord.

My feet feel heavy, my mind almost absent. Vaguely, I wonder if I'm in shock.

My foot hits the bottom step and I almost lose my balance. I grab onto the banister for support and Polly chuckles, amused at my lack of control. Anger rises inside me, and a surge of adrenaline floods my veins. I welcome the abrupt gush of energy stirring up my blood but stay silent as I walk toward the kitchen and my drugged son.

Chapter Sixty-Two

Michael's still sitting on one of the dining room chairs in the kitchen, dead to the world.

"What're you going to tell him when he wakes up and finds me dead?" I say, stopping in the kitchen doorway.

"Easy. I'll be gone. He never even saw me arrive here. I messaged him last minute saying I didn't want to see him anymore and to never contact me again. He'll never suspect a thing. And he's not a prick. He won't hassle me. Not that he'll be able to given I've tossed my burner."

The knife pricks my spine. I enter the kitchen slowly, scanning the room for anything I can reach out and grab.

"Go through to the dining room and fetch a couple of chairs," she says.

Surprised by her instruction, I do as she says. The chairs are heavy so I carry the first one in on its own.

"Where shall I put it?"

With the knife she gestures for me to put it next to Michael. I obey, wondering what she's up to now. A smirk plays at her lips. She's enjoying my confusion. I try to keep my expression bland to conceal the anger and adrenaline building up in my body. I managed to take her by surprise before; perhaps if I act docile, I can do it again.

I pick up a second chair and carry it through into the kitchen. She gestures for me to put it a metre away from Michael facing him. I do as instructed and turn to look at her.

"Sit there." She points to the chair I've just moved.

I sit down and let my shoulders sag. "What now?"

She smirks and places the kitchen knife on the counter beside the knife block. The nail scissors are nowhere in sight. She withdraws a tight coil of black cord from her back pocket. She unwinds the cord, picks up the knife and cuts off a length of about thirty centimetres. She tosses the cord onto my lap.

"Tie your right ankle to the chair leg. I want to chat for a bit longer, and I can't have you trying to attack me again."

As I bind my leg to the chair, she watches closely, scrutinising my work. "Tighter. Triple knot it."

I do as she says, pulling it tight but not tight enough to hurt.

"Now do the other one," she says throwing me another piece of cord.

Again, I follow her instruction, hating the increasing feeling of impotence attached to the act of tying myself up.

"Sit on your hands and don't move," she says.

Puzzled, I say nothing and obey. With the knife directed at my face, she walks over, crouches down and checks each ankle.

"Good," she says, giving my knee an appreciative pat.

I hold back the urge to spit in her face and think about whipping my hands out from under my bottom and grabbing her neck, but she's already moving towards the kettle, which she lifts, carries to the sink, fills, replaces and flicks on with her gloved hands.

"Thought we could have a nice cup of tea and I can finish my story."

I remain mute and placid as she busies about making two cups of tea. She selects a Little Miss Naughty cup and raises it at me then points to herself with a grin. For me, she chooses a cup James gave me for Mother's Day, on which is printed an adorable photograph of James and Michael aged three and six cuddling on the beach.

"How cute," she says mockingly.

I grit my teeth behind my lips and battle a shudder of fear.

She leaves her tea on the kitchen counter beside the kettle and hands me mine, the knife pointed at my eye –

probably in case I decide to throw the hot tea in her face.

A thought suddenly occurs to me but I don't say what I'm thinking. Right now, she's settling in for a talk and seems calmer. If I voice my challenge, she might snap out of this mood and get on with her plan, so I stay quiet.

She places the knife on the counter and picks up the Little Miss Naughty cup then sits on the chair next to Michael. To my disgust, she places her free hand on my son's thigh and strokes his leg with her finger, making a continuous circular movement. She sees me watching and says, "He loves this, you know."

I sip my tea and say nothing.

"Giving me the silent treatment? Oh well, that's okay. I'm going to carry on with my story anyway. Make sure you don't miss out on anything important. So…where did I get to? Yeah – that's it. So I'd sorted out Little Miss Chavvy. My next port of call was my father. I thought I'd give it a while for the police to forget about poor missing chav girl, but during those months, I organised my plan of attack. That was almost as fun as the execution, to be honest. I'm a planner not a pantser."

She shrugs, sips more tea. I sip mine too and nod as if in agreement. I don't want to hear this, but there's no way I can stop her and it's impossible to tune her out. I need to pretend I'm listening to every word with interest; she loves the sound of her own voice as true narcissists do, and her eyes keep flicking to mine as if she's trying to gauge my reaction. Angering her is the last thing I want to do, though scalding comments lie on the tip of my tongue waiting for an opportunity to burst forward and wipe the smirk off her face.

"I used Tyler again – oh, yeah, did you enjoy his little witch act? He told me about your reaction – made me laugh out loud! He was supposed to knock on your door and chase you through your house but when he saw you coming out, he switched up the plan. Very clever for him, really.

Messed with your head, didn't it? Tyler's a coward and a dimwit, but he was useful. And if push came to shove, I thought I could frame him for the murders. I kept evidence to plant, and I've already orchestrated my alibis. Not that it will come to that. I've thought of everything."

She smiles and downs her tea. Michael moans and shifts in his seat and we both look at him, but his eyes remain closed. In sleep, he looks even younger than normal. I long to hold him, make sure he's okay.

"Looks like I need to get a move on," Polly says calmly, "but I have to tell you about Father first. Apart from you, he's the one I'm most proud of."

"How does pride have anything to do with it?"

She gives me a piercing stare. "Pride is a feeling of deep pleasure or satisfaction derived from one's own achievements. I'd saying getting away with murder is a pretty big achievement, wouldn't you?"

"It depends how you define achievement. Most people would probably view an achievement as something that's hard to attain, so on the one hand, yes, I suppose getting away with murder could cause someone to feel pride, but most people would never derive pleasure or satisfaction from that because it has such negative connotations associated with it."

She nods. "Most people wouldn't see killing as an achievement because society's labelled it a negative practice. But killing for survival is a primal instinct; being able to protect and defend yourself is something to be proud of, isn't it?"

"Would you say that's what you were doing? Protecting or defending yourself?" I try to keep my tone bland, but the scepticism is there, and she's no fool.

"I don't need to justify my actions to you or anyone else for that matter. I did what I did to them and I'll do what I do to you, and I have my own reasons, reasons people like you can't possibly understand. You're too narrow-minded and fixated on these ridiculous notions of what's right and wrong, what's lawful and unlawful. Free choice doesn't exist for people like you, but it does for me, and I can tell you one thing with absolute certainty: when you allow yourself to embrace free choice it's the best feeling in the world. It's truly liberating. All the shackles imposed on us by 'civilisation' fall away and it's possible to be who you really are. All that bullshit conformist crap disappears, and the world becomes your oyster. And yes, I'm proud of being bright enough to see through this façade of what makes us human. I'm proud of being able to carve out my own path. I'm not afraid of anything or anyone and I do what I want, how I want, when I want, and it makes me feel insanely good. I'm powerful and free and proud and fearless – you're weak, inhibited and terrified of stepping outside what society terms 'normal'. I ought to feel sorry for you and everyone like you but, fortunately for me, I don't waste time and energy on feelings like that. I spend time and energy on identifying and achieving my goals. It's a hell of a lot of fun. You should try it some time."

I suppress the urge to roll my eyes and argue back. How all of this ties in with punishing people for adultery is something I'll never know.

She stands abruptly and carries her cup to the sink where she deposits it beside the kitchen knife. She seems frazzled and I notice her hands are shaking. Her jaw is clenched when she turns to face me, eyes unfocused as she walks over and reaches for my empty cup.

I raise the cup as if to hand it to her but instead of passing it over, I smash the cup up into her chest bone. It connects with a resounding crack. She gasps and staggers backwards clutching her chest.

It takes her a few moments to recover, during which time I throw myself onto my side, still clutching the cup, and drag my body towards the kitchen door. My ankles are still tied to the chair legs making it slow work, but I'm making progress. I hear a scraping sound and I know she's picked up the kitchen knife. I'm only inches from the doorway but I know I'm not going to make it in time. I glance back and she's striding over, knife glinting in her hand, free hand against her chest. Colour flushes her cheeks and her eyes shine oddly.

"Bitch," she says.

I stop trying to drag myself away and meet her hot gaze as she raises the knife, intention clear. Then she tilts her head and lowers the blade. Her free hand slips into her pocket and she withdraws the nail scissors and holds them up in front of her face, gazing at them fondly.

"You know what, Doc? I respect you a little bit for trying to fight for your life. You might be a lying, thieving whore but at least you've got balls."

Taking a wide berth of me, she slams the kitchen door closed and tells me to push the cup across the floor toward her. I do as I'm told; I've lost my chance. I've failed again.

She places the cup in the sink and walks back over to me. "Aw. Isn't failure a bitter pill to swallow?"

Terror explodes in my chest as she raises the knife. With a sly smile, she draws back her booted foot and kicks me in the stomach.

The pain is unimaginable. I hunch over and cover myself with my arms, fearing another attack but she laughs and returns to her seat beside Michael. I watch through tears as she plants a soft kiss on his lips.

Chapter Sixty-Three

I watch her from my position on the floor. My neck and right shoulder ache like crazy and my stomach feels like it's on fire. The cuts on my back and side burn, especially the one in my side which is pressing into the ground. I bend my arm and lean on it to lessen the pressure on my side, but it does little to ease the pain.

Polly drops her hand onto Michael's thigh.

The motion is proprietorial and natural, like she's done it a hundred times before. It's possessive, a display of power. I want to scream at her to stop touching him but daren't speak. I feel weak and shaky. Tears threaten but I hold them in, determined not to give her the pleasure of my fear and despair. Even though she says she won't hurt Michael after I'm gone, she could change her mind, and I would never know.

"How did you kill your father?" I say, desperate to keep her talking. Anything to postpone the inevitable.

She looks me straight in the eye. This time there's no smile, only a cold stare. "I lured him to the farmhouse, knocked him unconscious then buried him alive."

I swallow dryly and shift my weight, trying hard to dispel the horrifying slideshow of suffering rampaging through my mind.

She shrugs and yawns. "It was easy. Too easy really."

I raise my eyebrows, feigning curiosity. "No tricks for him then?"

She looks away, stands and wanders to the window. Déjà vu flitters across my mind. With her back to me, she says, "He needed to be punished but not in that way. Not in the way you do."

When she turns back to face me, the kitchen knife is

pointed at my face. Michael stirs again. A groan escapes his lips, but he doesn't wake.

I panic, blurt, "That scar on your neck. How did you get it?"

A slow smile curls her lip. "Been wondering that for a while haven't you, Doc?"

"I thought Richard might have done it. Heather told me he hit her once. I thought he was abusive."

She snorted. "My father couldn't hurt a fly." Her gaze darkens. "He was a lover, not a hater, as you know."

"Then how did you get it?"

Her fingers move to the scar, stroke it tenderly. "When I was little, I liked to play with cats. My mother caught me one day. I was about to do an experiment. I wanted to see if I could make our neighbour's kitty scream. Unfortunately, my mother came along, saw what I was doing and shouted at me to stop. I yanked back the knife and cut myself by mistake. I don't think she ever forgave herself. There was a lot of blood."

Horror curdles my blood. She's been harming animals since she was a little girl. An early sign of psychosis. Heather must have lied to herself, told the frightened voice inside her that Polly was just a curious little girl getting carried away. If Heather had acted then, would things have turned out differently? Could all of this have been avoided or would Polly have gone on to become a killer anyway?

I try to come up with another question, but my mind is a whirlwind, wild and broken, too torn by fear to function.

Polly moves to stand behind me, bends over and holds the knife under my throat. In my ear, she says, "Don't move."

I smell sweet sweat as she crouches down behind me, unties my ankle from the chair then frees the other ankle.

"Don't stand up. Crawl into the middle of the room."

I do as she asks, each limb trembling so much it's hard to make my body cooperate.

"Sit cross-legged and don't move an inch," she says.

I stop in the centre of the room and move onto my bottom. Wincing, I stare up at her, wanting to say something that will make her stop but knowing there's nothing I can say to change her mind.

"I'm going to throw you the nail scissors and you're going to slice open your left wrist then your right. Little tip, go down the vein, not across. It's faster. If you try anything, I will kill Michael. If you don't slice through your veins, I'll kill Michael. Plans can change. I'm flexible. Remember, it'll be your fault if Michael dies. If you do as I say, he'll be fine. I promise."

I open my mouth to speak, but she says, "Kiera doesn't exist and I'm wearing gloves. No-one will suspect poor little Polly George. Hey, Doc, you know that murder ballad I told you about? Well, Pretty Polly comes back and gets her revenge. Rips the murdering bastard to pieces. Isn't that great?"

Totally confused, I open my mouth to blurt another question – anything to keep her talking.

A noise makes us whip our heads in the direction of the kitchen door.

Polly says, "What the fu -" as Mark appears in the doorway connecting the kitchen and dining room.

He hesitates only a split second then runs into the room and launches himself at Polly.

She jerks her body around and plunges the knife into his chest. He cries out and staggers back. I lunge forward and yank Polly's ankle out from under her. She screams and crashes to the ground. Her head smacks Michael's knee as she falls, but she's still clinging to the knife and scissors which she stabs in my direction, even as she's falling.

I dart back and the knife slices air an inch from my eye. Mark's fist flies past my face and smashes into Polly's cheek. Her head jerks back and her eyes widen. Blood spurts from her mouth but her lips curl into a grimace and she lunges at

Mark and slices his cheek with the scissors, forcing him to shuffle backward.

With a cry, I grab her long blonde hair and pull her into me. She thrashes from side to side, stabbing wildly with the knife and scissors. I hook my arm around her slim neck and tighten my grip, keeping my face out of reach of her flailing hands. As I squeeze harder, she begins to stab my forearm, but I hold on to her neck, never loosening my grip, never letting go.

After three or four stabs into my arm, her attacks slow and weaken. Her thrashing legs still. The knife and scissors slip out of her fingers and hit the floor.

Her head flops onto her shoulder and I loosen my grip and shove her away from me where she drops to her side like a doll.

For a moment I stare in wonder at her beautiful face, too shocked to move.

"Jess? Jess, call 999," Mark grunts.

I look up, barely able to register what just happened or what he said. A moment later I find myself in a shivering heap in the hallway dialing the police.

Sure that the police and an ambulance is on the way, I dash over to Michael and untie him. He looks at me blearily. Confusion squinches his brow. He's pale and weak, but unharmed. I help him into the living room and guide him to the sofa.

"What happened? Are you okay? Is Kiera okay? What's she doing here? I thought she broke up with me."

"I'm sorry but I can't explain properly now. Just trust me when I say stay away from the girl on the floor. She's not Kiera. She's a very unstable patient of mine. She attacked me and Mark. I need to sit with him until the ambulance arrives. Stay here."

Michael nods and buries his head in his hands as I hurry out of the room. Blood drips onto the floor from my injuries but I'm too wired to feel any pain.

No. That'll come later.

"Mark? Can you hear me? Mark?"

He's out cold. Blood drenches his chest and his breaths are short, shallow gasps.

I grab every tea towel I can find and press them to the wound, terrified the paramedics will be too late.

Epilogue

Six Months Later

Heather George glances my way as she heads up the stone steps to the courthouse. I meet her eye and she gives me a nod, expression grim, face even greyer than I remember.

She's stood by Polly these last six months, I hear, visiting her whenever possible.

Though I know Polly feels nothing for her mother, the poor woman clings to the belief that her daughter loves and needs her. Polly, of course, will be maintaining her manipulative ways, charming Heather into the belief she's innocent, because she will need her for something later along the line, most likely money or a place to stay.

Heather admitted to finding a bag of syringes hidden in Polly's bedroom wardrobe, which, once tested, were revealed to contain traces of a strong sedative, so it seems bizarre that the woman still believes in her daughter's innocence. Then again, I wonder how I would react if James or Michael were accused of something so heinous. Could I ever abandon my faith in them, no matter how much the evidence stacked up? I don't know. I really don't, and I hope I never will.

Being a minor, Polly has been confined to a juvenile offenders' institution, where I can imagine she's worked her deceit and charm on as many of her fellow offenders and institute staff as possible. It's the way psychopaths work. They manipulate, charm and deceive. And they enjoy it.

Today, the judge will review her case and give a definitive sentence. I'm not going to lie. I'm nervous. Polly George is not the sort of person to let things go, and even if she receives a life sentence, she will only be forty when she gets out.

I stand on the bottom courthouse step and shield my eyes from the sun. Mark, Michael and James are halfway up the steps chatting in low voices to Eimear. I smile as I remember Eimear's hospital visits; every time she came she brought me a different type of sweet – retro sweets from our younger days. Candy sticks. Love Hearts. Flying saucers. Pippa, Rosie, Eimear and I would chat nonsense while snacking on sugary rubbish. The sound of the girls' gerbil-like giggles felt like the best therapy in the world. To my surprise and relief, Eimear didn't judge me for what I did. She said she loves me for being me, warts and all. After Christmas, she began pestering again and I finally caved in, making it my New Year's Resolution to give the dating website a proper go. I know it's time I stop beating myself up for what I did. Finally, I feel like I deserve to find love again. I just hope someone else does too. Someone who shares my love of salted caramel ice cream.

My sons slip their hands into mine. Mark is well on the mend. We've stayed in touch, but merely because I'm grateful to him for his bravery. If he hadn't popped by to persuade me to go out with him again, I dread to think what would have happened. I still have nightmares about Polly gutting my son in front of me then draping his intestines over my shoulders.

Michael starts telling me about his new girlfriend, a Harry Potter fanatic called Maeve. He's mid-word when he trails off. I drag my eyes away from his startled expression and stare up at the courthouse as a hush swells around us. People stop moving and talking.

At the top of the stone steps, Polly has stilled. Touched by sunlight, her hair looks like gold silk. A pretty, pink headband holds baby-soft tendrils off her face. Her neck is a swan's, elegant and balletic, her back as straight as a mannequin's.

She is, on the outside, a china doll. Inside, she is a serial killer. Brutal, sadistic, alive.

Many say that someone that young and that beautiful can't stay bad forever. They say that, in time, given the best treatment, she will reform and repent. This young girl will no longer pose a threat to society.

Only a handful of people know that Polly George is beyond rehabilitation. She will never get better. She has killed again and again and again. She is not sorry for her crimes and she will never repent. She does not feel guilt, only joy when others suffer her warped version of justice. A justice designed to somehow validate her thirst for blood.

Heather tugs on her daughter's hand, but Polly slowly rotates to look back down the courthouse steps.

Journalists go mad, thrusting themselves forward like hungry bloodhounds, eager for a shot of her exquisite face and – hopefully – a few pretty tears.

Polly parts them with a wave of her hand, and then there's just her and me, five steps apart, me below, her above.

Our eyes lock. She gives me a smile and nods, eyes glinting playfully, as if she has a secret I need to know. She holds my gaze a beat longer, turns and goes inside the courthouse.

I feel my sons' worried eyes on me, Eimear's hand on my back. Mark's awkward pat. I reassure them I'm fine. I even use the word 'lit' which earns me a hearty laugh.

Feeling more self-conscious than before, I slip my hands in my pockets. My fingers touch something crisp. Puzzled, I pull out a folded piece of paper. My heart pounds as I read the handwritten message.

And she stabbed her in the heart and the heart-
blood did flow,
Into her grave Pretty Polly did go.
She threw a little dirt over her and started for
home,

Leaving nothing behind but the wild birds to
moan.

And it's debt to the devil, and Jessie must pay,
For failing pretty Polly and running away.

My hands shake. Polly's message is loud and clear.

She's coming back to haunt me, and she won't stop until she has her revenge.

Thanks for reading *Pretty Polly*. I would really appreciate it if you could leave a review on Goodreads and Amazon.

Want to try another of my books or enter bookish giveaways? Go to my website and subscribe to my newsletter at:

www.abbydavies.com

Acknowledgements

Firstly, I want to thank you for reading my book. I hope you've enjoyed it and that it hasn't creeped you out too much! I'd be over the moon if you could share your review with others.

As always, my mum, dad and husband have been amazingly supportive throughout the writing and production of this book, giving excellent feedback on everything, from the first draft to the front cover. That said, Olly Bennett at More Visual, deserves huge praise for another beautiful cover design. I'd also like to thank my friends Derryn and Vix for their brilliant notes and ideas, and my ARC readers for helping to spread the word.

Once again, Vic has pulled out all the stops with her excellent blog tour (instabooktours), helping to build excitement and exposure for my sixth thriller.

Thank you to my special little girl, Heidi, for sharing her vital opinions of the front cover. I went with a black title instead of white/yellow, because she said, 'Black represents that it's a thriller better, Mummy.'

This book is dedicated to my gran, Gwen Richards. Throughout my life, she has been so loving, kind, generous and supportive. Every time I visit her, she asks me where I get my ideas from, and I never grow tired of telling her!

THE CULT

A hidden community…
Thirty years ago, in the English countryside, a commune was set up. Led by Uncle Saviour, it was supposed to be a place of love, peace and harmony. But what started out as paradise turned into hell.

A shocking abduction…
Now, two young children have vanished from their home in the middle of the night. Their parents are frantic, the police are at a loss.

A twisting case…
DI Ottoline is leading the search – her only clue a mask found in the woods. Could the key lie in events that took place decades ago, when a dream of a new way of life became something far more sinister?

'I had many a late night whilst reading, desperate to read just one more chapter.'
Amazon Reviewer, 5 stars

Available now

www.amazon.co.uk/dp/B08ZXYF77S

HER
No.1 FAN

Rachel Brown plays Doctor Elouise Sparks in the popular TV series 'Emergency'. Though successful in her career, Rachel has just learned that her chance of conception is small, and she is devastated by the information.

That's when Mikey Bell takes Rachel from her home to a remote mountain cottage. But Mikey's motive isn't 'normal'. He has a strange request. The good news is that if Rachel can deliver by Christmas Day, he'll let her go.

But someone else in the cottage is not on the same page as Mikey. This person has different designs for Rachel, and the bad news is that this No.1 Fan has no intention of ever letting her leave.

'This book is so fast paced I flew through it. There were lots of twists and I had no idea how things were going to turn out.'
Amazon Reviewer, 5 stars

Available now

www.amazon.co.uk/dp/B0CCK48ZGW

Printed in Great Britain
by Amazon

41244835R00148